THE WRONG PRINCE

Heirs of Cornwall
Book One

Veronica Crowe

ARE YOU SIGNED UP FOR DRAGONBLADE'S BLOG?

You'll get the latest news and information on exclusive giveaways, exclusive excerpts, coming releases, sales, free books, cover reveals and more.

Check out our complete list of authors, too!

No spam, no junk. That's a promise!

Sign Up Here

www.dragonbladepublishing.com

Dearest Reader;

Thank you for your support of a small press. At Dragonblade Publishing, we strive to bring you the highest quality Historical Romance from the some of the best authors in the business. Without your support, there is no 'us', so we sincerely hope you adore these stories and find some new favorite authors along the way.

Happy Reading!

CEO, Dragonblade Publishing

Dedication

To Oliver, my gorgeous, dashing, childhood friend, who was every girl's dream and the light of my life. You are always in my heart, though I still hold a grudge with you leaving me so soon without saying goodbye. If I could, I wish to God I could turn back the hands of time and bring back yesterday. May the angels in heaven keep you safe under their wings and keep you company, until we meet again. I miss you.

Your "little brat,"
~VC

CHAPTER ONE

Miss Cassandra Carlyle's Wedding
Cornwall, England
Fall 1807

"I'LL TELL PAPA you're being mean to me!" eight-year-old Cassandra Carlyle cried in the elegant drawing room of Rose Hill Manor. A stately cream-colored structure originally built in the past century, it served as the countryseat to generations of viscounts in the Carlyle family.

The heir, Cassandra's older brother Allayne, exchanged worried glances with his best friends, Richard and Jeremy. The three young men, all fifteen years of age, grew up together in neighboring estates.

"Papa!" Cassandra wailed louder.

Allayne peered out the window facing the side yard, adorned with a flower box full of roses on the sill, before hastily shutting the windowpane.

Cassandra knew he wanted to ensure the commotion would not reach the ears of their father, Viscount Rose, who was strolling about the garden conversing with the Duke of Grandstone.

"Whatever is the matter with you?" Allayne turned to her with a glower. "You've known we were leaving for Oxford today!"

Yes, Cassandra knew about their plans, and she felt excluded. And now that the big day had finally arrived, she was not quite ready to accept the reality of Richard leaving her just yet. "You and Jeremy can go, but I want Richard to stay!" Cassandra pursed her trembling lips and crossed her arms defiantly on her chest.

"All three of us have to go to University," Allayne said in an exasperated tone. "We can't stay here forever. That's just the way it is done."

"But I want to marry Richard when I grow up!" Cassandra exclaimed tearfully, her new large front teeth peeking halfway through her gums. "If you go, I'll never see him again!"

Allayne glanced sideways at his friends and rolled his eyes toward the ceiling. "Don't be ridiculous! Richard will be back sooner than you think. You'll see."

"Don't lie to me!" She pointed at the elaborate light fixture awkwardly tilted on one side. "I'll tell Papa you broke Mama's lamp and that you're hiding all those pamphlets with naughty drawings under your bed!"

Allayne gaped at her. "Who told you that?" He narrowed his eyes and thrust a forefinger at his sister's nose.

She clamped her mouth shut, but her eyes darted to the dark-haired young man standing next to him.

Allayne muttered a curse and turned to glare at Jeremy, currently the Earl of Calverston and heir to the Marquisate of Waterford, the estate which bordered Rose Hill to the left.

"What?" Jeremy raised his shoulders and blinked his dark eyes innocently at Allayne.

Richard, the heir and future duke to neighboring Grandstone Park, placed a soothing hand on Cassandra's shoulder. "Cassie, come now. Do not be so cross. I'll be back during the holidays, and who knows, I might even be able to visit you in a fortnight."

"I don't believe you!" Her eyebrows snapped together. "You'll go there and meet some girl with a big round bum and large bubbies, and then you'll forget all about me!"

Jeremy threw his head back and burst into a guffaw.

"Good Lord, Cassandra!" Richard stared at her in shock. "Where in Hades did you learn to speak like that?"

"Jeremy taught me," she declared with a tilt of her chin. "He said you like girls with big bottoms and fat melons." She splayed her hands with the palm side facing a foot away from her chest to demonstrate the exact size.

Richard swallowed and colored into a beet red.

"The hell he did!" Allayne pinned reproachful green eyes on Jeremy, who abruptly stopped laughing and feigned a saintly expression.

"I'll tell Papa you said a bad word!" Cassandra's face crumpled. "Papa!" she shouted.

Allayne hastily pressed his hand over her mouth and held her tight. "Stop this—now!" he hissed in her ear. "If you do not, I will chain your hands and stuff your mouth with filthy rags, then lock you up in the attic! Do you understand me?"

Cassandra nodded vigorously, looking utterly petrified, her curly red pigtails bouncing.

Satisfied that he had frightened his sister enough, Allayne loosened his hold and released her. Cassandra instantly bolted, elbowing her way past him and Richard.

"Damn it!" Allayne tried to grab her skirt but missed.

"Papa!" she cried as she dashed across the room.

"Come back here, you little—" Allayne hit his shin on a chair and uttered an oath, hopping on one foot as he rounded the furniture.

Cassandra darted under a table, crawled, and emerged on the other side.

Allayne launched himself across the tabletop, plowing through his mother's collection of small brass horses and various decorative trinkets.

"Papa! Help!" Cassandra raced toward the door. "Allayne is trying to kill me!"

Someone grabbed her at the waist and hauled her backward just as she reached for the doorknob.

"Cassie!" Richard deposited her flailing and screaming onto a chair, securely holding her in place. "Control yourself! This behavior is not acceptable!"

"But you're leaving me!" Fat tears slid down her pink, freckled cheeks. "I'll never, ever see you again—I just know it!"

"Don't be silly!" Richard pulled a handkerchief from his coat pocket and wiped her sodden face. "I'm going to school, not to debtor's prison."

"Oh, Richard, but I'll miss you so, and I'm going to die if you leave me!" she exclaimed between hiccups. "What if you marry someone else?"

Richard kneeled in front of her on the Aubusson carpet and chuckled. "Don't be absurd, Cassie. I am fifteen, and you are only eight. I have a long way to go, and so do you. A few more years from now, you will have young lads mooning over you and falling at your feet. You'll remember this ludicrous infatuation and wonder what you were thinking."

"I don't want other lads—I want you!" Cassandra smacked her hand on the mahogany armrest and began to weep again, prompting an argument between the three young men on how to keep her quiet.

A knock interrupted the hubbub, and Morton, the Rose Hill butler, entered.

"Lord Sunderland, your carriage is ready," he addressed Richard by his honorary title of Marquess of Sunderland in his usual formal manner, casting a sympathetic glance at Cassandra with a shake of his head, before bowing and retreating out the door.

"Well, we better get going." Jeremy checked his pocket watch.

Richard made a move to stand up, but Cassandra flung herself at him, clinging with her arms about his neck and her legs around his waist.

"Cassie, you fool! Let go of him!" Allayne yelled, doing his best to untangle her, but she fought him at every turn. She lost one shoe in the fracas, and her left ponytail became undone. The collar of her yellow dress twisted backward. In desperation, Cassandra grasped Richard's neckcloth and clung with all her might.

"Cassie! Quit pulling on my cravat!" Richard made a choking sound and peeled her fingers off, but she latched onto his shoulders instead.

Allayne pulled at her wrists.

"Ow! Ow!" Richard bellowed, clutching Allayne's arms to keep him from tugging on Cassandra's hands. "Stop that, you oaf! You are pulling the skin off my body! Ow!"

Cassandra kicked Allayne on his bruised shin. He howled and fell forward, knocking Richard, who was still on his knees, off-balance. The three of them tumbled in a tangled heap of skirts and booted limbs on the carpet.

"Good God, what a pickle!" Jeremy said with a hearty laugh.

"Well, don't just stand there, you dolt!" Allayne yelled at him over Cassandra's screams. "Help me get her off him!"

"Why didn't you say so in the first place?" Jeremy tapped Cassandra on the shoulder. "Cassie! Richard will marry you if you let go."

She immediately stopped bawling and released Richard from her grip. "Truly?" She blinked at Jeremy and gazed hopefully at Richard.

Allayne slapped his hand on his forehead and shook his head at Jeremy. "Now you really have done it, you half-witted buffoon!"

"I got her off him, didn't I?" Jeremy shrugged with a chuckle, merriment crinkling his dark eyes at the corners.

Richard rose to his feet and combed his fingers through his messy locks. "I think I've had enough excitement for the day. Let us get out of here before I lose my sanity." He smoothed his coat, walked to the mirror over the console table by the door, and fixed his cravat.

"But-but-but—" Cassandra's gaze flitted from one young man to the next. None of them were interested in proceeding with the wedding plans. She began to sob loudly.

"Enough of this, Cassandra!" Richard returned to her side and gently shook her by the shoulders.

She stifled her sobs with a shudder, sniffling as she fixed large, doleful green eyes on the love of her life. "You'll marry me, then?"

"Yes—by God!" Richard threw his hands in the air. "Anything to stop this madness!"

"Oh, Richard! I'm so happy!" Cassandra hugged him, then gaily skipped her way to the door. "Wait here. I'll go ask Morty to fetch the vicar."

"What?" Richard's eyes widened. "You mean—now?"

"That won't be necessary." Jeremy towed Cassandra by the arm back to the middle of the drawing room and threw a telling glance at his friends. "I can be the vicar by proxy."

Cassandra eyed him suspiciously. "Is that legal?"

"Absolutely!" Allayne interjected, shoving a lock of blond hair off his forehead as he surreptitiously sent a meaningful nod at Jeremy. "I'll even be your best man and witness."

"Shall we begin the ceremony?" Richard glanced at the grandfather clock in the corner of the drawing room as it sounded the hour with a bong. He frantically motioned for Jeremy to hurry up with their scheme and proceed.

Jeremy grabbed a book and a pair of spectacles that belonged to the viscount from the nearby desk, finishing the ensemble with Allayne's fine cashmere scarf draped over his shoulders. He gestured with his hands for Cassandra and Richard to stand before him.

"Dearly beloved," he began, looking up briefly from beneath the eyeglasses perched low on his nose, "do you swear to truly serve our Sovereign and do right to all manner of people after the laws and usages of this realm, without fear or favor, affection or ill will, so help you God?" He peered back and forth at their bewildered faces and then raised his eyebrows. "What?"

"That's one of my books," Cassandra frowned, pointing at the volume in his hand entitled *Spy Monk*.

Allayne rolled his eyes heavenward and scrubbed his palm along the length of his face.

"Reverend Jeremy, can we get on with this—please?" Richard said through clenched teeth. "We're a little pressed for time here." He flicked another glance at the clock and gave Jeremy a speaking look.

"Right." Jeremy threw *Spy Monk* over his shoulder and snatched the other book from the table. Allayne had been reading it earlier; it was entitled *Sins of a Gentleman*. He shuffled through the pages, nodded to himself with a grin when he found what he was looking for, and then cleared his throat to resume the ceremony. "Dearly beloved, by the power vested in me by the Constitution of Fornication and the Ladybirds of London, I now pronounce you husband and wife."

"Eh?" Richard's eyebrows shot upward with his mouth wide open.

"Reverend Jeremy." Cassandra raised a hand. "I have a question."

All eyes fixed on her.

"What is it, my child?" Jeremy leaned forward, asking in a preacher-like tone.

"What does fornication mean?"

"Bloody hell," Allayne mumbled under his breath.

Jeremy grinned. "Ah—my favorite word—"

"Reverend Jeremy!" Richard fairly snarled his name. "Can we just proceed—please?"

"Of course—let's see—where was I?" Jeremy peered at the naked cherubs painted on the drawing room ceiling and scratched his temple. "Ah, yes." He suddenly brightened and turned to Richard. "You may now kiss the bride!" he proclaimed, closing the book in his hand with a snap.

Richard's jaw dropped, looking thoroughly appalled.

"Actually," Allayne intervened quickly, "since the bride is under the age of—er—consent, a handshake would be more appropriate."

Cassandra stared at her hand. "But I don't even have a ring yet." Her mouth turned down at the corners, and her lower lip quivered.

"Oh—right—we forgot about the rings." Allayne hurriedly looked about the room. "Ah, there—give me a minute." He strode toward the broken lamp.

Allayne presented two brass rings from the lamp to Jeremy a moment later. "Reverend, can you rectify the ceremony so we can all move on with our lives in peace?"

"Of course, my son." Jeremy made a great show of blessing the rings before continuing with the matrimony in all piousness. "Miss Cassandra Carlyle, do you take Richard Christopher Radcliffe, Marquess of Sunderland, to be your lawfully wedded husband, to love and to hold—but only if he deserved it–and to obey—though you truly don't have to—forever and ever—but that's too long, and I won't recommend it—Amen?

"I do." Cassandra beamed in complete adoration at Richard.

Richard took the smaller ring from Allayne and tried it on her ring finger, but it was too wide, so he kept moving it on to the next one until it finally fit her thumb.

"Lord Sunderland," Jeremy went on, "do you take Miss Cassandra Carlyle to be your lawfully wedded wife, to love and to hold, to indulge and to spoil, to obey everything she asks you to do, with kindness and without a grudge, forever and ever, Amen?"

Richard snorted and cocked a tawny eyebrow at him. "Aren't you just a little bit partial?"

"Just answer the question, my son," Jeremy replied solemnly.

"I do!" Richard uttered in a sharp tone.

"You don't seem convinced, my son," Jeremy said in a serious tone worthy of a vicar and frowned at him. "Do you need a moment of contemplation?"

Richard pursed his lips and sliced his forefinger across his neck, narrowing his eyes at Jeremy.

Allayne coughed loudly and shuffled his feet as he tapped a fore-finger on his fob watch with a pointed glare at Jeremy.

"I suppose I can exorcise you another time." Jeremy spit on his index finger and drew a wet cross on Richard's forehead.

Richard swore and furiously erased it with his sleeve.

"Ha! You are possessed, my son. Let me pray for you." Jeremy dipped his hand in someone's leftover tea on the table and whisked the cold liquid across Richard's face as he muttered a blessing, ignoring Richard's angry retort, which included the word "bloody," the name "Jack," and the other term for a donkey.

"Ahem!" Allayne sidled closer and elbowed Jeremy sharply in the ribs.

"Assaulting the reverend is a mortal sin, my son." Jeremy grimaced, massaging his side. "But it can be forgiven with a petition and a generous donation." He extended his hand palm-up toward Allayne and waggled his eyebrows as he rubbed his thumb against his fingertips. Allayne reached into his pocket and begrudgingly slapped a half-crown onto Jeremy's hand.

"Bless you, my son." Jeremy stared at the coin and bestowed him with a condescending smirk. "But I fear your half-crown will only pardon half your sins—"

"What if I just slice the reverend's bollocks into halves?" Allayne growled. "Pray, will that absolve my transgressions?"

"I will pray for your blackened soul, my son," Jeremy quickly pocketed the coin and focused his attention back on the nuptials. "Please proceed, my child," he gestured at Cassandra.

Cassandra took the brass ring from Allayne and slid it on Richard's ring finger.

It fit perfectly.

"I now pronounce you husband and wife!" Jeremy replaced the viscount's eyeglasses on the table and deliberately threw the book over his head to land on Allayne's face, and then swooped down and kissed

Cassandra on the cheek.

"Richard is supposed to be the one to kiss me!" Cassandra writhed and giggled as Jeremy proceeded to tickle her.

"Forget this clumsy oaf!" Jeremy grinned crookedly. "He's not even half as handsome as I am!" He craned his neck and straightened his collar, then gave her a wink.

Cassandra stuck her tongue out and made a face at him.

"Quit dawdling." Richard glared at Jeremy before sending another concerned look at the clock, which began to chime the quarter-hour. "We are terribly delayed and must leave at once."

Cassandra's mirth faded. "You promise not to forget about me?" She clutched the tail of Richard's coat, her eyes filling with tears.

Richard smiled and ruffled her hair. "I promise," he said with a chuckle, pinching her cheeks and giving her face a playful shake. "Be good, all right?"

Cassandra tried her very best not to cry and nodded.

Then Richard was out the door with Jeremy and Allayne, running down the cobblestone path, bordered with a profusion of colorful blooms swaying in the breeze, to the waiting ducal carriage.

CHAPTER TWO

Ten years later…

CASSANDRA WALKED ALONG the deserted beach with her stallion, Apollo, absorbing the peace of her surroundings. She pulled on her horse's reins and coaxed him to venture with her to the very edge of the sea, where the water tickled his hooves, making him snicker.

She breathed in the salt-tinged air and smiled at the colors that blazed across the horizon. Ah, how she loved early mornings like this when all was quiet save for the birds and the sea. No one ever understood her penchant for such an ungodly hour, except for the one person who used to share it with her.

She heaved a deep sigh. Is he looking up at the same sunrise? Does he think of her sometimes?

Apollo nudged her cheek.

"I know." She patted his nose. "I shouldn't be moping, but I do miss him."

Her faithful mount bobbed his head before snorting in a manner that resembled disapproval.

"You know me too well." She laughed. "And I know you well, also, you colossal glutton. You don't care at all for my feelings and want to return home to your breakfast."

Apollo's ears perked up at the mention of food, and he started tugging on the reins she held.

"Oh, all right." Cassandra shook her head at his antics and mounted the eager stallion. They took off in a swift gallop toward home.

"Good morning, Morty!" she said as she passed the butler on her way to the breakfast room.

The butler's expression did not change on hearing this appellation, though a bushy eyebrow quivered.

"Good morning, Miss," he replied, his tone as stiff as the points of his collar. "And the name is Morton, the same one I have been using in my thirty years of service to the viscount."

"I know, Morty." She chuckled over her shoulder as she opened the door to the breakfast room. *Poor Morty.* She should quit riling him up every single morning.

"Mama, Papa, I'm home! Have you finished eating, or can I join you?" she said before coming to an abrupt halt upon realizing they had a visitor. Her parents looked up from their repast with broad smiles, but her attention focused on the third person occupying a chair facing away from her. Cassandra gasped at the sight of the man's wavy hair curling a few inches past his shirt collar.

"Allayne?" she said with a slight tremble in her voice.

Her brother swiveled in his seat. "Surprise!"

"Allayne!" Cassandra rushed to him and hugged him tightly. "I missed you so much!" She framed his face in her hands, laughing as she squeezed him again.

He looked taller and broader, and his hair was longer. His face was leaner, made even more handsome with deep dimples on his cheeks and stunning eyes identical to hers.

"Good God, look at you!" Allayne stood, lifted her up, and swung her around like he used to do when they were children. "You're all grown up! I can't lift you any higher—your legs are too long!" He pretended to fumble in mid-twirl, evoking the expected squeal.

"Of course, I am taller!" Cassandra chided as he set her down on her feet. "It's been three years since you last came home. What did you expect?" She smacked his arm for good measure.

"I'm glad you decided to come back home, son." Viscount Carlyle leaned back in his chair. "I have no inkling of how you can find European society so interesting."

"I was not interested in social life in Europe, Father. The history and culture of the places we toured were what fascinated me. I did write that Richard and I—"

The viscountess interrupted him with a loud cough, at the same time bestowing him with a speaking look.

"What is it?" Cassandra raised her eyebrows.

"Why don't you sit down and have some breakfast, my dear," her mother said, a large diamond ring winking from her finger as she waved her hand toward a chair.

A trim lady of mature years, she still retained the glorious titian tresses and clear complexion that had made her exceedingly popular with the gentlemen of the ton a couple of decades earlier. She was impeccably dressed in royal blue taffeta with not a wrinkle, a sharp contrast to Cassandra's saltwater-stained shirt and riding breeches.

As if reading her thoughts, a glint of distaste came into Lady Carlyle's eyes as she took in Cassandra's soggy attire and mud-encrusted boots. "After breakfast, I want you to go to your room and get rid of those ghastly breeches and that ridiculous man-shirt you're wearing. And—oh, Lord! You must have your maid do something with that hair! You will be the social death of me! I don't know how your father can tolerate seeing you like this."

"She looks fine to me." The viscount shrugged and took a sip of his coffee. Cassandra grinned at her father as she slid into the chair, facing Allayne.

"She looks like a stable boy!" Her mother straightened, planting her delicate hands on her waist. "And what were you thinking, giving her that monster of a horse?"

"Well, it didn't look like much when I purchased it from Tattersall's twelve years ago. How would I know it would grow to mammoth proportions?" Viscount Carlyle winked at Cassandra. "Besides, what my little girl wants, my little girl gets."

"She's eighteen, in case you haven't noticed," her mother glowered, her voice rising. "And she's overdue for her first Season in London!"

The viscount folded his hands over his belly and yawned, then rolled his eyes toward the ceiling.

"Did you see that, Allayne?" The viscountess pointed at her husband's bland expression. "This is the reason why your sister refuses to go! She should be dancing at Almack's, looking for a husband, but instead, she is galloping all over the countryside on that beast with that profligate friend of yours, Lord Waterford, and getting into all sorts of tomfoolery! She's turned into a hoyden, and it's all your father's fault!"

Allayne cleared his throat. "Mother, I think we all know why she's not interested in having her Season in London."

The viscountess harrumphed and glared at him but became mercifully silent, pushing the food around her plate with a frown.

Cassandra puckered her eyebrows. Her mother and brother seemed to be hiding something from her. Well, it was time to see what they were up to! She stood and placed her fists on her hips.

"All right. What are you not telling me?"

Allayne took a long sip of coffee and carefully set his cup back on the saucer before he addressed her in a serious tone. "We're invited to luncheon tomorrow at Grandstone Park. I—well, *we*—are back for good, Cassie."

"W-we?" Cassandra's heart began to pound. "Y-you mean—you—and Richard?"

"I'm sure you know that the Duke of Grandstone's illness has turned for the worst, and he is not doing very well. Richard is his only son and heir, and there are matters that must be settled and announced tomo—"

"Richard is here?" Cassandra whispered, barely paying attention to what her brother was saying.

"Yes, but—"

"Richard is here! Oh, I can't wait until tomorrow!"

"Cassie—" Her brother touched her arm.

"It might be best if you just stayed at home tomorrow, my dear." Her mother rose from her seat and went to her with a troubled expression on her face.

"Don't you worry in the least, dear brother and Mother! I wouldn't show up looking like this and embarrass you!" She glanced confidingly at her father. "Right, Papa?"

"Whatever you say, pumpkin." He grinned back at her.

"George Carlyle!" her mother yelled in a surprisingly booming voice, looking like she had finally reached the end of her tether. "Did you hear what your father said, Allayne? This is what I have to contend with! Is it any wonder that the girl is callow and spoiled beyond belief?"

Allayne propped an elbow on the table and rubbed his forehead wearily with his hand. "I think I'm going back to Europe," he lamented.

"I think I'm going back to my room." Cassandra strolled toward the door, humming a merry tune as she went. She had pined for Richard for years—and now, the waiting was finally over!

There were so many things she wanted to talk to him about, like University, his travels to Europe, America, and India! They could ride again in the mornings, and she could sit on the beach while Richard painted the sunrise. Then, in the evenings, they could play whist with Allayne and Jeremy and beat them soundly!

Cassandra wondered if Jeremy knew Allayne and Richard had returned. He had missed going to Europe with them because he was in mourning. His father had unexpectedly passed away three years ago, and he had taken over the title of Marquess of Waterford. Jeremy had been her only partner in mischief for the past few years, and sometimes she wondered if that had left him a tad lonely. But now, his old friends were back, and they would all be together again.

Cassandra ran up the staircase and burst into her bedchamber. She threw the armoire doors wide open and shifted through her clothes to select something appropriate for the luncheon. Several of the day dresses her mother had purchased for her had not been worn even once. She hated the frilly lace and fancy silks; brocades made her skin crawl.

She pulled out the pretty green silk with the least embellishments on the sleeves and shoulders. It had cream ribbon ties that would emphasize her waist and scalloped edges at the bottom that would bring the eye to her matching satin slippers. She sighed. For Richard's sake, she would wear it tomorrow—and try her best not to scratch herself, no matter how badly the fabric made her itch.

She hugged the dress to herself and stared at her reflection in the mirror. A slender young woman with large, vivid green eyes and tousled red-gold hair looked back at her. Her gaze slid down to her chest, and she turned halfway to look at her behind. *Oh, yes. She'd grown a round bum and nice bubbies, all right. Richard need not look elsewhere.*

Her full mouth curved into a smile. She tossed the dress on the bed and raised her left hand to contemplate the tarnished brass ring on her pinky finger. It had been ten long years since she had last seen Richard. Her mama would scold her time and again to stop being foolish and forget about him, and she tried, oh, how she tried!

She had accepted calls from suitors and even agreed to attend the local balls, but none of the gentlemen she met aroused her interest. None of them made her forget Richard. His image had always been ingrained in her heart.

Memories of Richard watching over her all through her childhood came flooding back. He was always there, protecting her from harm, patiently waiting when she lagged behind, soothing her after a scolding from Allayne or a tear-inducing bout of teasing from Jeremy.

He never failed to shower her with gifts of her favorite sweets or surprise her with much-coveted porcelain dolls to cheer her up whenever the other boys hurt her feelings.

She could still remember how devastated she had been when he left. Despite her tearful protests on that fine autumn day, she never genuinely believed that she would not see him again after he left for school—but that was exactly what happened. For the first few years, she had heard from Allayne that Richard spent his school breaks with his father, touring the duke's vast properties all over England to familiarize himself with the running of the estates. But after his father had become ill and returned to his ducal seat in Cornwall, oddly, Richard did not go with him. He never came back. Not for the summer or any of the holidays.

Richard had been gone from her life for ten long years. Even so, she had faithfully waited for him countless Christmases by the window. Still, every year, only a large white package with a big red bow arrived punctually at her doorstep, containing a brief note with the same holiday greeting, a new porcelain doll, and her favorite chocolate bonbons.

Her gaze drifted to the glass display cabinet where she'd kept every present he had given her. She cherished every single doll and even saved the fancy bonbon tins because they were all she had that was connected to him.

Oh, how she missed him! But now, he was home—and her world was whole again.

Oh, Richard, my dearest Richard, her heart chanted in silent prayer. "I'm all grown up now," she whispered and lowered her head, pressing her lips tenderly against the brass wedding band on her finger.

CHAPTER THREE

CASSANDRA SAT QUIETLY in the carriage on the way to Grandstone Park, watching Allayne and her mother from beneath thick lashes as she contemplated their strange behavior that had begun yesterday.

Allayne had been avoiding her since breakfast, even though he had loved spending time with her whenever he came home in earlier days. Her mother, on the other hand, acted even more furtive by contriving all sorts of excuses to discourage her daughter from coming. When Cassandra made it clear that she meant to go no matter what, her mama sulked in silence. Oddly, even her usually jovial father had lost his humor and looked a little concerned before they left.

Cassandra peered out the window of the moving carriage as it passed through the gleaming brass gates ornamented with twin griffins at the top and turned onto the long-graveled drive leading up to the palatial mansion beyond. Grandstone Park never failed to take her breath away, no matter how often she had been in and out of the estate. It loomed like a fortress, with turrets and fine stone carvings of Grecian gods, their blank eyes looking down at every conveyance approaching its entrance.

A sprawling labyrinth of towering boxed hedges occupied the front lawn, where she, together with Allayne, Richard, and Jeremy, used to play hide and seek as children. She recalled how she would become disoriented and lose her way. Richard always came back to save her.

As the carriage passed the perfectly manicured lawns, she spotted Old Ron, the groundskeeper, who paused from pruning a rose tree and waved at her. She stuck her hand out the window and fondly returned the gesture. After another minute or two, the coachman finally reined in the horses and eased the carriage to a stop in front of the manor.

The main entrance was in keeping with the rest of the place, impressively elevated from the drive by several broad stone steps leading up to the balcony-style landing. The residence certainly befitted the reputation of its owner.

The duke's butler, Gordon, greeted them at the threshold. "Welcome to Grandstone Park." He bowed to them with all the propriety of twenty-eight years of service. "Luncheon will be served at the Flower Garden." He beckoned a footman to show them the way.

Cassandra purposely lagged to let her parents and brother go ahead before she turned to the tall, thin, solemn-faced butler who had an uncanny resemblance to his cousins Morton, the Rose Hill butler, and Barton, the Waterford Park butler. Their employers had long ago foregone addressing them by their same last name to avoid confusion.

"Gordy, where's Richard?" she asked in her usual teasing way.

"He should be down soon, Miss, but in the meantime, Cook made your favorite strawberry-rhubarb pie. Would you care to have some in the parlor?"

"Thank you, Gordy, perhaps I shall have some later." She began to walk in the direction of the hallway leading to the garden.

"But—Miss Carlyle," Gordon practically stepped in her path. "Cook insists on serving the pie while it's fresh out of the oven. She is very particular that you be served a warm, generous slice."

Cassandra glanced longingly at the glass doors at the end of the corridor. Beyond them, she could see the other guests enjoying the beautiful day outside. However, she did not want to disappoint the motherly cook of Grandstone Park.

"Very well, Gordy," she sighed. "But don't bother to bring it into the parlor. I'll go down to the kitchen."

Several delicious bites later, not just of the pie but also veal cutlets in a rich gravy and potted lobster in a fancy porcelain dish with delicate thin crackers, Cassandra stood up from the table. "Thank you, Cook! That was superb!" She wiped her mouth with a white napkin and beamed at the doting cook. "Now, I must be off and mingle with the rest of the guests. Mother must be wondering where I am."

"But, Miss—don't you want to sample the roast beef, too?" Cook, a rotund older woman with plump cheeks, wiped her hands on her apron.

"I would love to, but I'm stuffed. Perhaps I can have some for a late supper—"

"How about some custard tartlets?" Mrs. Nell, the head housekeeper, asked.

"Thank you, Mrs. Nell," Cassie smiled fondly at her. "But I really must—"

The young parlor maid poured steaming liquid into her cup. "Have some hot chocolate, Miss Carlyle."

"Thank you, Mellie." Cassie turned her eyes to the timid girl who was looking at her expectantly. "Perhaps later, I can—"

"Ah, there you are, Miss Carlyle." Gordon stood in the doorway with a platter of scrumptious-looking confections. "May I offer you some sweetmeats?"

Cassandra opened her mouth to say something and then snapped it closed again. She looked between Cook, who immediately stared at her shoes, Mrs. Nell, who gulped and bit her lip, and Mellie, who wrung her hands and avoided her gaze. Gordon seemed jittery and unwell, glaring at the sweetmeats quite intently.

"What's going on here?" Cassandra arched an eyebrow at the staff, who had practically watched her grow up from a little girl in pigtails to a young woman. After the duke lost his wife some years ago, leaving him with Richard, their only child, the majestic house had become somber and hollow. The servants appreciated the cheer she brought into their master's life, doting on her so she would stay longer and call more often—which she faithfully did.

Even after Richard left, Cassandra kept up her calls to the elderly duke, who shared his son's fondness for her. She made him laugh and entertained him by playing the pianoforte, kept especially for her use in the parlor. In turn, the duke taught her how to dance, and she had learned to be quite proficient at it.

Lately, however, her visits had become more difficult due to his illness. Though she still managed to put him in a better disposition, he tired easily, and she always returned home with sadness in her heart. Richard had disappeared from her life, and now his father—her only living link to him—was about to do the same. Every day, the inevitable crept closer.

She narrowed her eyes at Gordon and placed her hands on her hips. "Is there anything you'd like to tell me, Gordy?"

Gordon's usual fine demeanor cracked. "I believe there's someone at the door," he announced to no one in particular and made his escape.

Cassandra lifted an inquiring eyebrow at Mrs. Nell, Cook, and Mellie, tapping her foot impatiently on the flagstones.

"Oh, dear, my roast is burning!" Cook took off in the direction opposite where her roast was grilling over hot coals.

"I should see to the other guests." Mrs. Nell swept out of the room, followed by Mellie, who mumbled something about lying, bumbling chickens, and God striking them all with lightning.

Cassandra shook her head. Whatever mischief was brewing in the kitchen had to wait. A luncheon was in progress, and she had no intention of missing it. She made her way out of the kitchen into the foyer, down to the hallway, and out into the garden. Beneath the arched trellis bountifully adorned with climbing roses in pink and white, she paused and surveyed the gathering.

The luncheon was well attended. Several people from nearby estates were present, and the others were aristocrats from London. She had never seen such a large gathering of fine-looking guests in all her life. But then again—what could one expect at a party hosted by the Duke of Grandstone?

She searched the crowd with her eyes. Richard should be somewhere with Allayne and Jeremy, waiting for her. She quivered inwardly, a mixture of anxiety and anticipation at the thought.

What would he think of her? What would he say or do when he saw her? Would he notice the pretty dress and the upswept style of her hair she had spent an hour fixing with her maid? Would he see her as a young lady, instead of the little girl he used to play with?

Cassandra stepped into the well-dressed coterie and wove her way through the lush, fragrant garden. She stopped and greeted the people she recognized until she finally reached the high end of the lawn, where the beautiful gazebo flanked on either side with marble maidens hoisting a clay jar, stood. Wide, flowing stairsteps tiled with colorful, intricate mosaic patterns graced the front leading up to the gazebo, where a make-shift stage with tables and chairs had been set.

"Your kind attention, please." An older but distinguished-looking gentleman, who sat next to the Duke of Grandstone on the stage, stood and shook a handbell.

The crowd quieted, and heads turned in his direction.

"As you well know, we are gathered here to share a most splendid occasion," the gentleman said. "But first, I would like to extend my delight in welcoming our beloved Marquess of Sunderland. It's good to have you back, Richard." He summoned him with a gesture of his hand.

The guests cheered and parted to let him through.

Cassandra craned her neck and pushed her way into the crowd as close as she could to the structure.

A tall gentleman with broad shoulders and longish, straight blonde hair climbed up the steps to the stage. "Thank you, Your Grace," he said in a deep, rich voice, shaking the older man's hand, before facing the waiting guests.

She held her breath in awe.

Gone was the youthful face, slim build, and easy smile of the boy she used to know. The person who stood before her was darker, his face defined by a strong jaw, high cheekbones, and a straight blade of a nose. He had a powerful physique; his long sinewy legs encased in tight breeches. His fine coat hugged his broad shoulders like a second skin, tapering down to emphasize his lean waist.

The Richard she knew had changed. Not a trace of her old friend existed in this new version. This person was confident, sophisticated, and devastatingly handsome. A certain air of mastery and dignified deportment commanded respect from his peers. This person was no longer a boy—but a man.

Clapping and whistling rang from the crowd, offering him a warm welcome home. He expressed his appreciation with a slight bow and accepted well wishes from the people nearest him.

"Excuse me. Pardon me." Cassandra squeezed her way to the front, murmuring her apologies to people she had to nudge aside so she could attain a better view. When at last she reached her destination, she looked up, just as the object of her affection suddenly turned, his piercing sapphire eyes meeting hers across the short distance that separated them.

His eyes lit up in recognition, and he gave her a dazzling smile.

Cassandra's heart somersaulted. She took a step forward, beaming with happiness and excitement, but someone from behind moved past her and crossed the narrow patch of grass toward him.

"Darling." An elegantly dressed woman climbed the stairs and reached out to take Richard's proffered hands.

She stood next to him, refined and graceful, a perfect complement to the sophisticated man Richard had become.

"My dear friends and family," he said, wrapping an arm around the stunning light-haired, blue-eyed goddess at his side. "To those of you who haven't met her yet, may I introduce my lovely betrothed—Lady Desiree Lennox, daughter of His Grace, Arthur Lennox, Duke of Glenford."

CHAPTER FOUR

JEREMIAH DEVLIN HUNTINGTON, Marquess of Waterford, plunged his fingers through his dark hair in consternation as he watched the entire scene unfold before him. He was standing with Allayne, not far from where Cassandra stood rooted to the spot, oblivious to the well-wishers brushing past her to congratulate the happy couple. She looked so pale, so helpless, like a lone wet duck shivering in the eye of a hurricane.

"Dear God, Allayne!" He whipped his head reproachfully at her brother, who seemed torn about what he should do. "You didn't tell her?"

A look of regret marred Allayne's face. "I tried to—but I couldn't bear to break her heart. I didn't know how to—" He shook his head and sighed. "Bloody hell, Jeremy, I have no excuse."

"You're damned right, you don't!" Jeremy strode off, then stopped halfway, jabbing a finger in his direction. "Do you think this is any better? Leaving her to find out in a public manner? Look at her, damn you!" Cassie stood, her hands trembling as she rubbed them over her chest, seeming to appease her broken heart.

Allayne grimaced. "I should take her home." He began to walk toward his sister.

"No." Jeremy raised a hand, bringing Allayne to a halt. "I'll do it. You, my friend, have some thinking to do. You'd better be ready to explain yourself to her." Utterly heedless of the curious stares his outburst had elicited, he stomped to where Cassandra remained motionless in shock.

Jeremy muttered a silent curse. Damn Allayne for letting her go through this! It was cruel and uncalled for—easily prevented if the milksop had the balls to warn his sister! He would have told her himself if he had heard the news yesterday, but he was just as flabbergasted to discover Richard's sudden engagement from Barton, the Waterford Park butler, this morning. Besides, who would have thought that not a single soul had mentioned this particularly important detail to her? Even the servants in all three houses knew.

"Come on, brat." He took her arm gently and dragged her away from the festive crowd. "Let's get out of here."

Cassandra calmly acquiesced. They walked toward the front of Grandstone Manor by way of the cobblestone pathways in the gardens.

Jeremy sent a footman to have his coach brought around, glancing at her with concern. Her eerie silence bothered him. The Cassie he knew was never like this. She had always been spirited and carefree, and her sharp tongue could slice and dice any man who dared leer at her. Her feistiness, not counting the profanities he had taught her, would be quite sufficient to induce her mother into a dead faint.

But this Cassie, who stood mutely beside him with her head hung low and her proud shoulders slumped, was a stranger. She looked defeated and confused, and his heart ached for her sorry state. Jeremy had to concede, however, that in spite of what she had just gone through, she shed not a single tear, nor did she launch into hysterics and make a scene. He did not know of anyone among his acquaintances who could boast of similar fortitude—men included.

His carriage arrived, and he handed her inside, taking his seat across from her.

"Pretty dress, brat," he ventured, flicking the end of a dainty ribbon trim on the edge of her skirt, hoping he could wangle a smile out of her.

She appeared not to have heard what he said because she looked out the window and remained speechless. She seemed far away, lost in her thoughts.

An unfamiliar wave of protectiveness besieged him. What could he do to fix this? What could he say to make her feel better? There must be something in his power to put everything to rights, damn it!

"Who did your hair?" he persisted, refusing to let her wallow in her misery. "I like it. You should show off that elegant neck of yours more often."

Jeremy waited for her reaction. God knows he was a Corinthian and a rake, and he had had plenty of practice in flattering the opposite sex. Cassie, however, knew him too well to bite at his bait. Either that, or she was not aware of him at all.

She kept silent and continued to gaze outside, her face expressionless and her eyes fixed on nothing in particular.

Jeremy shifted in his seat. Her aloofness disturbed him. Yes, she was sitting not more than two paces away from him, but she was not there. He felt like she had shut a door on his face and disconnected herself from him. A twinge of anxiety lanced his chest. He did not relish the thought of being cut-off from her at all. It felt unnatural not to hear her laughter and sarcastic quips, and even more depressing to feel emotionally excluded from her inner musings.

What was she going through? How much hurt was she dealing with? Why wouldn't she let him in?

Perhaps what she needs is a little respite, he convinced himself. For the sake of his own sanity, he had to believe that her pain would recede with time. With some effort, he refrained from any more attempts at conversation and quietly watched her profile instead.

She had grown incredibly beautiful during the last few years. Gone was the freckled girl with plump cheeks and an endearing, little button nose. Her countenance had transformed into a heart-shaped, angelic visage, with those stunning long-lashed ld eyes, full lips the color of sun-ripened cherries, and a complexion akin to peaches and cream. Her physique had likewise matured into a lovely hourglass shape that turned heads at every gathering she attended. The local lads had been—ironically, as Richard had once predicted—falling at her feet.

But unlike other young ladies her age, Cassie never showed any interest toward any of the gentlemen who had come to call on her. Yes, she would patiently sit and converse with her admirers as was politely necessary, but she would also bolt out the door and escape on her horse at the first chance she would get. To her mother's eternal vexation and her father's ceaseless amusement, she would rather gad about with him all day long than sit in a roomful of fawning young bucks.

Of course, it did not help that he purposely terrified most of her suitors with a cold, haughty stare if they even thought of touching a single hair on her head. He made it quite clear that no one—but no one—was allowed to hold her hand unless they wanted to meet the blade of his sword at dawn.

Consequently, many speculated and gossiped on why Cassie frequently spent time without a chaperone with a rogue like him, whose mere name could be detrimental to her reputation. But as luck would have it, he was a well-known close friend of the Carlyles, and that somewhat tempered any unsavory conjectures about their remarkably devoted friendship. Even her mother could not resist his charm and was very fond of him, despite her disapproval of his incorrigible ways.

As for the viscount, he did not seem to mind his unusual amity with his daughter, and Cassie, in turn, never gave the impression of caring one jot about his reputation as a rake. She had always enjoyed his company and flaunted their camaraderie, no matter how much her poor mother worried about the talk it may provoke and complained about the inferred impropriety.

Well, the gossipmongers could all go to the devil! He was very fond of Cassie—his little brat. And if a young man fancied himself in love with her enough to woo her, he would have to pass through Jeremy's rigid scrutiny first. He would never let any dandified dimwit near her—not because of his concern over Cassie, but simply because he knew a lesser man would never be up to snuff. His deceptively innocent-looking little brat could mince a lily-livered weakling in his own fat and eat him for breakfast—most probably while the poor lad was still alive.

Jeremy studied her face. She looked so sad. Her hands were folded on her lap, and he doubted if she could even see the beautiful panorama rushing by outside. A ray of sunlight shone through the glass and caught the pool of tears that had gathered in her eyes, making them glitter like minuscule stars.

Jeremy drew a sharp breath. *Good, God!* She had been trying to hold them back, trying to be brave and not break down in front of him the whole time! He suddenly wanted to murder Richard and throttle Allayne.

"Cassie." He leaned over and reached for her hand.

She bit her lip but did not make a move to look at him.

"Come on, brat, look at me," he said in a teasing tone, tugging at her fingers, endeavoring to lighten her mood.

A minute passed before she turned to him with large, doleful eyes.

"He looked right through me," she said in a small voice, her lips quivering.

Jeremy squeezed her hand and swallowed the sudden explosion of anger in his chest. What the devil was he supposed to say to that? Convince her that Richard probably did not see her—when he had witnessed everything that had happened? "Cassie—" he began, hating himself for having to appease her with a lie. "I'm sure he didn't notice—"

"He just looked right through me, Jeremy," she interrupted before he could finish, her voice scratchy and barely audible, as if she meant to repeat the words to herself.

Jeremy swore and pulled her onto his lap. Her faltering composure broke. The tears she had been trying so hard to contain fell in torrents.

He offered his handkerchief and drew her head to rest on his shoulder, wrapping her in a comforting embrace and letting her pour out all the bitterness in her heart. She wept nonstop while he soothed her with kind words the rest of the ride home.

"Perhaps Richard failed to recognize you," Jeremy said as the carriage approached Rose Hill, hiding the revulsion in his voice for making up another excuse to alleviate her pain as he rubbed her back.

"Do you think so?" She raised hopeful eyes.

"I know so." Jeremy nodded and forced a smile, pleased that he had finally succeeded in making her stop crying, yet at the same time, disgusted with himself for giving her false hope.

Cassie wiped her face with his handkerchief and leaned her head back on his shoulder without saying another word.

Jeremy clenched his teeth as he held her in his arms in silence until the conveyance stopped in front of her home. He may not know what to say to make things right, but he knew exactly what to do. There is no way in hell he would ever let anyone hurt her like this again.

CHAPTER FIVE

Cassie and Allayne...

CASSANDRA STAYED IN her room for the rest of the day, refusing to go downstairs to dine with her family. She was angry at all of them—her Papa included. Why had they kept the truth from her? Why had they let her show up at Grandstone Park, brimming with hope and dreams, only to have her expectations slaughtered by the grim reality that Richard—her first and only love—belonged to another?

The humiliation of being blindsided by her own family was beyond anything she could ever imagine. She felt like a laughingstock—for believing that Richard would keep his promise; for having faith in an oath he'd declared over a joke of a marriage when she was eight.

What a naïve, gullible twit she had been!

"Cassie? Can I come in?" Allayne's voice sounded from the other side of her door.

"Go away!" she shouted, her voice harsh with anger. How could Allayne come here and show his face after all that had happened? He should have been the one who broke the news to her in the first place. Instead, he had let her wander straight into the lion's den, not knowing what to expect.

The doorknob turned, and Allayne walked into her bedchamber, carrying a tray of supper, a glass, and a decanter of brandy. He set it down on the table by the window and sat on the edge of her bed.

"Why can't you just leave me alone?" Cassie pulled the sheets higher up her chin. She should have known that Allayne could never be deterred. He had always been the most indomitable, annoying person on the face of the earth—especially when he was intent on accomplishing a particular assignment.

"Cass—I'm sorry. Truly, I am. That was badly done of me." Allayne touched her arm, looking genuinely sad. "Do you think you can forgive me?"

Cassandra sighed and averted her gaze. Allayne would never leave unless he said what he had come to say—and gotten what he had come to gain. She could never manipulate him like Richard and Jeremy, nor shoo him away if he had decided to stay. Besides, what could holding a grudge against him and the entire family accomplish anyway? What was done was done. She could not turn back the clock and erase what had taken place.

"How long have you known?" she asked in a voice hoarse from crying for hours. The note of accusation was apparent in her tone, and she made sure he had noticed.

Allayne swallowed and stood up, massaging the back of his neck. "Before we left for Europe," he replied quietly.

A short silence ensued before she regained the nerve to speak again.

"T-that long?" she gasped. "And you never took the time to mention it in your letters?"

"I never thought anything would ever come of it. Richard has always been his own man and is not coerced into anything so easily." Allayne strolled toward the table and poured himself a drink. "It was prearranged. Grandstone and the Duke of Glenford were old friends. At the time of their agreement, both were recently widowed. Glenford had one child, a daughter, and Grandstone had Richard, the last scion of the Radcliffe clan. Grandstone needed an heir to keep the ducal fortune within the family, and Glenford wanted to make sure Lady

Desiree would marry a man who was in a position to provide her with the life she was accustomed to—who would not squander her money. He had bestowed on Lady Desiree a substantial dowry and an inheritance consisting of all the unentailed monies and properties he owned in the event of his death. The alliance would be one of the most prosperous in the kingdom." He turned to look at her, his glass hoisted halfway to his lips. "It was a brilliant match, Cassie."

"And Richard agreed to this?" She sat up straighter on the bed. "This cold-blooded, loveless—"

"No, of course not! Not right away, anyway." Allayne shrugged and took a sip of his brandy. "But with the two old dukes' machinations, Richard was obliged to dine with the Lennox family and meet Lady Desiree." Allayne stared into the crystal goblet in his hand and swirled the liquor in it. "He—ah—he liked her, Cass. The first time he saw her, he was quite taken by her."

Cassandra inhaled sharply and squeezed her eyes shut, the pain of knowing that Richard—her Richard—had fallen for Lady Desiree ripping a hole in her heart.

"But he wasn't prepared to get married," Allayne added, the bed dipping with his weight as he sat next to her on the mattress. "He may have been smitten with Lady Desiree, but he was too young at the time. He valued his freedom and wanted to see the world outside of England. He was not ready to be tied down. That was the reason why I never told you. Richard was angry at his father for forcing his hand. Why do you think he went to Europe with me and stayed there for so long?"

Cassandra opened her eyes and searched her brother's face. "But he came back because of her. He's ready to marry her now." She bit her lip and looked away. What a moon-eyed ninny she had been to assume that he had come back because he remembered and missed her and all the things they used to do together! Wouldn't he have come back sooner if that had been the case? But no—she did not think—she only believed.

"Well, no, not exactly." Allayne placed the crystal goblet on her bedside table and took her hand in his.

"What do you mean?" She swung her head toward him, unable to dampen the glimmer of hope that swiftly invaded her heart.

"His father is dying, Cass. He must return home. Richard could not delay the inevitable any longer. It was his father's most fervent wish for him to settle down and produce an heir, so he could go peacefully to his grave, knowing that the Radcliffe family line will live on. He does not have much time, and Richard loves him dearly. He did not want to disappoint his father. As soon as our ship docked in London, we set out to Lennox House in Mayfair, and Richard asked for Lady Desiree's hand in marriage."

"He must have secretly loved her to do that so effortlessly." She choked back the tears that threatened to overwhelm her once again. After all, what man would not desire the goddess she had seen today? Lady Desiree was perfect, a Venus de Milo to Richard's Adonis. One would be blind not to see how fine they looked together.

"I don't know—" Allayne shook his head and pursed his lips. "I don't think so. He has only known her a few days."

"But the way he looked at her—"

"She's very beautiful, Cassie. Any man would be enamored of her. Whether they will suit together and fall in love—I have no answers for you. All I know is—" Allayne squeezed her hand, and his expression turned somber. "You must forget Richard." His voice was kind but markedly firm. "He's not the one, Cass. Let him go. Open yourself to new possibilities and find another."

They stared at each other in silence until finally, Cassandra dropped her gaze to her lap. Deep inside, she knew Allayne was right. She had been holding on to an impossible dream, a ridiculous notion of a childhood promise that had no merit.

The moment had come for her to accept reality. Richard had never been *The One*. He was certainly fond of her—like a little sister—but he had never loved her the way a prince loved his princess, or a knight cherished his damsel in distress.

Richard, the man of her dreams, would always stay that way—just a dream—unattainable, untouchable, a figment of her imagination.

And if she had some sense left in her, she would heed her brother's advice and forget him, bury him in the past.

Richard, Richard, Richard, as always, his name swirled like a stubborn ache in her head even as she mentally admonished herself.

He is not yours, you pathetic fool! She smothered his image from her mind, then she covered her face with her hands and cried in her brother's arms.

CHAPTER SIX

Letting Go...

C ASSANDRA WATCHED THE ocean waves roll in, towering and churning in the distance before tapering down into feathery frothed fans of cool gritty water as they reached the gleaming sand on the shore. *Just like me,* she whispered, hugging her knees to her chest as she reflected on the many hours she had spent coming to terms with wave after wave of anger, disillusionment, and regret at her appalling foolishness.

After the river of tears she'd shed and the heartbreak she'd suffered, a certain peace had come over her. The mysterious kind of calm that dwelled in one's heart when all hope was gone, and one must accept defeat.

She felt the sting of the sun on her skin and realized she had been sitting on the beach for hours. For the first time in her life, she failed to notice the magic of the sunrise, the briny scent of the sea, and the beauty of the natural surroundings she had always loved.

Apollo stomped his hooves on the sand and shook his mane impatiently.

"Yes, I know, it's time for us to go home." Cassandra stood up and brushed the sand from her breeches, then mounted the restless stallion, riding him all the way back to the stables of Rose Hill Manor.

Benny, her father's stable hand, took the reins from her as she dismounted. She had no cheerful greeting for him this morning, breaking their little ritual for years. He touched the brim of his hat with a smile and said nothing to her, but she caught the concern in his eyes as he walked Apollo to his box. "Ye 'ave to do a better job o' cheerin' 'er up," she heard him murmur sternly in the horse's ear.

Apollo snickered and bobbed his massive head before getting distracted by a tempting bucket of apples placed just out of his reach.

Cassandra deliberately took the rear door to the servants' stairs to reach her bedchamber. She had to avoid her mother, who undoubtedly would throw another fit if she saw her disheveled state. Cassandra had no desire to participate in any arguments at present.

As she tiptoed along the second-floor hallway, she overheard several voices from below. Curious about their morning visitors, Cassandra inched toward the banister along the upstairs balcony that had a partial view of the drawing room on the first floor and peeked down.

Her heart went to her throat. From where she was, she could see Richard standing in the middle of the drawing room with her parents and Allayne.

"Where's Cassie?" Richard asked. "I didn't see her at the luncheon yesterday."

"She went riding," her Papa replied.

"Ah, yes," Richard chuckled. "I remember how she loved riding along the beach. We used to go every morning to watch the sunrise."

Cassandra's hand flew to her chest. He remembered, and he had come to see her! A sudden burst of joy obscured the misery she had endured throughout the night. With alacrity, all her suffering vanished. Richard was here—and that was all that mattered.

She ran toward the winding stairs to go to him. Elation filled her to bursting. She wanted to shout to the high heavens and thank God for answering her prayers.

"Do you suppose she will be back soon?" She heard Richard ask as she hurriedly descended the carpeted steps.

"Er—we can't tell for certain," her mother answered. "In the meantime, come, let us have some tea."

"Thank you, my lady," Richard replied. "I do hope she'll be back soon. I am really looking forward to introducing her to Desiree."

Cassandra grabbed the balustrade and skidded to a halt halfway down the staircase. Her gaze fastened on the blonde woman whose back was now visible from where she stood.

Lady Desiree exuded sophistication and elegance in her pale rose day dress, her skin as smooth and white as alabaster. A dainty hand rested upon Richard's arm, and Cassandra could not help but notice once again just how perfect they looked together. Both were splendidly dressed and immaculately groomed, the ideal picture of a lady of quality and a gentleman of high birth.

She caught her own reflection in the gilt-framed, mirrored panels that hung parallel to the wall abutting the stairs. A shabby girl with large eyes, tanned, sunburned skin, and mussed hair looked back at her. She appeared ridiculous in her wrinkled muddy breeches and soiled white shirt.

"I am very eager to meet her," the woman said in a cultured, melodic voice. "Richard told me so much about her." She gazed up at him, and they smiled into each other's eyes.

Cassandra saw her whole world spin and shatter into little pieces as a stab of intense jealousy besieged her. She covered her mouth with the back of a trembling hand and slowly stepped away from the railing. Her shoulders shook uncontrollably as she struggled to stifle the excruciating pain in her chest that felt like a thousand spears plowing into her heart.

From across the room facing her, her eyes met Allayne's concerned gaze.

"Go," he mouthed without a sound.

She swiveled and ran back up the stairs in a stream of blinding tears until she found herself in the safety of her bedchamber.

CASSANDRA WOKE UP to tapping on her door and saw that it was dark outside. Her head throbbed from crying, and she wondered how long she had been asleep. "Come in." She rose from her bed, rubbing her eyes and tugging at her hair to give it some semblance of order, before shrugging into her dressing gown.

Bess, her maid, came in with a tray of supper on one hand and a package in the other.

"Your friend Lord Waterford is downstairs having supper with the family, as usual. He is asking for you." She placed the tray on a table. "Also, Lord Radcliffe was here earlier. He left this for you." Bess put the package on her bed and bobbed her head, avoiding her mistress's eyes as she went to the door.

"Bess, wait." Cassandra took a step toward her.

"Oh, Miss," Bess said with a rueful expression. "I'm so sorry. Please do not be angry. We meant to tell you—I swear we did—but when the time came, we just couldn't do it."

"I see." Cassandra sighed with an inward wince. So, they did know. Everyone, including the servants knew—except her! But then, she should have guessed. The servants of the neighboring houses knew each other very well and were usually the first to hear about gossip regarding the occupants of the households.

"It's all right, Bess." Cassandra glanced at the white package with the big red bow on her bed. "Thank you for bringing this up for me. Oh, and will you please tell Jeremy—I mean, Lord Waterford—to come for luncheon tomorrow? I'll join him then."

"Yes, Miss." Bess did a quick curtsy and hurried out the door.

Cassandra picked up the box and sat on the chair by the fire. She unlaced the luxurious large velvet bow and lifted the lid. An expensive-looking porcelain doll stared up at her with wide glass eyes, and a tin container of bonbons lay next to it in a bed of pink satin.

She picked up the note with the Radcliffe family crest embossed on the wax seal and broke it open. There, in Richard's strong, flowing script, was the same message he had written year after year:

To Cassie, my little piglet.

R.R.

Year after year, she had held on to those words as if they were her very lifeline. She even envied the vellum he touched and wrote on. Like a silly, lovesick fool, she would kiss the note and hug it to herself for nights on end until the paper was close to crumbling. But now, as she read the note once again, she saw it in an entirely different light.

Piglet. Richard's memory of her was still that of a little girl with the chubby little hands that dimpled at the knuckles and pink round cheeks that he loved to pinch. To him, she was still the eight-year-old child who liked porcelain dolls and consumed an alarming number of chocolate cherry bonbons.

Piglet. Oh, how she hated it when he teased her with that name! To make him stop, she used to threaten Richard that she would start calling him a "prick"—the word Jeremy said meant an obnoxious person and something else he would not reveal no matter how much she implored. He simply assured her that Richard would abhor being called that word, and true to his promise, that threat always worked like a charm.

She took the tin container and transferred the bonbons onto a plate Bess had brought with the tray. Afterward, she returned the tin inside the box, replaced the lid, and retied the red bow. She refolded the note and placed it in a small wooden chest she kept beside her bed, along with the other notes that had accompanied every gift she received from Richard.

Her gaze settled onto the cabinet full of presents she had faithfully saved over the years.

Cassandra then stood up and went to her sitting room. She opened the large closet in the corner and extracted two large trunks. Carefully, she set one trunk on the table in front of the glass display case and the other on the settee next to it. She began to pack her dolls in the trunk on the table, taking care not to chip the fine porcelain or crease the lovely dresses they came in. After finishing that task, she packed the bonbon tins in the trunk on the settee.

IN THE DINING room downstairs, Jeremy eyed the empty chair Cassie normally occupied as he sat down for his customary supper with the Carlyle family. "Where is she?" he asked Allayne, who was seated across from him.

"Upstairs." Allayne picked up his soup spoon and sampled the steaming lobster bisque the footman ladled into the small bowl in front of him.

"Is she coming down to dine with us?" Jeremy quirked an eyebrow at his friend. Allayne's habit of using single words in a conversation could sometimes be annoying.

"Maybe," Allayne replied.

Jeremy hid his frustration as he snatched the napkin from his lap and dropped it on the table next to his plate. He pushed his chair back and stood up.

The Viscount and Lady Carlyle looked up from their soup.

"Pardon me—" He inclined his head at them. "But I must investigate what is causing Cassie's delay."

"Oh, but there is no need." Lady Carlyle set aside her spoon. "She won't be joining us. She's indisposed."

"Indisposed?" Jeremy tried not to sound incredulous.

He had known Cassie all her life, and "indisposed" was a word foreign to her vocabulary. The only times she refused to dine with her family were the days when the two of them quarreled, and she did not want to see his face. Even then, being "indisposed" was not her excuse. She simply sent her maid to announce that she would never, in a million years, dine with a mean, selfish bully, or a rotten, cocky scoundrel—her two favorite appellations for him—depending on his current offense.

"Yes, dearie." Lady Carlyle motioned for him to sit down. "Do not worry. She will be fine in a day or two. Why don't you try the soup? It really is superb. The rack of lamb will be served shortly. Isn't that one of your favorites? Morton, could you please pour more wine for Lord Waterford?"

Jeremy sighed and settled back in his chair as Lady Carlyle fussed over him, urging him to sample this dish and that, and asking the footmen to give him another serving of the rack of lamb. She might have some reservations about his friendship with her daughter and disapproved of his philandering ways, but the lady was genuinely fond of him and had treated him like her own son since his boyhood years.

Nevertheless, Jeremy had lost his appetite. He had been looking forward to seeing Cassie again after that fiasco at Grandstone Park, just to be certain she was taking everything in stride.

Apparently, she was not.

Jeremy's mood darkened, and he pushed his unfinished plate of lamb away. He wanted nothing more than to see Cassie, but he could not disappoint his kind hostess by acting sullen. Christ, he could not wait for this particular meal to end!

The dinner soon concluded, and Lady Carlyle left the men to their port. Morton, the butler, came in and discreetly conveyed a message from Cassie's maid, whispering that Miss Carlyle requested his company for luncheon on the morrow. Jeremy nodded his acceptance with little consolation. He wanted to see her now, but if she did not feel like having company, then he would have to wait until she's ready.

The viscount inquired about the investments he had made in India and America with Allayne and Richard some years ago. Jeremy reported that the market had been brisk, and their money had quadrupled. Viscount Carlyle crowed with delight. Indeed, none among the three of them was reliant upon their inheritance. They were all independently as rich as Croesus, with unentailed wealth earned from their own fastidious business sense, regardless of how much running a commercial enterprise was frowned upon by the upper ten thousand.

As their discussion came to a close, Jeremy stood up and bid his thanks and farewell, declining to join the family in their usual after-dinner game of cards. His temperament had not improved even with the viscount's excellent port.

Allayne walked him to the door.

"How is she, really?" he demanded as the footman assisted him with his coat. "And don't give me a damn one-word answer, or I swear, I'll barge into her bedchamber and see for myself."

Allayne's eyes glimmered with humor.

Jeremy bit his tongue. Cassie's brother was the only man he knew who could never be intimidated. He might be a person of a few words, but he feared no one. And no one in his right mind would dare challenge him to a duel.

"She's fine," Allayne drawled.

A two-word answer. God help him if he had the sudden urge to strangle his friend, but the man was a comic!

"Damn you, Allayne!" Jeremy scowled at him, angrily yanking his gloves on.

"Damn you, too, Jeremy," Allayne chuckled and gave him a heavy-handed slap on the shoulder before he let him out the door.

UPSTAIRS IN HER bedchamber, Cassie had finished packing away the entire contents of the cabinet. She pulled on the bell designated to summon the butler.

Five minutes later, Morton knocked on her door.

"Come in." Cassie looked up from her desk, where she had just completed writing notes to the headmistress of the orphanage and the Vicar's wife.

Morton walked in and glanced at the trunks in the middle of the room.

"Morty, see to it that this is delivered on the morrow to the orphanage." She handed him one of the notes and pointed at the trunk where she had packed the dolls. "And this one, have it sent to the vicarage." She indicated the trunk with the tin containers and gave him the other note. "The Vicar's wife can use the boxes for gift giving."

"As you wish, Miss." Morton's eyes darted to the bare glass case behind her. "Let me call some footmen to help take these down."

"Oh, and Morty?" Cassandra grabbed the plate of bonbons from the tray.

"Yes, Miss?"

"Share these with Gordy and Barty." She handed him the plateful of sweet-smelling confections.

"My cousins' names are Gordon and Barton, Miss," Morton replied primly.

"I know, Morty." Cassandra followed him to the door.

Morton paused before stepping into the hallway. "Miss Carlyle, if I may be so bold," He swallowed and dropped his gaze with a frown to the sweetmeats on the plate, "I truly am sorry. I—"

"Don't be." Cassandra shook her head. "It is for the best—really. I know that now."

"Very good, Miss." Morton cast another glance at the display cabinet and trunks.

Cassandra patted Morton's arm fondly. "Where is my family?"

"They have retired to the library, Miss." He held the door open for her.

"Is Lord Waterford still here?"

"No, Miss. He did not seem to be in his element and left as soon as he had his port."

Good, Cassandra thought as she preceded Morton out the door and made her way toward the stairs. It would be better if Jeremy did not know about her plan—at least not yet. She went down the flight of steps and crossed the drawing room, pausing for a moment to brace herself before veering off into the library.

At her sudden entrance, her father and Allayne looked up in surprise from the books they were reading. Her mother set aside her embroidery.

"Are you all right, my dear?" the viscount asked as he rose and moved toward her.

Allayne closed his book with a snap and placed it on a nearby table. "Feeling better, Cass?" he asked with concern.

"What is it, my dear? Do you need anything?" Her mother rushed to her and took her hands.

Cassandra drew a long breath, released it with a hiss, and straightened her spine. It was now or never.

"Cassie?" Lady Carlyle peered at her with apprehension.

Cassandra raised her chin and looked her mother directly in the eyes. "I'm done, Mama."

Her mother gaped at her. "Done with what, dear?"

"Waiting."

"Waiting?" The viscountess gave her a puzzled frown.

"It's time, Mama."

"Whatever do you mean?" Her mother's fine eyebrows lifted.

"I'm ready now," Cassie said with sheer determination in her voice.

"Er—ready for what, dearie?" Lady Carlyle tilted her head and peered at her with a mixture of anxiety and impatience in her expression.

Cassandra turned her gaze to her father, who stood by her mother's side. "Papa, will you take me to my first season in London?"

Viscount Rose burst into a hearty laugh and ruffled her hair, the way he always had since she was but a wee girl. "Whatever you say, pumpkin."

"God help us." Allayne scrubbed his face with his hand.

"Mama?" Cassandra raised questioning eyebrows at her mother, who still had her mouth suspended halfway in shock.

The viscountess moved her lips, but no sound came out. Then, she turned white, and her eyes crossed as she fell into a dead faint—conveniently, into her husband's waiting arms.

CHAPTER SEVEN

The London Season...

> *Dear Jeremy,*
>
> *Forgive me, but I shall not be riding with you to the village tomorrow and the rest of the coming weeks. I have decided to concede to my mother's wishes and have my first Season in London. We are leaving at first light.*
>
> *P.S.*
>
> *Don't you dare show up in London, Jeremy Huntington, and make fun of my frivolous new ballgowns or terrorize my soon-to-be suitors. I swear if you do, I will hang you by your toenails and gouge your eyes out.*
>
>

Yours most affectionately,
Cassie

JEREMIAH DEVLIN HUNTINGTON, also known as the Most Notorious Rake in all of England, stood smiling to himself at the top landing of the grand staircase in the Earl of Farthingale's impressive ballroom. He had just finished re-reading Cassie's letter, and he could not wait to see her reaction once she discovered his presence in London.

Ah—she would probably get mad and kick him on the shin when no one was looking, but he simply could not resist vexing her. He was in too much of a jovial, devil-may-care mood to be wary of what she might do. Moreover, he had come because he really missed her. Cornwall was agonizingly dull without his little brat pestering him every single day.

He folded the letter and tucked it inside his dark blue tailcoat, then swept his gaze around the ballroom. Numerous crystal chandeliers hung from the ceiling, casting a golden glow over the glittering, bejeweled crowd. Lively music emanated from the orchestra on a marble podium at the far end. In the center, several couples were dancing to the beguiling tune.

He caught sight of Lady Libbey, one of the more pertinacious matchmaking mamas, heading toward him with her daughter in tow. Not far behind her, he could see Lady Hadley frantically waving at him, dragging her eldest daughter with her. Jeremy pursed his lips. *Good God!* Five minutes into the blasted ball, and the hounds were already sniffing at his heels. He subtly slipped into the crush in an effort to lose them, only to be accosted by Lady Campbell and her two silly, simpering chits.

"Lord Waterford." Lady Campbell planted her plump self in his path, blocking his escape. "I am thoroughly delighted to see you back in town."

"Er, yes, I'm sure you are." Jeremy glanced about to look for any acquaintance of his, who could provide him with an excuse to make a swift exit. "If you'll pardon me, my lady, I have to—"

Lady Campbell practically seized his arm. "My lord, surely you'd like to meet my daughters before you remove yourself to the card room." She gestured for her girls to come closer. "May I present Lady Henrietta and Lady Georgia." Both girls curtsied and fluttered their lashes at him.

Jeremy stared at them. They both had bushy eyebrows that connected at the center spot between their eyes and a trace of a mustache beneath their thick noses. *Henry and George*, the peculiar thought struck him. The one named Henrietta had the gall to wink at him and lick her lips. Not to be outdone, her sister, Georgia, blew him a kiss while their mama, unaware of their antics, prattled on about non-sensical things. Jeremy's eyes nearly popped out of their sockets as he watched them flirt outrageously with him behind their mama's back. He suddenly wanted to put bags over their heads and run screaming from the ballroom.

"My daughters would be charmed if you would sign their dance cards..." Lady Campbell was saying.

"Waterford! Is that you?"

Jeremy blew a sigh of relief at the sound of Allayne's voice rising above the din in the ballroom. *Salvation, at last!* "Excuse me, ladies." Jeremy hastily inclined his head and walked away, not waiting for Lady Campbell to formulate a reply.

"What are you doing in London?" Allayne asked as he met him near the refreshment tables.

"Cassie sent me a note." Jeremy snared a glass of champagne from a tray carried by a passing footman. "She said she'd decided to have her first season and informed me, or rather—threatened me in no uncertain terms—not to show my face in London."

"I see." Allayne sighed. "Jeremy, this is really important to Cassie. She must find someone to make her forget Richard. I know you mean well, but—" He plunged his fingers through his hair. "Just go easy on her. She needs plenty of encouragement. She needs us—now, more than ever."

"Yes, I know." Jeremy nodded and patted Allayne on the shoulder. "That is precisely the reason why I'm here, old chap."

ON THE OTHER side of the ballroom, Cassandra carefully parted the spindly bush she had been hiding in to peek at the sea of faces around her. She had been keeping herself out of sight to avoid any more signatures on her dance card.

Her feet hurt, and she was ravenous, but her mother had particularly told her that it simply was not the thing to gobble up half the buffet. She had been handed a glass of watery lemonade and a piece of cheese, and that was that. Well now, her tummy had been growling like the very devil, and she suspected her stomach might be planning to eat her other organs for dinner.

A group of young debutantes giggled to her right as one of them pointed a discreet finger at someone whom Cassandra assumed must be one of the gentlemen in attendance nearby.

"Oh, but isn't he fine?" the girl heaved a dreamy sigh and placed her hand over her heart.

"I just adore that long, wavy black hair," said the girl in pink next to her.

"Oh—and those eyes!" another girl exclaimed.

More giggles rose from the group.

"My, but he's tall, don't you think?" the girl nearest to Cassandra, said. "And look! There are two of them. His friend with the charming dimples is likewise very handsome."

"Who are they?" the girl in the blue gown asked.

"The dark-haired one is Lord Waterford. Unfortunately, I am not acquainted with his friend," the girl who had pointed the finger replied.

Cassandra released the bushes with a rustle. So, Jeremy Huntington decided to show up and torment her after all! *The cad!* She squeezed past the group and stomped back in the direction where she had left her parents.

Allayne and Jeremy were standing next to each other with their backs to her. The girls were right, she had to admit. Both men looked very handsome in their evening finery.

With her brother Allayne's honey-blond hair, striking, chiseled features, and startling green eyes, he could have any girl in the room.

Jeremy, on the other hand, was the epitome of sin in the form of a deliciously gorgeous male with his tousled, longish black hair and eyes as dark as midnight. And if that weren't enough, the devil himself had most likely been responsible for lavishing him with thick, lengthy lashes any woman would kill for.

In Cassandra's opinion, Jeremy Huntington, with his looks and his gilded tongue's power of persuasion, was a danger to the entire female population. A veritable wolf disguised in a perfect gentleman's clothing—a philanderer and a rake, who must be castrated and locked in a cell with the keys thrown away.

Cassandra chuckled at the thought and regarded him and Allayne with genuine fondness. Even from where she stood behind them, both men looked very tall and very dashing indeed.

She suddenly remembered how they used to tease Richard when they were younger by calling him "Tiny" because, of the three of them, he was the shortest. But that epithet was quickly extinguished when he grew by leaps and bounds within a single year at the age of fifteen, quite remarkably surpassing both Allayne and Jeremy by an inch.

Cassandra bit her lip and smothered the echo of his name in her mind. *No more*, she reproached herself, pressing her lips in a rigid line. *Think of him no more.*

Just then, Jeremy turned and saw her. He bestowed her with a smile devastating enough to send every chit in the ballroom aflutter, which he followed with a slow, wicked wink. Cassandra just stood there, staring at him, astounded by how fine he looked in his splendid evening clothes. It was such a shocking change from his usual rugged attire when they rode around the vast countryside at home. Tonight, his princely countenance, impeccable grooming, and commanding physique took her breath away. She truly could not fathom what to say or do with this sophisticated, elegant version of him. Thankfully, from the corner of her eye, she caught sight of Lord Winterley, the next gentleman on her dance card, striding toward her.

JEREMY'S SMILE FROZE on his lips at the sight of Cassie. By God, she was beautiful! He clamped his teeth together to keep himself from uttering the words aloud. The pale aquamarine and gold gown Cassie wore highlighted her curves and suited her coloring becomingly. The low neckline exposed her shoulders and the creamy tops of her breasts. A choker of diamonds and emeralds adorned her throat, and a matching set of earbobs dangled from her ears.

He had never seen her so exquisitely attired before. She always preferred simple and comfortable cotton day dresses that did not do anything to flatter her figure. She never favored jewelry, either, and kept her hair confined in a long braid almost every day.

But tonight, in this ethereal silk confection, with her titian hair done in Grecian fashion, gathered high on the back of her head with half the length of it flowing in curls over one shoulder to her right breast, she stood out amongst the sea of debutantes.

He curbed the instinctive response his body made in the proximity of an alluring female. This particular female was Cassie—his childhood friend. *Keep that in mind*, he scolded himself.

"What are you staring at, brat?" He pasted a nonchalant expression on his face and cocked his head at the dance floor. "Come on. Let us dance."

"I believe Lady Carlyle owes me this dance, my lord." Lord Winterley, a young, pleasant-looking gentleman, who was as thin as a witch's broomstick and had an easy disposition, interjected.

Jeremy arched a dark eyebrow at the man and surveyed him up and down, demonstrating his displeasure with a marked frown. "Go away, Winterley." He glared mightily at him as if he were a little mouse that had escaped from under a cat's paw.

Lord Winterley's complexion colored into a bright scarlet, but he stood his ground, albeit on unsteady feet. "I say!" he exclaimed indignantly, the crimson stain high on his cheeks. "Not to be rude, my lord, but—"

Jeremy hoisted a finger in front of Winterley's nose. "Go. Away." he repeated in a sterner tone.

"Lord Winterley, please pardon Lord Waterford," Cassandra interrupted with a pointed glower at him, offering her hand to poor Winterley. "Of course, we can dance."

Lord Winterley darted his eyes at Cassandra and her outstretched hand, then made a cautious move to take it.

Jeremy bared his teeth and made a snarling sound.

Lord Winterley recoiled, casting Cassandra a helpless look before he swiftly scampered off, muttering under his breath.

"Oh, you detestable, boorish, oaf!" Cassandra stabbed a forefinger at his chest. "Look what you've done!" She fisted her hands on her hips and turned to her brother, who was observing the whole scene, noticeably trying to suppress his laughter. "Allayne! How can you just stand there and let this—this—"

"Handsome scoundrel?" Jeremy supplied with a grin.

"Shut up, Jeremy Huntington!" She slapped him on the arm. "Why are you here? I specifically recall informing you in writing that I quite clearly forbade you to come to London!"

"Cassandra!" Her mother stood up from the bench she was sharing with her husband. "Keep your voice down! Whatever is the matter with you?"

Cassandra pursed her lips and scowled.

"Come now." Jeremy nudged her with an elbow after her mother gave them a sharp lecture on proper behavior delivered in an undertone, before returning to her seat. "Don't be in such a snit. I just saved you from Winterley. He may look harmless, but he's a gambler, buried in debt up to his ears, and has no consequence whatsoever.

He's not a suitable match for you."

"Humph. This coming from you—the worst libertine in London."

"Yes," he replied on a serious note. "I know my kind, which is why I'm here—to see to it that you don't end up with one of us."

Cassandra stared at some vague point past his shoulders and remained quiet for a moment, seemingly weighing her reaction to what he had just said, before she turned her gaze back to him. "Jeremy, forgive me. I didn't mean what I said." She shook her head in frustration. "I was just—oh! I hate London and I hate balls! I am hungry and my feet hurt. I don't know what I am about anymore. I just want to go home!"

"It's all right, I had it coming." He shrugged and looked away. "You wouldn't want to be involved with a man like me, Cassie. You deserve better."

"Oh, Jeremy, I am so sorry. What I said was uncalled for." She reached out to squeeze his hand. "If anything, you've been a most wonderful friend to me for the past few years."

"And you to me." He offered his arm and gave her one of his most charming, crooked smiles. "Now, shall we dance?"

Cassandra chuckled and placed her hand in the crook of his elbow. "Ready when you are, my lord."

"Well then, let's hurry to the dance floor." He glanced over his shoulder. "Your mother is glaring daggers at me."

Cassandra let Jeremy lead her into the middle of the ballroom floor. They joined the other couples as the opening chords of a waltz flowed from the tantalizing strings of the orchestra. Jeremy put his arm around her and placed his hand on the small of her back, pulling her to him and pressing her breasts to his chest in an intimate and certainly less-than-decent manner.

Cassandra stiffened. "What are you doing?" she rasped angrily in his ear. "Release me, you oaf!"

"Be quiet and trust me." He took her right hand and held it in his.

"Put your left hand on my shoulder." He gathered her to him so closely that his breath fanned the little hairs on her temple and their faces almost touched.

"Jeremy Huntington, this is outside of propriety!" she said. "People are watching and talking!"

"I don't give a damn what they think or say." He twirled her around the dance floor. "But I do have a plan that would be highly beneficial to you."

"What plan?" Cassandra knitted her eyebrows. "I do hope this is not another one of your demented schemes."

"Far from it." Jeremy darted his eyes about the room. "Look at them—they're observing us closely—whispering, wondering. By the time this dance ends, Cassie, you will be the talk of the ton. The women will be speculating on why I singled you out, and the men will be formulating various conjectures on what aroused my interest in you. I may have a notorious reputation when it comes to the opposite sex, but the fact remains that I am still one of the wealthiest and most eligible bachelors in all of England with a high-ranking title to match. The women will want to know your secret for snaring an excellent catch, and the men will view you in an entirely different stratum simply because you have attracted my attention."

"And the whole idea behind this deranged ruse of yours is—?" Cassandra lifted skeptical eyebrows at him.

"To take the quest for your hand to new heights and raise the bar of rivalry to a more select and befitting group of gentlemen." Jeremy bestowed a besotted expression upon her.

"You are beautiful, Cassie. You come from an excellent family and have a sizeable dowry. Fortune hunters like Winterley, and social climbers like Bosworth over there, who has been ogling you for the past five minutes, by the by—will come after you in droves." He glowered fiercely at the gentleman in question. "In the meantime, the titled gentlemen in the very upper echelons of society will snub you because your father is a mere viscount, and they couldn't care less about the value of your dowry." He spun her in a graceful circle in the center, in tandem with another dancing couple.

"So, you're saying that the likes of you will ignore me simply because I am beneath your station." Cassandra frowned at him.

"Precisely. As much as possible, we prefer to form alliances that are above or equal, but never beneath our rank." He gazed at her with what one would postulate as a love-struck twinkle in his glorious eyes.

"Why are you looking at me like that? You're making me uncomfortable."

"Because I'm breaking the rules for you, my dear little brat." He gave her a heart-stopping grin and brought her right hand, the one he held, to his lips.

"This is not funny, Jeremy!" Cassandra gawked at him in shock and snatched her hand away, but he caught it right back in his again.

"Be quiet and stop fighting me." He lowered his long thick lashes and raked his dark, devilish eyes over the exposed creamy expanse of the tops of her breasts. "Very nice indeed."

"Jeremiah Huntington! I swear I'm going to gouge your eyeballs right this very second!" she hissed, stepping on his toe on purpose.

"Good." Jeremy buried his nose in her hair and inhaled deeply. "The more indifferent you are to my charms, my dear brat, the more intriguing you'll come across. They're already fascinated by you, Cassie." He raised his head and swept his gaze about the room. "I can see the Earl of Bristol and the Duke of Kingston hovering, circling like vultures awaiting their prey."

Cassandra gasped and swiveled her head to look in the same direction he had fixed his eyes on. Two fine-looking gentlemen stood not more than three yards apart and were watching her with interest. She also noticed that many of the ladies were whispering behind their fans and looking their way.

The waltz ended, and Jeremy released her gently from his hold, save for her hand. He bent his dark head over her fingers, right there in the middle of the dance floor—in full view of everyone—and planted a warm, lingering kiss on her knuckles.

Cassandra stared at him slack-jawed, flustered at his blatant show of affection.

"Welcome to your first—and last—season in London, Cassandra Carlyle," he whispered with smoldering eyes, before he placed her hand in the crook of his arm and led her back to her mother, who was gaping in horror, and her brother, who looked ready to murder him.

Thankfully, her father stepped in.

"Well done, Jeremy, my boy." The viscount beamed. He took Cassie's hand from Jeremy's arm and gave the younger man an approving pat on the back.

"I am delighted to have pleased you, sir," Jeremy drawled, bestowing her with another intense gaze and a devastating crooked smile, before melting away into the crowd, leaving a roomful of whispers and hot speculation in his wake.

CHAPTER EIGHT

Richard Christopher Radcliffe
Marquess of Sunderland

A Fortnight later...
Almack's Assembly Rooms
St. James, London

RICHARD CHRISTOPHER RADCLIFFE, heir to the Dukedom of Grandstone, had it all figured out. For the past two weeks, he had worked with his father's chief steward and solicitors to acquaint himself with the current operations of his father's various holdings and estates. He had fulfilled his father's wish for an alliance with the Duke of Glenford and had announced his betrothal to Glenford's daughter, Lady Desiree, to bring finality to their arrangement.

He never once faltered in his decision to ask for Desiree's hand once he had returned home. After all, she was a diamond of the first water—so excruciatingly beautiful that he would be foolish not to agree to the match. Everything was perfect. They were an ideal couple of equal social standing, excellent lineage, and each with an enormous fortune to their names.

Richard glanced over his shoulder at his betrothed, surrounded by adoring gentlemen who were endlessly showering her with praise. She had been basking in all the male attention for the past hour, enjoying herself, while he had been standing next to the refreshment tables with an empty lemonade glass in his hand.

Good Lord, but he was bored out of his mind! After their guests had left three days following the luncheon, Desiree and her father stayed for another week for the sole purpose of encouraging the two of them to spend time and get to know each other better. It would have been a wonderful idea—if only Desiree had the ability to experience some satisfaction derived from the simple pleasures of country life.

Richard frowned at the thought of the agonizingly long, lackluster week he had with Desiree. She had refused to go with him to the beach for fear of burning her ivory skin under the sun. She had stayed inside the coach and declined to mingle with commoners when he took her to the village to visit some of the tenants. When he asked her to go riding with him, she obliged—but only to let her horse go at a slow trot. He had almost fallen asleep on the saddle by the time they reached the gates of the estate.

As the fourth day of the week rolled by in her company, he had been in such a state of disappointment that he felt as restless as a tiger in chains. He was not used to idleness and inane conversation. He was a man who loved to spar with intelligent discussions with his friends, explore the nature around his father's lands, and pursue several types of sport, testing his physical prowess to its extreme and bask in the thrills of daring adventures.

To relieve his tedium, he had sought out Jeremy at Waterford Park only to be told by Barton, Jeremy's butler, that he had left for London twelve days earlier. He then proceeded to Rose Hill Manor to call on Allayne and Cassie, to see if they might want to go riding with him along the coast or perhaps indulge him in a stimulating game of charades, but Morton had told him that the entire family had decided to spend the season in town and closed the door in his face without further ado.

If it were not for his father's scheduled visit to his physician in

London at the end of the week, he was quite certain he would have pulled his hair out from the monotony and lack of physical activity that his betrothed seemed to favor.

Richard threw another look at Desiree and stifled a yawn with the back of his hand. As to why both of them were even in attendance at Almack's, otherwise touted as the "Marriage Mart," was beyond him. He would much rather go to White's with Allayne and Jeremy than escort his intended to this insipid ball that he had allowed her to drag him to.

He decided to stroll about the ballroom, looking for acquaintances that might entertain him with the latest goings-on in parliament. He also kept an eye out for Jeremy and Allayne, though, for the life of him, he knew not why they would be interested in attending Almack's—unless they were looking for their future brides. *The two of them would probably rather hang themselves than get leg-shackled*, he thought in amusement.

Richard continued to wander around the room, nodding at acquaintances and muttering polite greetings at the dowagers who had stopped to congratulate him on his betrothal. The room was a crush, particularly in the direction where he was headed. A large cluster of gentlemen seemed to have congregated together in one corner, transfixed by a single point of interest. The group was quite impressive. He recognized a couple of dukes, a few earls, three marquesses, and four viscounts, not counting the rest whom he was not familiar with—but who nevertheless exuded the aura of good rank and consequence.

He caught sight of the Earl of Bristol and the Duke of Kingston. Richard blew a sigh of relief. Ah, he had finally found good company. They were probably discussing some important recent developments on the implementation of new irrigation systems for farmlands. He strolled with enthusiasm toward the men.

"Why, if it isn't Sunderland." The Duke of Kingston, a tall, handsome, well-dressed man with blond hair and pale blue eyes shook his hand.

"Your Grace." Richard inclined his head at the duke, then turned to shake the Earl of Bristol's hand.

"We heard you've gotten yourself affianced." The earl, a man of average height with brown hair and warm brown eyes, said.

"Er, yes," Richard nodded with slight embarrassment. His recent engagement had become the talk of society ever since the banns had been published in the papers.

"Brilliant match, old chap." The Duke of Kingston patted him on the shoulder. "My felicitations."

"And mine," the earl added with approval.

"Thank you, Your Grace, Lord Bristol." Richard shifted his gaze toward the other gentlemen in the crowd. "What is the meeting all about? I see half the lords in parliament here."

The Duke of Kingston chuckled and shook his head. "There's no meeting, Sunderland. All of us are simply vying for the attention of a very special young lady."

"Is that a fact?" Richard raised his eyebrows in disbelief and craned his neck over the gentlemen's heads. Even Desiree had not attracted such a sizeable and illustrious audience, apart from the young bucks who all but did nothing other than fawn and prattle some drivel at her.

"You won't look so skeptical once you see her," the earl said. "You might even momentarily forget about your Lady Desiree, if you'll pardon my presumptuousness. For this jewel is as beautiful as your betrothed—if not more so, and charmingly clever, too."

"All in good humor—no offense taken," Richard shook his head and shrugged. "But I do doubt the veracity of your claim, Bristol," he continued with a laugh. "If what you say is true, then she must be an angel descended from the heavens who brought her gifts of wisdom for the consumption of mortals. A mere woman cannot embody such perfection."

"Prepare to be astonished, then. Why don't you go see for yourself?" The duke jerked his chin toward the middle of the crowd in an invitation for him to take a closer view of their subject.

"Very well." Richard wove his way through the group of men who seemed mesmerized by the ongoing discourse coming from the center of the crowd.

As he came nearer, the first thing he saw was a glimpse of red-gold hair. It shone beneath the lights of the chandeliers and cascaded in loose ringlets from the top of her head down to her nape, snaking into a mass of silky curls on the side of her neck before disappearing over her shoulder.

Richard felt the sudden urge to twine his fingers in the rich, gleaming locks and bury his nose in its softness. Who was this woman who held captive such an impressive audience?

Intrigued, he pushed his way closer.

From where he stood behind her, the elegant line of her neck came into view, tapering into feminine shoulders exposed for male appreciation by the scoop neckline of her dress. The same neckline plummeted several inches at the back to display the gentle curve of the top of her spine. Richard followed the slight indentation the column made on her smooth skin, from the base of her hairline to the place where her dress concealed the rest of its length. Her complexion was silky and glowing with health, which made it apparent she loved spending a little time under the sun.

His interest peaked.

He shouldered his way to the front where he might behold her face. His build and stature gave him the advantage he sought to carve his place among the worshipping men.

"But, Lord Cavanaugh, I beg to disagree," she was saying to one of his peers as he strained to his full height for a better view. "If your standard for a wife is that of beauty and docility alone, surely you aren't thinking of thirty years with her down the road. What would you do once her teeth fall out and her chin drooped to her knees? Now—if we were speaking of a horse, then I would agree with you completely. Nothing could be more pleasing than having a mount that is beautiful and docile at the same time."

"Cavanaugh, I believe you just got yourself bested," the gentleman next to the dashing, fair-haired young lord elbowed him amidst the snickers.

Lord Cavanaugh inclined his head and laughed good-naturedly. "Which is why, my dear, I am here before you with my heart on a silver platter. I have added intellect to my list, and only you can fill all the requirements."

A mellifluous laugh flowed like honey from her lips. "I regret to disappoint you, my lord, but alas, I prefer gold over your silver platter."

Loud guffaws sounded from her enthralled audience.

"Have mercy on my poor heart." Lord Cavanaugh clutched his chest in a dramatic fashion. "Don't let it wither and die, for it is only you that it seeks."

"And what about your brain, my lord?" she cocked her head to the side. "Doesn't it have any say in the matter, or has it been sleeping all along?"

"Cavanaugh's brain hasn't been sleeping, Miss," Lord Edmonton, the tall, handsome heir to an earldom, stepped forward from the crowd. "It's been swimming in brandy since this morning!"

Laughter erupted from the gentlemen as the two lords engaged in pleasant banter and endured friendly ribbing from their peers, as Richard squeezed his way only a few steps apart from the young lady. Amid the merriment and without warning, she turned away from Lord Cavanaugh's bewitched gaze to look directly into his eyes.

Richard's breath hitched in his chest.

He had never seen such stunning green eyes, veiled by the longest lashes that curled outward to emphasize their size. Her face was heart-shaped, her nose, small and straight. She had full lips shaped in a gentle cupid's bow, undoubtedly made for nothing else but kisses. His gaze slid down to her generous breasts.

Good God, she truly was an angel! He feasted his eyes over the rest of her curves before he dragged them back to the jeweled green depths of her gaze.

What he found there, unexpectedly, was recognition. His heart leapt and began to pound. Had they met before? If they had, he certainly could not recall when, where, or how. What was he supposed to do? How was he supposed to act? Should he feign an acknowledgment?

He offered her a small, tentative smile. No, they had never been introduced before—he was quite sure of it. Moreover, he did not wish to appear fresh.

But then, as quickly as he saw the look of recognition in her eyes, it was extinguished—shadowed by some semblance of uncertainty before annoyance replaced it completely.

The smile disappeared from her lips, and she averted her face, flicking her fan open, obstructing his view with the wedge-shaped silk, painted with roses and butterflies.

Richard Christopher Radcliffe, the heir to the Dukedom of Grand-stone—could not believe it.

The innocent-looking angel who made his blood boil and his heart pitter-patter in a rhythmic symphony had just given him the cut-direct—in front of not just anybody—but half of London's most prestigious peers!

CHAPTER NINE

An encounter at Almack's...

S HE HAD SEEN him—*Richard*—as she parried Lord Cavanaugh's ardent suit. Oh God, but she was not ready to encounter him just yet! Her shock in finding those piercing blue eyes in the crowd had completely paralyzed her. Cassandra had stared at him, rooted to the spot like a moon-eyed ninny, and she knew he had noticed. Despite everything that had happened, her affection for him still thrived in her heart, even if the dictates of her brain alerted her to flee. It had taken all her willpower to do just that.

"Gentlemen, if you will please excuse me." She turned away from him, holding her fan up like a shield to hide the rush of warmth in her cheeks.

"May I escort you to a seat?" Lord Cavanaugh immediately offered.

"Would you like something to drink?" Lord Winterley asked.

"Perhaps I can procure you a slice of cake," the Earl of Bristol said from behind her.

"Oh no—thank you, all of you." She feigned a grateful smile as the men parted to let her through, and she began to walk away on shaky legs. "I simply need some air."

"Allow me then, to escort you to the balcony." A large hand caught her arm. Startled, she whipped her head sideways and found herself looking into the bluest eyes she had beheld in her life.

Without waiting for a reply, Richard took her hand and placed it in the crook of his arm, securing it there with his hand firmly on top of hers. He swiftly led her away from the rest of the bewildered gentlemen.

"My lord, if you please—" Cassandra attempted to ease her gloved hand from his grasp, struggling to keep her composure. "I truly am in no need of an escort." She had not expected this—not from the Richard she knew, who had always been considerate and well mannered.

This man, who obviously could not take no for an answer, and whom she had somewhat offended by refusing to acknowledge his wordless, but amicable, greeting in the form of a tentative smile, was not to be trifled with.

Goosebumps rose on her skin, and beads of sweat erupted on her forehead as the winds of caution enveloped her.

"I simply wish to speak with you." His voice was firm, and his hand closed over hers more tightly as he guided her into a nearby alcove.

They stood face to face in the small space that concealed them from the ballroom and provided them with some semblance of privacy. His gaze roamed over her features, searching her countenance with an expression of curious interest.

Cassandra found herself arrested once again by those intelligent eyes. No—she could not be alone with him like this! She was not prepared to deal with him, to stand this close, to feel the dense muscles on his arm beneath her fingers and the warmth of his hand touching hers through her glove. He still affected her like an enraptured fool, leaving her agitated, trembling, and mesmerized under the gaze of an Adonis.

"What do you want?" She feigned irritation, lifted her chin, and made an effort to look brave, even as her knees shook beneath her skirts.! The breadth of his shoulders almost filled the alcove, blocking the light and the noise, and he smelled so wonderful that she yearned to crawl inside his coat.

"I need to know if we've met before—"

"No, never. I don't know you," she abruptly cut in, pulling her hand away almost regretfully from his loosened grasp. She had delighted in the feel of those strong fingers encircling hers.

Richard regarded her thoughtfully and took a step closer. "Are you certain? Something about you seems familiar—"

"No," she interjected even more vehemently. "I've never seen you before in my life."

Richard searched her face for a moment, then the corners of his mouth curled. He took another lazy step toward her and propped himself on his hands on either side of her head.

She shifted her attention to his impeccably tied cravat, and tension filled the air.

Richard's eyes slid down to her bosom and lingered there. Without even touching her, she could feel the intensity of his hot gaze. For a moment, Cassandra thought her knees would give way. He was such a virile man that his mere nearness could elicit titillation in any female. She leaned against the wall at her back for support.

"If that's the case, then, allow me to introduce myself," he drawled in a deep, sultry voice.

He lowered his head until his breath fanned on her cheek, their lips separated only by a mere inch. *Oh God, he is going to do it—he is going to kiss me!* Cassandra stared at his chiseled mouth that she had imagined kissing countless times in her dreams. She could almost taste its sweetness, feel its firmness against her own. By its own volition, her tongue darted out and wet her lips.

Richard's eyes instantly dropped to her mouth.

Oh, how she wanted him! She craved him so badly; she could feel the burn of submission in the marrow of her bones. But she was not going to. No—she could not give in. He was not hers to covet. He was never hers to begin with.

"Please, my lord," she managed to croak over the thunder of her heart.

Richard's gaze met hers. "Please what?" he whispered as he inched even nearer until she could swear his mouth was but a hairline from touching hers.

Cassandra shook her head. She could talk no more. She could not even think. Not with him standing this close, not with the tips of her breasts brushing against his chest, not when every nerve in her body was screaming for his caress. She could only look at him and plead with her eyes.

Then, he drew a deep breath and exhaled it slowly before the corners of his mouth lifted. "Lord Sunderland, at your service." He brought her fingers to that sensuous, masculine mouth of his. "And you are?"

"I, my lord," Cassandra snatched her hand away before her resolve crumbled, and she made a complete twit of herself, "am leaving."

She ducked under his arm and sidled past him, swiftly striding toward the well-heeled crowd to separate herself from him. As to how she had gathered the strength to make her legs move and carry out her escape, she could not remember.

CHAPTER TEN

Finding Prince Charming at the masquerade
Two days later…

C ASSANDRA WOVE HER way through the throng of guests in the crowded ballroom at Countess Libbey's masquerade ball. This unconventional affair was not exactly what her mother considered appropriate for a young debutante, but after much arguing and begging, Cassandra had finally worn Lady Carlyle down and succeeded in persuading her to allow her to attend. Her mother had reluctantly granted her permission on the condition that Allayne must accompany them as an extra chaperone.

Predictably, her older brother, who disliked overly frivolous socials that required guests to wear silly costumes, took some convincing. He only conceded when he learned that Jeremy would be meeting them there. By the time he grudgingly agreed, however, it was too late in the day. As a result, Cassandra did not have enough time to acquire a proper costume. Fortunately, her mother had found a beautiful Venetian mask at a shop in Bond Street that would go perfectly with an elaborate shimmering gown that Bess had managed to dig up in the attic.

So here she was, disguised as an ice princess, looking ethereal and utterly out of place in white and silver, amidst a sea of Medieval Royalty, shepherdesses, dominos, highwaymen, and God knows what. Nevertheless, that did not dampen her enthusiasm for the occasion.

Truth be told, this was the first gathering that had excited her in weeks. Even now, as she surveyed her surroundings with her mother and Allayne, she could not contain her delight at the darkened ballroom decorated with torches and medieval arches rising to the high ceilings, transforming the place into a magical castle of old. Giant faux-winged serpents clung to the towering pillars on all four corners, baring their sharp fangs at the festivity below. After all those tedious balls she had been attending and the proper façade she had to put on for the sake of appearances, she was quite ready to kick up her heels, have some fun, and do some serious mischief.

She searched the crowd for Jeremy, her partner in all things exciting and forbidden, but he was nowhere to be found. Either he was late again, as was his wont, or she had overlooked him in the heavily disguised crowd. Of course, it did not help that she had been so empty-headed lately from her encounter with Richard two days ago that she'd forgotten to ask what costume he would be wearing tonight.

"There's Countess Libbey," her mama said as she waved at their host, who was sitting with a group of dowagers near an open window. "Come, let us congratulate her on the success of her masquerade."

"Mama, may I be excused?" Cassandra touched her mother's arm to gain her attention after a half-hour of sitting and listening to all the on-dits her mama and the dowagers were tattling about.

"I'll go with her," Allayne quickly added, sending her a serious look.

"All right, my dear." Her mama patted her hand and then turned to her brother. "Allayne, do be certain not to let your sister out of your sight."

"You need not escort me," Cassandra said under her breath as they walked away. "I'm going to the ladies' retiring room!"

"We both know you're not." Allayne looked sideways at her.

"Oh, Allayne! Must you be a bore?" Cassandra exclaimed, abruptly stopping in her tracks and facing her brother. "If I spend another minute listening to all that tittle-tattle, I swear, I am going to scream! I am dying to explore this townhouse and take part in the festivities. Now, if you do not wish to accompany me, then let us just go back and sit with Mama again."

Allayne took a deep breath and let it out in a long-suffering sigh. "You're my responsibility. If anything untoward happens to you, Mama and Papa are going to have my hide."

"It's just a party, Allayne, and we practically reside three houses down from here. I am perfectly capable of looking after myself." Cassandra threw her hands up in exasperation when her brother seemed unconvinced. "Listen. I simply wish to admire the decorations and perhaps look for something to eat. Look! There is the card room. Don't you want to join your peers and enjoy yourself, rather than sitting with Mama for the next three hours?"

Allayne grimaced at her mention of the length of time he would have to endure with the dowagers. He gazed longingly at the revelry going on in the card room before his resistance crumbled. "All right." He hoisted a forefinger in front of her face. "One hour. Meet me by the refreshment tables. If you are not there, I swear I'll not let you drive my phaeton for a month!"

"Oh, Allayne! Thank you!" Cassandra hugged him tightly and kissed him on the cheek.

"Good Lord, what did I do to deserve a lovely, maddening sister like you?" Allayne said when they parted from their embrace. "One hour, do you hear me?" He gave her a warning glare over his shoulder as he turned and strode toward the card room.

CASSANDRA CIRCLED THE perimeter of the opulent ballroom. The footmen, bearing trays of wine in silver chalices, were garbed in leather armor mimicking ancient gladiators. The ball was in full swing, and the guests were lively and daring. They laughed, drank, cavorted in dark nooks and—good heavens—even in plain view! Lord help her; she did not even want to know what went on in the gardens below.

Oh, but this was all so scandalous! She shivered in shocked delight. She had never thought she would say it, but she preferred this event over any of the formal balls she had attended. The anonymity afforded by the masks permitted everyone to enjoy the ball freely, without cause for worry over decorum for once.

Cassandra squeezed between a fairy and a courtier and peered at the dancing couples in the center of the room. Where the devil was Jeremy? She giggled at the kissing couples. Lord, they were doing it even in the middle of the dance floor! This really was a bit too much. And speaking of Jeremy—she would not be surprised if he was flirting in some dim corner with a milkmaid—the wretch! He had probably forgotten all about their plan to pour soap powder in Countess Libbey's Grecian fountain in the garden.

A glimpse of the large marble and bronze clock with a reclining maiden attired in a golden robe made her squirm when she saw that the time Allayne had allowed her had ended. She was about to turn around in the direction of the refreshment tables to return to her brother, who was most likely going mad looking for her, when a tall, magnificently garbed prince bowed before her.

"My princess, may I have this dance?" he drawled in that familiar voice, making her insides constrict into a tight knot.

She tilted her head up and saw brilliant blue eyes behind his gold mask. His thick, straight blonde hair was tied at the back with a black ribbon, and he bestowed her a dazzling smile that made her knees weak.

Richard.

She suddenly lost her tongue, and all she could do was stare at him like a simpleton.

"Such silence, my princess." He reached for her limp hand and kissed it. "What could it mean? Should I take it to mean, yes?"

Cassandra's mind raced. Richard was asking her to dance! How many times had she imagined herself in his arms, twirling in time to heavenly music and with eyes only for each other? Should she accept? Would it be proper? Where was his fiancée?

She swept her gaze around the ballroom. None of the ladies present approximated Lady Desiree's description, but then again, this was a masquerade. People were not supposed to be recognized.

"It is but a simple dance, my princess," Richard whispered. "I beg you not to break my heart and run away from me again."

Cassandra stiffened at his words. Could it be possible that he recognized her from Almack's? Her hand went up to touch her mask, which was intricate but also covered only her eyes and not the rest of her countenance. It would be easy enough for her to be recognized if one had seen her face up close and knew the distinctive shade of her hair.

"You do remember who I am, do you not?" He answered her unspoken question. "I must apologize for my previous behavior, but you have captivated me with your wit and beauty. I must plead my enchantment with you to forgive my audacious assertions. I confess, I felt more than inclined that night to offer you my heart on a gold platter to supersede Lord Cavanaugh's silver."

Cassandra frowned. How dare he allude to his feelings for her when the whole of London was *au courant* with his betrothal? "Yes, I remember who you are," she retorted curtly with a lift of her chin. "I am also aware that you, my lord, are betrothed to a fair lady of the ton."

"So—you've been paying attention." His eyes held a satisfied gleam. "But she is not here now. If I may speak plainly, I have lost some sleep thinking if I might have made a rash decision and made the wrong choice. For I must confess, ever since I saw you, my mind has been filled with no one but you. You have bewitched me, my princess.

I came here solely to try my luck in finding you and perhaps spend a few moments in your company."

His words took her breath away. Cassandra could not quite believe what she was hearing. He had said everything she had always wanted him to say, declared with utmost conviction his feelings for her. But nothing changed the fact that he was a man betrothed. He may have come here to be with her, but he had not yet broken his engagement—a fact he had revealed himself.

No. She could not possibly allow herself to be involved with him. Her heart pounded so forcefully that her ears rang, and her breathing quickened. Somewhere in the background, she heard the beginnings of a waltz and felt his fingers gently tug on her hand.

"Please, princess." She detected the note of appeal in his voice. "Would you grant me the honor of a dance?"

She hesitated. Did he sincerely mean what he had said about his sentiments for her—or was it just some cruel jest at her expense? Was he trying to charm her into submission so he could get her into his bed? She looked into his eyes and saw nothing except a sincere, open plea to dance with him. Her contrived imperviousness to his charms disintegrated.

"Very well." She allowed him to lead her onto the dance floor, all the while assuring herself that there was no need to fret overmuch.

As they took their places in the center of the room, she suddenly remembered her brother. He would surely box her ears if he caught her dancing with Richard! She furtively peeked over his shoulder at the people milling along the perimeter of the ballroom. A sigh of relief escaped her when she ascertained that Allayne was nowhere in the crowd. He may have missed the passage of time, or he may have seen Jeremy in the card room and decided to linger a bit longer. Either that, or he may have chosen to remain at their meeting place, imagining himself wringing her neck as he waited for her.

Anxiety over her brother's wrath made her pulse race, but she gathered herself and smiled up at Richard as the orchestra played the first notes of the waltz. Really—there was no need to fuss. For it was only a dance. Richard could rejoin his betrothed afterward, and she could return to her murderous brother.

However, as soon as Richard swept her into the graceful movements of the waltz, she realized how mistaken she was. The heat of his hand warmed the small of her back, and his broad chest obscured others from view, leaving her secluded with him, locked in a magical ballroom; a prince and a princess isolated from the rest of the kingdom.

And God help her, but he danced effortlessly, flawlessly, gracefully! They glided and twirled in unison on the dance floor, with fluid steps guided by his expertise.

His eyes never left hers, and Cassandra realized with a jolt of awareness, that this was not just a dance. This was the beginning of a courtship—one that, both of them were well aware—was forbidden.

Cassandra suppressed the seed of disappointment that bloomed in her belly. Why could not fate be kinder? Why couldn't she have him to herself when here he was, offering himself to her without reserve? What had she done that had been so wrong as to offend the gods in heaven and bestow such inevitable doom upon her head?

"I don't even know your name," Richard whispered in her ear. "I'd like to see you again, princess, if you will let me."

Cassandra snapped her head up, alarm rising in her throat. She had almost forgotten. They might have spoken to each other at Almack's, but she had never given him her name! He did not know who she truly was, nor did any of the guests in this house. Both of them were just nameless painted faces in a sea of costumed guests.

Could it be possible for her to be with him for just one night, shrouded under the protection of anonymity? To delight in his embrace, to lose herself in his kiss for just a few stolen moments before he was gone? Could she have Richard, at least once, before he was taken away from her forever?

Cassandra's heart lurched in earnest at the thought. He could never be hers—what else was there for her to lose? Life was too short to spend wondering about what could have been. What difference would it make if she took her chances with him now? One night was all she needed to share an embrace and a few kisses—a treasured moment in time where each of them belonged to no one but each other.

"Meet me by the fountain in the garden," she said with a slight tremor in her voice as the waltz ended. Then, she slid from his arms and disappeared into the festive throng with a mixture of excitement and trepidation at her brazenness.

A few minutes later, she emerged from the veranda and made her way into the dimly lit gardens below. Lanterns lined the path and flickered from the trees as she wandered deeper into the hedges. Around her, concealed from view, she could hear the giggles and murmurs of couples out on a rendezvous.

She wrinkled her eyebrows as she came upon a centerpiece with the statue of Aphrodite on a pedestal. From where she stood, the pathway divided into three lanes. She wondered where the blasted fountain could be before deciding that the most practical way would be to take the middle. However, as she neared the end of the trail, she heard the gush of water not just from the path up ahead but also from either side of the tall hedges separating the pathways.

She paused in her tracks, uncertain of what to do as she realized there was more than one fountain. The garden on this part of the property was the farthest from the house, and it was very dark, save for an occasional flickering lantern spaced a good distance apart from each one than those nearer to the residence. Only the silken light of the moon served as the other form of illumination that washed over the landscape, turning everything it touched into a somber shade of silver and gray.

Everything in the landscape appeared grotesque and mysterious, even somewhat sinister, inciting a spurt of uncertainty and apprehensiveness in her bosom. An eerie silence pervaded the unfamiliar surroundings, and she had the unnerving feeling that unseen creatures hiding in the shrubbery were watching her every move.

Cassandra hugged herself, rubbing her arms, and wondered if she should just give up and turn around. At the unexpected echo of strange noises and rustling coming from the trees, she whipped around this way and that, peering into the darkness, straining her eyes to see. Maybe this was a mistake. Perhaps she should return to Mama and Allayne.

She began to back away and retrace her steps, but then, from the corner of her eye, she caught a distinct movement to her right. Spinning in that direction, she caught a glimpse of the prince of her dreams, resplendent in his magnificent royalty costume. *Richard.* He had his back turned, facing the enormous fountain—waiting for her.

A renewed determination shot through her veins. Her heart began to pound. She could do this. She would not miss it for anything. Sweat broke upon her brow, and she wiped hands that had suddenly turned clammy on her skirt. But then, a crackle broke the stillness as she stepped on a dried leaf, and he turned swiftly at the sound to face her. On impulse, she swiftly rose on her tiptoes and wrapped her arms around his neck, pulling him into a passionate kiss before she completely lost her nerve.

And dear God, did he match her passion with his own! Despite her inexperience, she took his lead, mirroring his movements, receiving him wholeheartedly without hesitation.

Their tongues twined, and he explored her mouth with such skill it made her moan and melt in his arms. He was a wonderful kisser, just the way she had imagined him to be.

The kiss went on and on until she felt his hand slide up to cup her breast and squeeze it gently. She gasped as his thumb rolled her nipple over the thin silk of her dress. Then, he plundered her mouth some more in a demanding kiss that swept the air from her lungs.

Cassandra's knees turned to jelly at the intensity of the rapture they shared. She leaned heavily against him, lost in her own slice of heaven on earth. His arms tightened and fastened her possessively against him, crushing her breasts into his hard, muscled chest. Her mind deserted her when suddenly, his mouth left hers and skimmed over her throat, gliding downward in a lazy course until his tongue found the cleft between her breasts and dipped inside with wet, slow strokes.

A surge of warmth flooded the triangle between her thighs, and she closed her eyes at the overwhelming desire she felt, allowing him to feast on her bosom. When she couldn't stand the sensations he aroused any longer, she clutched his hair to bring his mouth back to hers. She wanted to keep on kissing him forever! She wanted to remember his taste, his scent, the feel of his mouth and hands on her. She wanted to imprint his whole person in her memory so that when this dream ended, she could play it in her mind over and over again whenever the wretchedness of missing him overtook her.

A small protest escaped her lips when he pulled abruptly away, breaking their fervent kiss and yanking her unceremoniously out of her magical fantasy.

"I see you've been practicing," he drawled in that unmistakable voice Cassandra would recognize even on her deathbed.

"Oh!" She gasped in shock and sprang away from him like a frightened rabbit, still panting from the heat of his bold advances. A feeling of horror slowly stemmed in her gut and snaked up to her flaming cheeks.

"J-Jeremy?" she managed to say in a small voice.

"Who the devil did you think it was?" He pulled off his mask and gave her that heart-stopping, crooked smile of his. "Prince bloody Charming?"

Chapter Eleven

Afterglow from the kiss…

ASSANDRA HAD NEVER felt so utterly mortified in her life.
"Oh my God! Jeremy, you lecherous oaf!" She shoved him away from her, shocked beyond words at her gaffe and his presumptuousness. How dare he kiss her like that and fondle her—her—

"Did you remember to bring the soap powder?" he asked blithely as if nothing significant had happened between them.

"What?" she exclaimed in dismay, feeling the gradual burn of anger rising in her throat.

"The soap powder for—" He pointed over his shoulder with his thumb at the enormous fountain decorated with frolicking cherubs and half-naked maidens a few feet away from where they stood.

"I heard what you said, you dolt!" She didn't know what to think. "How can you just stand there and ask for the stupid soap?"

"Why? Weren't we supposed to soap the Libbeys' fountains just like we always did at their seat in the country? You do remember that the countess always anticipated and adored the amusement." He pursed his lips and raised a dark eyebrow. "Don't tell me you forgot to bring some."

"You just had your tongue in my mouth, and your paws on my breasts, you lascivious ogre, and all you can think about is the soap?" Cassie yelled at him through clenched teeth.

"Oh—that." He grinned.

"Yes, that!" she fairly screamed at him, closing her hands at her side. He had better have a sufficient explanation for his actions, or she swore, she would plant a shiner on those gorgeous, wicked eyes of his.

"Where did you learn how to kiss like that?" He waggled his eyebrows at her, annoying her even more.

"Nowhere!" She felt the blood rush to her cheeks and was thankful that the darkness hid her embarrassment. "What sort of idiotic question is that?"

"Just wondering." He shrugged and inspected his nails.

"Wondering?" She placed her hands on her waist and glared at the vexing, incorrigible swine. "Wondering about what?"

"Nothing, really." He blinked in all innocence—which fueled her ire even more.

"Nothing? That's all you can say—nothing? You're not even going to apologize for molesting me—you shameless, insensitive beast?"

"Why should I?" He snorted with a twist of his lips. "You started it."

"I—what?" She gaped at him with disbelief. Did the galling, tactless fiend just say what she thought he had said?

"You—" he reiterated by pressing his forefinger on her forehead with a little jolt as if to juggle her brains on the correct order of things, "started it."

Cassandra was at a loss for words. Yes, she had sort of—started it, hadn't she? And he had, sort of—played along with her, hadn't he? Her anger melted into a puddle, and she would have admitted her gaffe right there and then, and been done with it—if he had just shut his mouth and waited for her to extract her way out of her faux pas to save face.

But oh, no—this was Jeremy, the King of Unmannerly Louts, and he had to mumble something about her attacking him with a lewd kiss, like some lusty tart, compromising *his virtue* as a proper gentleman.

After that audacious retort, she failed to hear the rest of what he was saying. Her wrath had thundered back with a vengeance worthy of the Norman Invasion! To describe her state of mind at that very moment—well, to put it bluntly—she simply exploded The devil himself must have possessed her sensibilities because the expletives that spewed from her mouth shocked even the jaded Jeremy. She had thrown a tantrum so furious that the next thing she knew, her fan had broken in two, Jeremy had ended up in the fountain, hands clutched on his groin, and for some reason, she had lost a shoe.

All she could think of, as she marched off in a huff minus one slipper without looking back, was how dare he act so dense and unmindful of her feelings after what had happened between them? Didn't all that kissing and touching affect him at all? Did he see her as just another one of the many women he had debauched without remorse? *Ha!* The conscienceless brute! He should thank his lucky stars that she still had to deal with her brother, Allayne, or else he would be swinging by his toenails, with his eyes gouged out and fed to the elves in the Libbeys' garden! But she'd never tell her brother.

Later that night, she was still ruminating about the same questions as she lay on her tester bed staring at the canopied ceiling. She could not understand her reaction to his kiss and his caresses. He had woken something she was unfamiliar with—a yearning, a need to experience all those things she had covertly read about in those naughty pamphlets hidden under Allayne's bed. Despite her resentment and vexation at what Jeremy had done, she could honestly not find it in herself to feel violated, no matter how much she thought she ought to be.

On the contrary, she was more disappointed when he nonchalantly dismissed the episode. She had been waiting for him to bestow that crooked smile on her—and tell her how amazing their kiss had felt, how different she was from all the other girls, how wonderful, how special it had been. But instead, Cassandra frowned in the darkness.

Apparently, the cad did not feel the need to reassure her. He was as bland as a boiled potato and as romantic as a side dish of turnip. She pounded her pillow and pulled the sheets up to her chin, willing herself to cease thinking about the infuriating, wicked man, as she drifted off to sleep.

CHAPTER TWELVE

The spectacle at the Templeton soiree
Two days later...

J EREMY STOOD WITH a flute of champagne in his hand next to a large
pillar on the stairway landing, watching Cassie hold court in the
ballroom below. She was dressed in a pale lavender and silver gown
instead of the tawdry, virginal white that debutantes favored. Tonight,
her hair was piled on top of her head, held in place with diamond-
encrusted combs on either side, loose ringlets framing her heart-
shaped face.

She looked gorgeous.

Her court was impressive as usual, composed of high-ranking
peers of the realm and a few others who had the gall to pay their suit,
despite the intimidating rivals. His plan of increasing her chances for a
good match had certainly worked. Her suitors now included the most
eligible bachelors of the ton.

Jeremy slid a little farther back into the shadow of the pillar to
conceal himself not just from the matchmaking mamas, but also from
Cassie. She had been utterly furious at him for what had happened at
the masquerade ball and had since refused to see him.

Jeremy smiled to himself as he took a long sip of the bubbly liquid.
She had been vexed to the extreme when, after she had recovered
from her shock, he asked her if she had remembered to bring the soap
powder for the fountain—as if nothing of import had occurred in the

past ten minutes. Truth be told, that was simply his way of distracting her, for he had lost his self-possession, agitated at the gravity of how she had affected him during their encounter.

What a nasty fit she had thrown! Kneeing him in the groin and breaking her fan over his head, not to mention all the horrid names she had called him—which he had taught her when they were children, by the by. And then, when he had told her she was the one who had started it, kissing him like a tart in the first place—he was clobbered with a shoe and pushed into the fountain without further ado.

Ah, so what if he had gone home dripping like a wet rag, his costume smudged with slimy moss, to the dismay of his coachman and discomfiture of his valet, Percy? In all honesty, that was the most fun he had had in the last fortnight! Jeremy chuckled as he swirled the last of his drink in the glass.

However, after three days had passed and still Cassie refused his calls, he had begun to miss her. He'd even worried that he might have overstepped his boundaries this time, for even though he'd meant to just play along at the beginning, the moment their lips touched, he was made aware of the fact that his little brat—was no longer little. In fact, she was a full-grown woman with luscious curves and a coquettish streak that had both astonished and aroused him.

It had not been his intent to get carried away—no—certainly not at all, but his libido had taken over his brain, and everything had gone quite hazy and fervid from there.

Jeremy tipped the champagne flute to his mouth and drank its entire contents. Tonight, he planned to grovel at her feet to gain her favor back. He had likewise promised himself to remember that Cassie was Allayne's little sister. If even a peep of what he had done to her reached her brother's ears, he would be facing a duel opposite Allayne's gun barrel at the first crack of dawn.

He sobered at the thought. Allayne's aim was so damned sharp, he could blow anyone's brains out with his eyes closed. It would be in his best interest if he kept his hands to himself and maintained a respectful relationship between them.

Jeremy handed the flute to a passing footman and emerged from his hiding place, striding with purposeful steps toward the group of men surrounding Cassie. An unfamiliar pang of regret clutched him in the chest as he neared, for he knew that one of them would someday claim her, and he would lose her forever. He frowned and shoved the thought aside. None of them deserved her, except perhaps the Duke of Kingston, who was the paragon of excellence in all things, in which he, Jeremiah Devlin Huntington, was not.

"Jeremy!" He paused and swung around at the sound of a familiar voice calling his name.

Richard waved at him from a few yards away and began to walk toward him.

"It's good to see you, old chap!" Richard patted him on the shoulder as soon as he reached him.

"Same here." Jeremy returned the warm gesture. In spite of the hurt Richard had unknowingly inflicted on Cassie, he did miss his old friend and was glad he was back in town. "I didn't see you come in. Have you been here long?"

"No, we've barely arrived." Richard cocked his head toward Lady Desiree, who was in a conversation with a group of gentlemen.

Jeremy glanced at the blonde beauty basking in all the male attention and wondered how Richard could stand the constant swarm of fawning men around her. "I thought your father was ill. What are you doing in London?"

"My father was due for his regular visits to his physicians, so here we are," Richard spread his arms wide. "Who is with you? Have you seen Allayne?" He craned his neck to look over the crowd.

"Yes, he's over there." Jeremy turned and raised his hand to beckon Allayne, who immediately excused himself from the group of gentlemen he was speaking with and headed toward them.

"Ah, but if it isn't the blushing groom." Allayne gave Richard two forceful smacks on the back. "So, how has life been treating you, old boy? Do you feel the noose gradually tightening around your neck?"

RICHARD CHUCKLED AND picked up a glass of champagne from the tray a footman offered to them. He took a leisurely sip from it, watching the tiny bubbles as they rose to the surface. When he looked up again, he saw that Allayne and Jeremy were eyeing him with interest, eagerly awaiting his response. He sighed. They had been friends for so long that they could almost figure out each other's thoughts.

"Would it be ridiculous if I told you—" He only had two best friends in the whole world, and both of them were standing here, waiting for an the truth. "I—ah …" He chuckled again and shook his head. Now—if he could only get past the damned lump wedged in his throat!

"What is it, old chap?" Allayne gave him another heavy-handed smack on the back, which was probably what he had needed to dislodge whatever was blocking his windpipe.

"I suppose—what I was trying to say was—I met someone else," he said in one breath, and even then, he could not keep himself from smiling.

True, the lady had rejected him not only once or twice—but thrice, God help him! However, he simply could not disabuse himself of the notion that she was not indifferent to him. Lord, just the way she looked at him made his heart croon! And despite his greatest efforts, he could not deny a certain connection he felt with her—a deep, natural affinity that both fascinated and mystified him.

"You're jesting!" Allayne's eyes widened.

"No, he's not." Jeremy smirked and twirled a forefinger around and around his ear. "He's gone daft, that's what."

Richard felt the heat rising on his cheeks. He most definitely was not jesting, but Jeremy was probably right. He had most certainly gone mad. "I am dead serious." He looked both men in the eyes. "I feel troubled—and trapped at the moment."

"Good God!" Allayne scrubbed his hand on his face. "You feel trapped—with her." He pointed in the direction of Lady Desiree. "One of the most beautiful, desirable, best-dowered ladies of the ton."

Richard let Allayne's words sink in before he replied, "I know it's hard to believe, but yes. That's exactly how I feel."

"I'm intrigued." Jeremy narrowed his shrewd dark eyes at him. "Who is this special lady who made you lose your head? Have you slept with her? Did she possess some special skill you enjoyed in bed?"

"Damn you, Waterford!" Richard admonished him under his breath, stealing a quick glance around them in case someone might be eavesdropping on their conversation. "Must everything always be about sex with you?"

"Of course." Jeremy raised his shoulders and gestured with his hands. "What else is there? I can hardly believe that men would be charmed by the way a lady pours tea or wears a ball gown. Honestly, I prefer them in my bed—naked."

Richard chuckled and shook his head with an exasperated sigh. Jeremy would always be Jeremy. Nothing much ever interested him in women but for that.

"So—who is she, then?" Allayne cut in with earnestness. "Pray, do tell!"

"That's just it." Richard drained his glass before he continued, "I don't even know her name."

"Balderdash!" Jeremy exclaimed and looked at him as if he had lost his mind. "You've met her, and you think you might be falling for her—but you didn't remember to ask who she was?"

"Of course, I did!" Richard snapped his eyebrows together in exasperation. "What do you think I am, an idiot?"

"Most of the time." Jeremy grinned.

"Wait—" Allayne raised both hands. "The sense in all this escapes me. I am quite certain that I have a good idea of the inventory of available females of the ton, and it confounds me to imagine that I have failed to notice one that would surpass Lady Desiree's attributes. Wouldn't you agree, Waterford?"

"Er—yes. Of course." Jeremy hid a smile and nodded vigorously in assent. "Hard to miss those attributes."

"Where exactly did you meet this chit?" Allayne cocked his head at Richard.

"Well, I first saw her at Almack's." Richard's eyes took on a faraway look as if picturing that blessed day. "Not only is she beautiful, but she is intelligent, too. She was holding court with the most impressive group of men I have ever seen, holding her own and thwarting the best of them with clever and amusing retorts."

"Now, that's novel." Allayne looked bewildered. "I didn't think you'd be drawn to a quick-witted chit. I—well—Lady Desiree certainly did not come across to me as the sharpest knife in the block when we went to see her after we arrived from Europe. All she nattered on about was the weather and the latest fripperies. And do not deny it—I observed you swallowing a yawn more than five times over dinner. Pray, do excuse my bluntness."

"Don't trouble yourself." Richard lifted his shoulders. "I know what you mean. I never thought it would matter, but after spending an entire humdrum week with Desiree, I realized now that it did. I was going out of my mind with tedium, and Papa's appointments with his doctors in the city were the only things that saved me from drowning myself in brandy. Accompanying Desiree to the various balls here in London may not have completely rescued me from the doldrums, but at least it enabled me to socialize with other people. And when I saw her—this girl—sparring with astuteness with the brightest members of

Parliament—"

"You found a way to introduce yourself to her." Jeremy crossed his arms over his chest.

"Well—yes! But she gave me the cut direct! Twice—would you believe it? She was angry at me for some reason. But I could not rest until I saw her again, so I attended one of the most popular events of the season, the Libbeys' masquerade, in the hopes of finding her there."

"And, did you find her?" Allayne asked.

"Yes. She was wandering around the ballroom unescorted, so I assumed she might have been looking for her companions. I followed her for a little while just to be sure it truly was her, and I was not mistaken. When I asked her to dance, she granted her consent. I had an odd notion that she knew who I was. But when I asked for her name and if I could see her again, she hesitated, and then, the waltz ended." Richard shook his head and sighed.

"And she left you standing in the middle of the dance floor without telling you her name?" Jeremy gaped at him.

"Yes—but not before she requested a tryst by the fountain in the gardens outside."

"My God!" Allayne exclaimed. "How utterly risqué and romantic!"

"MORE LIKE RECKLESS and idiotic, me thinks! Did you, by any chance, have the decency to mention that you are betrothed before you agreed to an assignation?" Jeremy's eyebrows snapped together while mentally cursing in all the languages he knew, as Richard protested that it was not what they thought at all. The meeting never came to fruition because he had gotten hopelessly lost in the Libbeys' vast gardens. When he finally found the fountain, the lady never showed. Either that, or she had left by the time he had arrived. Richard lamented that he may have had completely misunderstood or misheard her instructions, for it was quite lively in the ballroom at the time because he discovered several other fountains situated in different areas of the garden.

Jeremy need not hear any more of Richard's account of what had happened next or who the lady in question was. He knew perfectly well who she was and what had transpired—and at the moment, he had a distinct inclination to wring a certain brat's neck. The little twit! Had she lost her senses? Luckily, he was there, waiting for her to bring the soap powder at that fountain, instead of Richard! She could have ruined herself in the hands of a soon-to-be married man!

"Richard." Jeremy nodded in the direction of a large gathering of men not too far away from them. It seemed to him that the only solution available to settle this problem was to give both of them a much-deserved jolt in their pudding-filled heads. "Why don't you say hello to Cassie?"

"Cassie?" Richard broke into a grin. "She's here? I haven't seen her even once since my return!"

"Yes, she's in attendance," Allayne said in a nonchalant tone, but Jeremy caught the reproachful look he darted at him. "Come, let me take you to her. I'm sure she would be delighted to see you."

RICHARD FOLLOWED ALLAYNE and Jeremy, feeling the excitement of seeing Cassie again after all these years. Though he was not a letter-writing sort of fellow, she nonetheless faithfully sent him numerous correspondences while he was still in school and abroad, and they were his most favorite things to receive.

At first, her missives were simple drawings of stick figures of a boy and a girl holding hands, signed with a giant heart with both their initials inside. But as the years went by and she had learned to write better, she would post him lengthy notes about the goings-on in Cornwall, including news about his father. Sometimes, when he felt homesick, he would re-read her letters and laugh at the stories of her latest antics with Jeremy.

He had looked forward to returning home three and a half years ago, but then his father had announced his agreement with his friend, the Duke of Glenford, for him to marry Glenford's daughter. Ah, he may have been fascinated with Desiree when he met her, but his father's heavy-handedness in controlling his future had angered him, and he had wanted to rebel against the old man. So, he fled to Europe on a whim—as a means of escape.

Cassie's letters and Allayne's company had thankfully seen him through during those long years of exile when all he did was pursue his painting and drown himself in vice when the longing for home was beyond what he could bear.

Richard nodded at a few acquaintances as they squeezed through the crowd, which included the Earl of Bristol and the Duke of Kingston, who were standing with the other men. He was more than elated—he fairly thrummed with eagerness in seeing his childhood friend again.

Cassie meant home to him. The embodiment of everything important he had been forced to leave, the little sister he had always wished for but never had. She was the sunrise, the sea, the heavens above, and the fresh, salty breeze. She was laughter and innocence, and all things true, where troubles were far away, and joy was all there was to share.

Yes—to him, Cassie was the memory and heart of home. The place he had always wanted to be, the kind of life he had always wanted to live.

"Ah, here we are." Allayne leaned forward and placed his hands on the shoulders of a lady with her back to him, slowly turning her around with a kiss on the cheek.

Richard waited patiently behind Allayne as they exchanged greetings, anticipating the surprise on Cassie's face when she saw him.

Finally, Allayne turned aside and urged Richard closer. "Cassie, you do remember Richard, don't you?"

Richard stepped forward with a big grin on his lips, then froze, as the stunning lady with hair the color of rose-gold slowly lifted her gaze and stared at him. The pudgy cheeks, sprinkling of freckles, and button nose he remembered were all gone. The woman who stood in front of him was slender with full breasts, deliciously rounded hips, a narrow waist that he could span in both hands, and a face that could have belonged to an angel. She was the same woman he had cornered in the alcove at Almack's and waltzed with at the Libbeys' masquerade.

"Piglet?" he blurted without thinking, belatedly regretting the volume with which he had uttered the word, which had consequently garnered the other men's attention.

Her smile vanished, and her cheeks went red as the conversation around them halted, and everyone settled into an awkward silence. Her humiliation at his uttered appellation for her seemed to shine like a beacon from every part of her body for a moment. Then, a wicked gleam flashed in her narrowed eyes, and she gave him a devious smile, replying at a decibel that carried her voice clearly across the room, "Well, hello again, *tiny prick!*"

CHAPTER THIRTEEN

The Templeton soiree (Part 2)
One minute later...

JEREMY COULD NOT quite fathom what to make of the entire blasted scenario. He had meant for this reunion to unravel the dilemma of the two nitwits involved, but instead, both had managed to muddle what he had planned to resolve!

Allayne had choked on the champagne he had been drinking and spewed it at—of all people—the immaculate Duke of Kingston's fine brocade waistcoat.

And as if that weren't enough, hard-of-hearing Lord Bhramby elbowed to the front and demanded to know if Cassie had said, *tiny tick or shiny prick—or was it, tickly prick?*

Murmurs and laughter rose from the illustrious crowd, and before long, everyone in the ballroom was scandalized and exclaiming out loud.

Devil be dammed! Jeremy rubbed his chin as he assessed how he could salvage the rapidly deteriorating situation. What was a rakehell to do?

At present, Richard and Cassie were glaring at each other fiercely, neither willing to back down, while Allayne was on his knees before the duke, frantically wiping his waistcoat—which appeared somewhat perverted and abominably lewd.

It did not help either that Richard had chosen that exact moment to stir the already overflowing pot and rise to Cassie's god-awful taunt.

"Believe me, my dear Miss Carlyle—there's nothing *tiny* about me," he stated boldly, straightening his spine to his full height as if demonstrating to the public how long, tall, and well-built he was so that one might suppose every part of him was constructed likewise.

Cassie colored to a deeper scarlet, but not to be outdone, blurted, "Well, my lord, if you insist, then—we'll just have to see." She dropped her eyes to his groin and lifted a daring eyebrow.

Stupefied gasps emanated from the slighted but fascinated mob.

Jeremy rolled his eyes heavenward to ask for guidance from above. He was not a religious person, and he was quite sure God held him responsible for all the sins that blackened his soul. But, if the Almighty could just set aside their grudge for a while and help him fix this fiasco for once, there could not be a better time for divine intervention than right now. Jeremy waited with bated breath for the Lord's help to materialize.

And it came—in the form of a blonde, blue-eyed goddess, which was not exactly what he had in mind but would certainly do for the moment.

"Darling, I've been looking all over for you," Lady Desiree said in a melodic, somewhat inappropriately sensual voice. "What are you doing here?"

When Richard did not give her an immediate reply, hard-of-hearing Lord Bhramby volunteered to enlighten the beautiful but self-important lady by holding a quizzing glass against an eye and lowering it to examine Richard's crotch. "Miss Carlyle was just saying that Lord Radcliffe couldn't pee. How queer, don't you think, my dear?"

A barrage of muffled laughter burst from the avidly attentive, eavesdropping crowd.

Lady Desiree lifted a haughty brow and darted her eyes between Richard and Cassie, before regarding the latter from head to toe with obvious disdain. "You must be Richard's childhood friend. Miss Cassie, is it? The one he refers to as Piglet? Goodness!" Her hand alighted on her abundantly endowed bosom. "How suitably amusing!" She tilted her head in sardonic laughter.

Jeremy saw Cassie's eyes narrow and wished he had been more specific with his request for help from the Lord God Almighty. Next time—and he hoped there would not be another one—he would mention that he'd rather have the devil come to his aid than a beauty with a maggot-infested brain.

"Am I correct in assuming you're Lady Desiree?" Cassie cocked her chin and regarded her without blinking.

"Precisely." The flaxen brow rose condescendingly once again. "One hardly forgets a memorable name like mine."

"I most certainly agree." Cassie nodded with a suspiciously artificial grin. "As a matter of fact, I have a *goat* named Desiree."

"Bhaaaaa!" Jeremy heard Allayne cachinnate from somewhere behind him. As to why her big brother would choose to emulate a goat at this very moment when all was about to explode in a society quarrel of gargantuan proportion was beyond him.

Another round of choked guffaws and snorting rose from their enthralled audience.

The practiced smile congealed on Lady Desiree's lips, and a look of outrage replaced her well-rehearsed aristocratic façade.

"Cassandra, is everything all right, my dear?" Lady Carlyle emerged from the throng with her husband in tow.

Jeremy pinched the bridge of his nose and shook his head. Of all the temporal order of things in the world, why must Lady Carlyle be punctual at this particular point when this circus was about to unfold?

"Everything is perfectly fine, Mama," Cassandra replied with a satanic smile that Jeremy hoped did not reflect what was brewing in her mind. "I was just giving Lady Desiree a most stimulating account of my goat. You know, the golden-furred one with the odd blue eyes that constantly craved attention from the billy goats and had a penchant to have her—uhm—her—"

"Arse," Jeremy supplied instinctively and wondered what in Hades was wrong with him for condoning Cassie with this odious display in public.

"That's precisely the word," Cassie continued as if they were having a conversation about the weather over a cup of tea. "She did have a peculiar fixation on getting her—ahem—*arse*—licked by all the billy goats wherever she went. You do remember that one, right, Papa?" She turned adoring eyes to her papa, who was listening attentively to her drivel.

"Whatever you say, pumpkin," her papa declared proudly, nodding at the lords and ladies who clapped and chortled at his response.

"George Carlyle!" Her mama's jaw nearly dropped to the floor, and her eyes practically popped out of their sockets.

"Bhaaaaa!" Someone from the crowd who resembled their host, the Earl of Templeton, bleated loudly.

The long-suffering, tautly repressed spectators eagerly joined the earl with relief and imitated into a noisy bleating herd of cattle.

"My lady, if you would forgive my daughter's indelicacy," Lady Carlyle sputtered amidst the commotion.

"Indelicacy?" Lady Desiree's mouth tightened into a thin line. "Your daughter, madam, has insulted me beyond measure! Clearly, you have not brought her up to snuff with what is expected of a young lady! But I bear no regret, for now, the crème of the ton have witnessed her most insolent behavior. I daresay no sane gentleman would be temerarious enough to pay court to her!"

"Oh!" Lady Carlyle turned beet-red and covered her mouth with her hands in discomfiture.

"Pray do hold your tongue, Desiree!" Richard bit out with a warning glare at his betrothed.

Hell, Jeremy exhaled in disgust as he watched Cassie's expression change, her hand forming into a fist at her side. He had better get his posterior over there before she planted a colossal shiner on the dimwitted chit's eye.

He placed a hand on her arm just in time as she lifted it to do exactly what he had thought she would do. After a discreet shake of his head and a quelling look directed at his little brat, he turned his attention to the belligerent fair maiden.

"Lady Desiree," he drawled in his deep bedroom voice, bestowing her with a heart-stopping, pantalette-dropping smile. "I don't believe we've been formally introduced. Jeremiah Devlin Huntington, Marquess of Waterford." His dark eyes not leaving hers, he brought her gloved hand to his lips, and instead of kissing it, he bit her knuckle lightly and winked.

Lady Desiree blushed a healthy shade of rose and fluttered her lashes at him, seeming to forget her outburst of a few moments previous.

Jeremy proceeded to regard her with a steamy, heavy-lidded gaze, ignoring Richard, who seemed more fascinated with Cassie than his betrothed. Ah, he could not blame the poor old chap for letting his desire lead him by the nose. Lady Desiree certainly more than made up for the lack of a functioning brain with her ample breasts and delectable derriere, which he would happily lick if he were a billy goat.

As the goddess before him showed signs of pleasure under his blatantly salacious scrutiny, Jeremy decided it was time for him to deliver the ax. "Forgive me, my lady, but I could not help overhearing your tirade against Miss Carlyle." He glanced at Cassie, who was scowling at Richard. "I beg to disagree with your forthright judgment of her character. In fact, all these perfectly sane gentlemen here are besotted with her charms and are paying her the most ardent suit."

Lady Desiree tossed her head and laughed, commanding the attention of their audience once again. "How honorable of you to come to Miss Carlyle's defense, Lord Waterford. But do any of these gentlemen truly have the gall to offer for her hand?"

A brief silence ensued. The wench was right. After Cassie's colorful reference to Richard's genitals, she had inadvertently provoked the ton and damaged her sterling reputation.

Jeremy pondered for a moment. This situation seriously demanded his clever ingenuity to reach a satisfactory resolution. Would the scheme he had been toying around in his head succeed in redeeming his little brat's honor?

A slow, self-satisfied, crooked smile formed on his lips. "My dear Lady Desiree, you've put me in an awkward predicament. But I confess—I am delighted, so I might as well take the opportunity." He wrapped an arm around Cassie's waist, well-nigh dragging her to his side and successfully prying her attention from Richard.

She turned to him with a questioning gaze.

He looked into her eyes and took a deep breath. "Ladies and Gentlemen," he began, his eyes never leaving hers, "let it be known that I have asked for Miss Carlyle's hand in marriage, and she has accepted." He swiftly cupped her face in his hands and kissed her on the mouth in front of everyone before she got the chance to realize what he had done and dismember him on the spot.

Shocked murmurs filled the ballroom. From the corner of his eye, he caught Richard's stunned expression, Allayne's open-mouthed stare, and Lady Carlyle dropped into a swoon, conveniently—as always—into her husband's arms.

Good God, what a pickle! he thought, as he gently pulled away and smiled into his newly betrothed's mortified face.

CHAPTER FOURTEEN

The newly betrothed
Waterford House
Mayfair, London

A DANGEROUS AND murderous Allayne had dragged Jeremy with the entire family to his carriage, hissing something about an urgent private meeting through clenched teeth. Once inside, Allayne ordered the coachman to take them to nearby Waterford House, after which everyone bellowed their respective opinions about this unexpected situation all at the same time, save for Cassie, who had looked out the window and ignored the pandemonium with a resigned sigh.

As soon as they entered the Waterford House library, Allayne picked Jeremy up by the collar and well-nigh guillotined him with an asphyxiating twist on the knot of his cravat before demanding an explanation. At the same time, Lady Carlyle went into hysterics in the middle of the room. Her husband, on the other hand—thank God for his cheerful demeanor—settled onto a fat chair to enjoy his stock of excellent port, perfectly content to watch the drama unfold.

"Jeremy, what have you done?" Cassie finally wailed from the corner, where she had collapsed onto a chair in front of the fireplace, drawing everyone's attention to herself.

She had been noticeably quiet during the ride home, much as she had behaved when she discovered Richard's betrothal. Even now, as the glow from the fire illuminated her beautiful angelic face, she looked older than her eighteen years. A certain anxiety haunted her eyes, and Jeremy could not help but blame himself for being the most likely cause.

He calmly pried his collar from Allayne's death grip and sat down on the cushioned footstool in front of her, gently reaching for her hand. "I'm sorry," he whispered, clasping her cold fingers in his warm ones. "But it was the only way for me to protect you. You must see that."

"I don't need you to watch over me." She slipped her hand away from his and tucked it underneath her skirts.

"I know you don't." Jeremy winced inwardly at her refusal to hold his hand. He brushed a wayward curl from her face instead. "But tonight, Cassie, was different. The ton is as fickle as the weather. You can be cast out without a second glance if you fall out of favor. That spectacle at the soiree would have had tongues wagging for weeks— you would have been ruined. I had to think of a way to divert everyone's attention."

"By announcing our so-called engagement?" she snapped angrily at him. "How could you, Jeremy?"

"How could I not? Believe it or not, news of a betrothal to a high-ranking peer is a more favorable topic of conversation than your show of boorish behavior. The ton is more likely to forgive and forget your misstep because of your alliance with me. I saved you, brat—accept it and stop complaining."

"How could you have saved me? I'm mistakenly engaged to you, you oaf!" She pointed at him. "I am ruined!"

The note of revulsion in her tone rendered Jeremy speechless. He gaped at her, shocked at the unexpected hurt he felt. Did she really have that low of an opinion of him?

The mist clouding his brain suddenly lifted, and he realized the truth of this epiphany. She might like him well enough as a friend, but

Cassie thought very poorly of him as a prospective husband. Why else would she have reacted with such repugnance at the mere idea of becoming his betrothed?

He clenched his jaw and abruptly stood up, turning away from her to prop an arm on the mantelpiece as he struggled to hide his bruised feelings from the others. Unfortunately, his reaction did not escape Cassie.

"Jeremy—" she uttered his name with a tinge of contrition, her skirts rustling as she crossed the distance between them. She wrapped her fingers around his arm and gently turned him to face her, but he sullenly averted his eyes, refusing to meet her gaze.

"Jeremy, I'm so sorry," she said, reaching out to cup his cheek with her hand. "I didn't mean what I said. Please forgive me." She searched his face with large green eyes and then hugged him tightly, laying her head against his chest. "You know I adore you."

"I know, brat. It's all right—no harm done." Jeremy sighed and kissed the top of her head before fixing his gaze on the smoldering tongues of flame greedily lapping on the fragrant logs in the fireplace. What was he moping about, anyway? He had always known he was not good enough for her and did not deserve her. Of course, she had the right to be offended by his audaciousness in taking the upper hand and spinning a betrothal out of thin air!

Jeremy placed his hands on her shoulders and pushed her away from him, ignoring the impulse to return her affectionate embrace. "If it makes you feel any better, I suggest that we simply maintain the charade for two more fortnights. By that time, you will be back into society, and you can cry off from our betrothal. I don't give a fig what you tell them." He shrugged, trying his damnedest to sound insouciant. "Perhaps you can concoct a story that I've been a scoundrel and slept with other women while we are engaged. No one will question you—my reputation precedes itself."

Cassie regarded him with a startled stare, visibly distressed before she lowered herself slowly onto a nearby chair.

Lady Carlyle blew her nose loudly in the silence that briefly descended on the room.

"He's right, Cass." Allayne broke the awkwardness and walked over to her, squeezing her shoulder. "After you cry off from your betrothal using the excuse Jeremy suggested, you'll earn the sympathy of the ton and will be welcomed back into its fold. Your engagement will be brief enough to be unremarkable. Your chances of finding another good match will be propitious again."

Cassie swiveled her head toward her brother with a concerned expression on her face. "What about Jeremy? What will happen to him?"

"Jeremy will be unaffected and forgiven as always." Allayne sat on the chair opposite hers and leaned forward with his elbows propped on his knees, clasping her hands in his. "It's different for men, Cass. Society is more tolerant of our misconduct—especially if one is wealthy and well-connected."

"I agree," Jeremy said. "Don't concern yourself about me. I will manage, as always. You must know, however, that for this plan to work, we must keep up with the pretense that we are truly betrothed. The eyes of society are on us, and they are not easily fooled."

Cassie lowered her gaze and became pensive.

Jeremy watched her furtively, bedeviled by his conscience. She looked so sad. He made her so sad. He wanted to shoot himself.

After a moment, she heaved a deep sigh and nodded. "Very well."

Jeremy restrained himself from rushing to her side to reassure her that everything would be all right. "No one must know about this ruse," he uttered, giving everyone in the room a pointed look. "Not a single word of it must be spoken outside of this room. If we betray our confidence and word gets out, we will all suffer the consequence of being ostracized from society. You insulted a duke's daughter!"

Lady Carlyle flew into another round of hysterics, saying she would rather face the gallows than be shunned. "This is all your fault, George Carlyle!" She pointed a quivering finger at her husband. "You spoiled her into becoming a hoyden and let her spend too much time with this—with this—this—" She shifted and shook her finger frantically toward Jeremy.

"Favorite scoundrel of yours?" Jeremy smiled fondly at her. The viscountess might constantly nag about his friendship with Cassie, but in truth, she doted on him and had practically adopted him after he lost his mother at a very young age.

"Oh! You shameless profligate!" Lady Carlyle covered her nose with the handkerchief her husband offered. "If I wasn't so very fond of your late mama, who was the very epitome of kindness and moral uprightness, I would have skewered you with a poker and roasted you over the fire!" She glared at him and furiously wiped her nose. "Oh, if only she lived long enough to see to your upbringing. My poor, dearest Marjorie, God bless her soul!" Lady Carlyle wailed as she folded and refolded the square piece of linen in her hands. "Lord knows, I and that loyal butler of yours, Barton, tried to keep an eye on you and bring you up to snuff—but did you ever listen?"

Jeremy opened his mouth to respond.

"No!" the viscountess went on. "You twirled poor Barton around your little finger, ignored my lectures, and did what you wanted! Did you ever stop to reflect whether your behavior upset me—your poor mama's one true friend, who only wanted what is best for you?"

"Ah—"

"No!" the viscountess prattled onward. "You philandered about town, chasing any living thing with two legs and a skirt! And did your scandalous behavior end there?"

"Er—" Jeremy thought about it. "No?"

"No!" the viscountess reiterated in a huff. "You had to concoct this madcap scheme with the entire family involved! Oh!" She touched the back of her hand to her forehead and heaved an exaggerated sob. "I give up! May your poor mama forgive me for failing her, but I don't know what to do with you anymore!"

"There, there, Mama." Cassie stood up and went to her mother, sitting on the chair next to her and rubbing her back. "You must gather yourself together. This situation is only temporary and will be over before you know it. Be brave now. Remember, we must all pretend that Jeremy and I are engaged, or else—"

Lady Carlyle smothered a sniffle with the handkerchief. "God in heaven, but we're all sinners! Lying and deceiving society like a bunch of devil-worshipping criminals! I will never be able to look at the vicar straight in the eyes again! My lord husband, have you anything to say about this?"

"Indeed, my dear. I think this ruse far surpasses the opera!" The viscount held up his glass of port in the semblance of a toast. "Well done, Jeremy, my boy!"

"George Carlyle!" Lady Carlyle flung the wet handkerchief at her husband's face.

"Don't worry, Mama, it will be all right," Cassie squeezed her mama's hands. "In fact, I do wish to go home as soon as possible. I don't think I could walk into another ballroom again."

"On the contrary," Jeremy interrupted, and they all turned to look at him. "I propose we stay in London for the next five days. We shall have to fulfill our duty and call on my grandmother. I also expect to see several invitations from friends and acquaintances who would wish to meet Cassie and the whole family. We must endeavor to make our relationship look authentic."

"I agree." Allayne inclined his head.

"Do I gather that we are all of the same mind?" Jeremy swept his gaze around the room. He waited until everyone had concurred, whether willingly or otherwise, before pushing himself upright from the fireplace. "Well then," he said as he made his way toward the door. "If you will excuse me, I must retrieve something from upstairs."

Back in his bedchamber, he removed the large framed oil on canvas and opened the safe concealed behind it. He took out what he needed, closed the safe, and hung the painting over it once again.

For a few minutes, he stood staring at the stunningly beautiful woman in the portrait. She looked back at him with dark eyes fringed with long black lashes, an impish smile on her full red lips. Her long hair tumbled down to her waist in thick, shining waves of black silk.

He looked so much like her. He could still remember the way she used to hold him in her lap and caress his hair as he drifted off to sleep on her shoulder. Her scent, a heady blend of roses and lilies, still wafted in the air to this day and enveloped him. And her voice—low-pitched, smooth, and vivacious—would sometimes echo in his dreams and wake him in the middle of the night.

Sadness swept over him and made his heart ache so badly, he thought it would explode out of his chest.

He reached out to touch the image of her delicate hand with the diamond ring on her finger. "I miss you, Mama," he whispered, blinking back the sudden onset of tears.

He returned shortly to the library, carrying the elegant red velvet box with the Waterford coat of arms embroidered in gold silk thread on its cushioned lid that he had retrieved from the safe.

His gaze went directly to Cassie as he entered the room, and somehow, the grief that had overtaken him upstairs evaporated into nothingness at the sight of her face.

He knelt before her on the luxurious Aubusson carpet and opened the box to reveal a magnificent ring with an exquisite round diamond surrounded by rubies.

Cassie covered her mouth with a gasp—a reaction echoed by Lady Carlyle, who sat next to her, as both of them riveted their eyes on the sparkling gem nestled in a bed of black satin.

"This was my mother's." He took the ring out of its luxurious cradle and paused to look at it for a moment, remembering the woman who had been the love and light of his life, the guiding beacon who illuminated his path—extinguished and gone too soon. "I want you to have this." Jeremy lifted his gaze to look into Cassie's eyes, the girl whose friendship brightened his dark, dreary days and whose unquestioning acceptance of his true self—both the good side and the bad—brought him back from the gloom.

"Oh, no, Jeremy—you can't—I can't—" She shook her head briskly and held her palms up. "That is meant to be worn by the lady you'll someday marry."

He smiled crookedly and took her left hand anyway. "Of course, you can." He poised the ring at the tip of her ring finger. For a split second, his heart lurched, and he felt suddenly nervous. *What the devil was the matter with him?*

"Jeremy—" Cassie gently tugged at her hand, but he tightened his hold on her fingers.

"You're my betrothed." He swept his long, thick lashes upward and met her wide-eyed gaze. "The girl I'm going to marry, at least for the next eight and twenty days."

And with that, he slid his beloved mother's ring onto her finger.

CHAPTER FIFTEEN

Coming home
Grandstone Park, Cornwall
Nine days later...

R ICHARD NEEDED SOME air. He inhaled the cool, salt-tinged breeze from atop his horse, Artemis, as he admired the breathtaking panorama before him.

"Ah, it's good to be home," he said to himself with a contented sigh. He needed to be here to clear his mind and revitalize his soul.

A few days ago, he had felt so suffocated that he left London with his father the day after that disgraceful scene at the Templeton soiree. Though most of the gentlemen had jovially patted him on the back and nonchalantly brushed off the incident as a jest, Desiree had fussed and yammered until his ears bled and his eyes glazed over. By the time they arrived at Glenford House in the heart of Mayfair, he was ready to bolt back into the carriage and leave the stale, foggy city in haste.

The walls of uncertainty closed in on him. He had returned to England on a mission to fulfill his father's dying wish—to oversee the vast responsibilities he had neglected, but which now awaited his attention. He had finally fulfilled his promise, embraced his fate selflessly, and bound himself to a future with a woman of his father's choosing, whom he barely knew. It had been so easy and right at the time, and he wondered why now—when everything was done and carved in stone—he was flooded with such an overwhelming shadow of a doubt?

Hence, he ran away to the only place he knew that could give him solace in the midst of the circus his life had become—Grandstone Park. What he wanted was his old self back—the one who laughed easily and did not take life too seriously. The person who used to notice the beauty all around him, who always thanked the Almighty for the bounty bestowed upon his family, and met each waking hour with zest.

Richard cast another admiring gaze at the slowly rising sun on the horizon.

He drew in the scent of the sea to find comfort from the tender stirrings of his heart. He had never expected this. Never in a million years did he anticipate he would fall in love so swiftly. The instant connection he felt towards her was amazing and inexplicable. It almost felt too familiar. He had always scoffed at the romantic notion of love at first sight, yet here he was, drowning in the sweetness.

Artemis suddenly bobbed her head with a warm neigh, swished her tail, and danced on the sand impatiently. Only the sight of Apollo—her brother—could elicit that kind of gleeful welcome.

There, bathed in the first rays of sunshine, several yards away, Cassie sat atop her horse, watching him.

CASSANDRA HAD BEEN dying to ride along the shore. She laughed as Apollo's hooves sent the water flying high up in the air, showering them both with fat droplets.

Oh, how she missed the glorious sunrise that signaled the beginning of a new day! London had been wonderful with all the splendid soirees and operas, but it was also cold and supercilious. That city was a place where she could never belong. She had done her part with her family, met and visited with the upper echelons of society who praised her engagement to Jeremy, but her affinity was for the home of her birth, with its abundant nature and the familiar people she loved.

She knew only one other person who delighted in riding along the shore at this unearthly hour. Only one who revered the legacy of God like this, grateful for the very air he breathed and the earth he stood on.

Apollo's ears pricked at the sight of his sister Artemis, who pranced in excitement at their first encounter in years. Startled, her rider turned, riveting his brilliant blue eyes on Cassie.

It was Richard.

For a moment, they stared at each other, neither saying a word, nor acknowledging the other with a wave, nor making a move to come nearer.

Then, suddenly, his face lit up with a radiant smile.

Her heart cartwheeled in her chest at understanding his way of reaching out for a truce. She smiled in return.

And just like that, the recollections of the past came pouring in, like a long-lost diary opened once more, its yellowed pages a litany of words and portraits playing in her mind. She was a little girl again, out with her hero at the beach, admiring the break of dawn.

Richard rode toward her at a canter. "Hello, Cassie."

The butterflies in her belly awakened at the sound of his deep, rich voice. Pins and needles tortured her nerves and made her hands tremble. He searched her face with something she could not quite discern in his eyes, and yet she could feel the warmth in them.

"Hello, Richard," she managed to answer with a slight quiver in her voice.

"You're all grown up," he said, his mouth tipping at the corners in that achingly familiar smile.

She lifted her chin and returned his gaze bravely, even if her heart was careening around her ribcage. "Yes," she whispered with eyes misting, not from the salt-tinged air, but from the realization that he had finally and truly seen her.

CHAPTER SIXTEEN

Return to my betrothed...

AFTER THE CARLYLES had left for Cornwall, Jeremy stayed in London for another three days to bury himself in vice and rid himself of the doldrums. He did every preposterous proclivity a rake of his caliber was expected to do. He drank, gambled, slept with not one, but five (or was it eight?) women, and now the last but certainly not the least, was Lord Wright's young wife, who was happily bobbing her pretty head as she knelt between his legs.

Hell, he had an erection as large as Mount Everest and had reached climax multiple times like Mount Vesuvius, but why the devil couldn't he feel any satisfaction from his release? After all the moaning, groaning, and rough, uninhibited sex, all he felt was emptiness, akin to a lonely stretch of desert.

And devil take it, but he was restless! He had been brimming with pent-up libido since that night at the masquerade ball. What he started as a jest had spiraled into a full-blown raging desire, and he had wanted her—Cassie, of all people—his partner in crime, the little brat he'd grown up with, the one he was supposedly protecting from lechers like him.

What in Lucifer's name had gotten into him that made him as randy as a damned billy goat? Ever since that night at the Libbeys' garden, he had not had a single night's sleep without dreaming of caressing Cassie's luscious body, of taking her time and again. His lust for her took over him, and every morning the evidence of his need screamed at him in the wetness blemishing his pristine white sheets.

How was he going to purge himself of this affliction? Drowning himself in alcohol and gambling away a small fortune certainly did not help—nor did sleeping with women.

His craving for Cassie had developed into such an obsession that he felt it necessary to distance himself from her—before he did something outrageously imprudent and forced Allayne into challenging him to a duel. No, that simply would not be acceptable at all unless he wanted an early death.

Cassie.

Only she could fill the void.

He must be out of his mind! Since when did he start babbling like a love-struck fool? He was Jeremiah Devlin Huntington, more often referred to as Devil, London's most notorious rake! He would rather hang himself than get leg-shackled—which, by chance, if he laid even a fingertip on her—would most certainly be his fate.

What was he going to do?

CHAPTER SEVENTEEN

Suppositions...

CASSANDRA DISMOUNTED FROM Apollo and handed the reins to one of the Grandstone Park stable boys. The estate was brimming with activity as it always did every morning, with numerous workers tending the horses and vast gardens, as far as the eyes could see.

"Mornin', Miss Carlyle." The lad inclined his head with a tip of his hat.

"Good morning, Peter." Cassandra beamed warmly at him. "Don't let him eat everything in sight." She patted Apollo's flank. "He's too fat for his own good."

Apollo kicked the dirt, giving her a horse's version of a disapproving look.

"I won't, Miss Carlyle," Peter replied with a grin as she turned towards the duke's house with a wave.

"Good morning! What lovely blooms you've grown this season!" Cassandra greeted the gardeners going about their work, who paused to return her cheerful compliments with sunny smiles.

She stopped to chat with Old Ron, who had been working at Grandstone Park for as long as she could remember, before continuing on her way. She knew every person who worked for the duke, from the lowly scullery maids to the many stewards who managed the vast ducal properties. In fact, she thought with a chuckle, she knew everyone who worked for all three neighboring estates.

She climbed up the marble steps to the manor's entrance and lifted the brass door knocker, tapping it vigorously. Today was her customary day to visit Richard's father.

Gordon, the butler, opened the door.

"How is he, Gordy?" she asked as they crossed the foyer.

"He seems to be in better spirits, Miss Carlyle. Lord Sunderland's presence has cheered him up considerably." He glanced at her as they reached the foot of the winding staircase.

She smiled fondly at the butler. "I'll show myself to his rooms, Gordy. You need not escort me."

"As you wish, Miss. He is expecting you." Gordon half-turned to leave, then hesitated. "By the by, Miss, allow me to express felicitations on behalf of the staff on your recent engagement to Lord Waterford. And if I may say so, we are relieved that you and Lord Sunderland are friends again."

"Thank you, Gordy. Lord Sunderland and I will never cease to be friends," Cassandra replied with delight, but her pleasure was short-lived as the butler's remark reminded her that she was, indeed, betrothed.

"That is good to hear, Miss Carlyle." Gordon bowed with a smile before walking away.

Cassandra frowned as she watched Gordon turn in the direction of the kitchens. How could she let her engagement slip from her mind? She stared at the enormous diamond ring surrounded by rubies on her finger, and her heart sank. Richard's company had completely occupied her attention, and her bliss at their reunion disguised all her troubles. Yes, she was looking forward to ending her betrothal to Jeremy, but she could not bear the thought of spreading hurtful, false rumors a⸍ ⸍o justify their parting. She wished there was a better ⸍ ⸍ut the dissolution of their betrothal ⸍⸍⸍ ⸍⸍⸍⸍ through all the drama associated with having to satisfy the wagging tongues of the ton.

Cassandra went up the steps to the second floor and turned toward the right wing where the ducal chambers were located. As she strolled along the carpeted corridor, she passed a room with the door opened halfway, the brightness of the afternoon sun streaming through the massive glass windows unadorned with draperies. She had never seen what was in that room before, so she paused out of curiosity and poked her head through the doorway.

The scent of turpentine assailed her nostrils as she gaped at the size of the spacious, rectangular room. It had wood floors and was devoid of furnishings, save for two chairs by the floor-to-ceiling windows and a table laden with pots of paint, brushes, palettes, rags, and a variety of liquids in sealed bottles. Propped against the opposite wall were numerous paintings of different sizes. Some sat on easels, and some hung from the walls displayed around the room.

The temptation to go in and investigate was irresistible. She glanced up and down the hallway to see if anyone was around, but the entire second floor was deserted. After another moment of hesitation, she finally gave in and carefully slipped through the door.

The first row of paintings braced against the nearest wall depicted familiar landmarks of various cities in Europe. Farther along the same wall, the second grouping portrayed everyday country life in the villages. The third collection displayed in large wooden easels near the windows illustrated the stunning panorama of the waterfront at sunrise.

Cassie recognized the setting as the beach bordering the east side of Grandstone Park that she and Richard frequented. She slowly surveyed each painting, admiring the way every piece captured the splendor of daybreak. As she reached the last few paintings, she paused in surprise. There, in front of her, in six large canvasses, were various portraits of a young boy with blonde hair ruffled by the wind and a little girl in curly red pigtails.

She and Richard.

There could be no mistaking the way they sat on the sand. Then, there was the portrait of the two of them building the huge sandcastle that took hours to construct, only to collapse from the rising tide in an instant.

Cassie traced her finger over the signature on the lower right-hand corner.

R.C. Radcliffe c.1814. The year Allayne and Richard embarked on a much-awaited grand tour of Europe, months after Napoleon Bonaparte finally succumbed to a devastating defeat in the Battle of Waterloo. The three of them had originally intended to visit the continent after finishing school in the summer of 1811, but the increasing tension in the Peninsula, which subsequently spread to the rest of the continent, had delayed their plans. Undeterred from the lure of adventure, they opted to sail for America instead.

She remembered they stayed in America longer than planned, reveling in the popularity afforded by their aristocratic titles amongst the American elite, which opened many doors to significant money-making opportunities. Though business was an odd pursuit for men of their standing, they nonetheless acquired an interest and fascination for financial matters. "Stock and Trade Investments," Jeremy wrote in his letters, explaining the fundamentals of wealth-building through investment portfolios and illustrating his brilliant mathematical calculations. She read his missives until her eyes crossed, her brain froze, and the numbers turned into fat sheep skipping over fences.

Clearly, their visit to the American continent turned out to be most profitable.

Cassandra strolled toward the rest of the paintings. Each piece was dated between the years 1814 to 1817. Three long years—the length of time Richard and Allayne spent in Europe. Allayne mentioned in his letters that he ventured into the lucrative buying and selling of valuable artwork from the continent, while Richard studied art under the tutelage of an Italian master. Jeremy never followed them in their adventure. He remained in Cornwall to assume his father's title as Marquess of Waterford and see to his financial affairs—a subject he declined to discuss.

A small smile tugged the corners of her mouth as Cassandra gazed at the portraits once again. They all depicted memories of their childhood, cherished moments frozen in oil and canvass, forever immortalized.

He had never forgotten.

Her gaze settled on the last painting swathed in white muslin. Unable to resist, she cautiously lifted the stained white cloth draped over it. As the unfinished rendering of Richard and she came into view, Cassandra gasped in amazement. They were sitting atop their horses, looking at each other against the backdrop of the rising sun. Both no longer portrayed as children but rather as a man and a woman meeting for the first time.

"Do you like it?" She turned abruptly at the sound of Richard's voice behind her.

"Richard!" She felt her cheeks flame in embarrassment at being caught nosing around where she should not be. "I'm so sorry—I didn't mean to—"

"It's all right." He took the muslin from her fingers and unveiled his work with an audible swish. "Another day or two, and it should be finished."

"It's beautiful," she exclaimed, as the full length of the painting was revealed.

"So are you," he whispered, and their eyes met.

Cassandra's heart jumped with joy upon hearing his words. The scent of his cologne replaced the vapor of turpentine. She found herself enthralled by his nearness, the sheer breadth of his shoulders, and the masculine perfection of his body, which might as well have been carved by a sculptor. He looked so handsome that when she was little, she always thought he was an angel sent from heaven to watch over her in secret. Four days ago, the first time she saw him again with his eyes closed and face upturned to the heavens—he looked exactly like an archangel in a conversation with the Divine.

But despite Richard's spirituality, he had never been religious. He was not one of those people who went to church every Sunday or memorized every bible verse like a preacher. He always communed with his God in a special way. In fact, everything about him was special. For her, he was the epitome of what an ideal man should be, and she adored him endlessly.

Someone cleared his throat loudly.

Startled out of her cogitation, Cassandra turned toward the doorway at the same time as Richard.

≫≫≪≪

"HELLO, SWEETHEART." JEREMY strolled in and flicked his dark eyes at Richard.

He had been standing by the doorway watching them, and he felt offended. No—he was *not* jealous by any means! Just *slightly upset* that Cassie was here alone with Richard, looking up at him like a besotted puppy, ready to lap on his—well, if that was not offensive, then he did not know what was. After all, they were supposed to be betrothed, and he had all the right to feel resentful—*did he not?*

"Jeremy!" Cassie's eyes widened.

Ah, how enchanting! Jeremy thought with satisfaction. Her reaction was exactly what one would expect from a blushing bride-to-be. He regarded her upturned face, with her large eyes and soft pink lips slightly parted, and he could not resist. The brat could slap him later when they were alone, but right now, he was determined to kiss her.

And he did—longer and deeper than he had intended.

Watch and drool, old chap! Those were his last thoughts before he felt Cassie lightly bite the tip of his tongue in warning. He pulled away and gave her his most charming crooked smile, ignoring the fury blazing in her eyes. "How are you doing, old chap?" He turned his attention to Richard, who looked every bit as uncomfortable as she did.

"Fine, and you?" he replied with a small frown.

"Never been better." Jeremy cocked his head to the side and smirked.

"And how was London?" Richard said in a tone that had a stern ring to it.

"Busy, what with all the—ah—*errands* and such. But I am glad that is all done and over with. I couldn't wait to get home, for I miss my sweet brat, ahem—I mean, my sweetheart." He wrapped a possessive arm around Cassie's waist and pulled her close, keeping her half turned, so her breast pressed nicely against the side of his chest.

Ah, and wasn't that just wonderful? No—he was *not* thinking that, because he liked it, but because they were betrothed, and he was *supposed* to feel like he liked it—*right?*

Richard's brow furrowed, and he glanced at the large diamond ring on Cassie's finger. "Congratulations on your engagement," he said in a voice that did not reflect his approval of his friend's good fortune.

"Thank you." Jeremy tightened his hold on Cassie and dropped a quick kiss on her lips, paying no heed to the heavy stomp she inflicted on his foot.

"How long have you two been courting?" Richard turned to Cassie with an intense stare.

"Er, ah—" Cassie averted her gaze and darted her eyes in every direction, fidgeting and flustered as Richard shuffled his feet to remind her that he was still waiting for an answer.

"A year," Jeremy cut in.

"A year." Richard narrowed his eyes at him. "Weren't you seeing Lady Bosworth six months ago, at the same time as Miss Darvis and Madame Le Bleu?"

Cassie gasped.

Jeremy's amusement faded. "I didn't know that news of my exploits was common-knowledge in Europe," he replied icily.

"No, in fact, they were not. It was Cassie who apprised Allayne and I of your adventures through her letters."

Cassie's cheeks colored a deep shade of red. "I-I—"

"Why don't you run along and see the duke?" Jeremy released her, angry now for being put on the spot. "Gordon told me you were here for a visit."

"Yes." Cassie immediately scampered away without looking back at either of them.

Jeremy watched her disappear through the doorway before he turned irately at Richard. "What are you trying to suggest?"

"I should be the one asking you that." Richard pinned cold blue eyes on him.

Jeremy clenched his jaw. Richard had always been a keen interrogator. Jeremy had been careless—he should have discussed details with Cassie and prepared for just these kinds of questions. Richard was the kind of man who would not be easily persuaded, especially if he suspected something was amiss.

"Are you trying to imply that I am unfaithful to Cassie?" Jeremy asked in a rigid tone.

"Are you?" Richard pressed, staring him down.

"Whether I am or not, I believe it is none of your business." Jeremy folded his arms across his chest and regarded his friend with undisguised indignation.

"Cassie's well-being is my business." Richard straightened to his full height—an inch taller than Jeremy.

"Is it—now?" Jeremy clenched his jaw and squinted his eyes into slits. "Did you even wonder about her well-being when you came home with your betrothed in tow? Do you know how much that hurt her?"

Richard's expression softened for a moment, and he appeared baffled by his remark. "I don't understand what you mean. Why would my engagement wound her?"

"Because she waited for you, you idiot!" Jeremy said. "Every Christmas, she sat by that damn window overlooking Rose Hill drive, waiting for you to come back! Ten years, Richard—she waited ten bloody years, and when you finally came home, you had Glenford's daughter with you."

"Good God." Richard shoved his fingers through his hair, thoroughly appalled at what he had learned. "I had no idea she would take a childhood promise so seriously."

"Yes, it's damn stupid—unbelievable even, but there you have it— she did." Jeremy threw his hands in the air in exasperation. "She was devoted to you, and she missed you terribly. And when you returned with another girl, she felt betrayed. In her mind, she thought you had forgotten her. It did not matter if she saw you as her best friend or her idol or if she was infatuated with you. When she saw that other woman by your side, she thought you had replaced her."

"Lord no—that isn't true!" Richard placed his hands on his hips and shook his head as he stared at the floor. "I would never replace her. She was like a sister to me. I have always remembered her as a little girl of eight years, who had an endearing childhood infatuation toward me, but I never dreamed that she would take that to heart and into adulthood. I admit I never pictured her as a grown young woman."

"Well, she is—now." Jeremy sighed.

"And you've asked to marry her, and she accepted," Richard said gravely.

"Yes." Jeremy nodded, steeling himself once more against Richard's oncoming interrogation.

"When did you decide to get leg-shackled?" Richard looked him up and down, giving him the impression that he did not believe a word he had said. "I didn't get the impression you were ready for a lifetime commitment."

"I am." Jeremy shrugged and tried not to squirm under his scrutiny. "I took the plunge, didn't I?"

"When did you ask her father for her hand?" Richard persisted, undeterred. "Did you get rid of all your mistresses before you began courting her?"

"As I said before, my affairs are none of your business." Jeremy could feel his temper begin to flare. He hated being grilled in such a fashion, especially when he did not have definite answers to counter Richard's pointed questions. All he had were lies and more lies, and he was starting to feel suffocated under the weight of his own fabrications.

"Do you love her?" Richard regarded him with a reproachful look that made him feel like a defiant adolescent.

"Yes," he replied without hesitation. Not that he was lying once again. He had meant what he had said—just not in that romantic, nauseous, disgustingly sentimental sort of way. He simply responded as he ought, he told himself—the way Cassie's future bridegroom *should* react to questions like such.

"Well, so do I." Richard looked him straight in the eyes.

Jeremy swallowed, and beads of perspiration formed on his forehead at Richard's declaration. What could he do? What could he say to that? His mind went blank, and there was nothing he could think of as a retort. And somehow, for the first time in his life, Jeremy felt the sting of fear and vulnerability of losing Cassie, deep in the confines of his *supposed-to-be-jaded* heart.

CHAPTER EIGHTEEN

The real Prince Charming...

RICHARD WALKED INTO his father's bedchamber with a bitter taste in his mouth. He was not in the least bit proud of confronting Jeremy. He had looked forward to seeing his friend and resuming their friendship after his long sojourn in Europe, but now it seemed their abrupt dispute could put a wedge between them.

"Ah, there you are," his father beckoned from the bed.

Sitting on a chair by his bedside, Cassie looked up from the book she was reading to him.

Richard took in the domestic scene, delighting in the fact that she had kept up her visits to his father during his absence. They had always been fond of each other—an unusual inclination for the usually somber duke.

"How are you today, Father?" Richard leaned over the side of the bed to kiss the top of his head. His handsome countenance was gone, replaced by the haggard face of a man who had gradually deteriorated over the years.

His robust and proud physique had become decrepit, and his hair had turned silver, making him look much older than he was. The guilt of having defied his father for so many years over his wishes for him to marry Desiree nagged at his conscience. He was too young back then; he was not ready. His father's heavy-handedness at managing his life had angered him and caused him to rebel. Now, he could see his father had the best intentions for him. He had never meant to alienate his son. The duke had made what he believed was an excellent match to secure his future after he was gone.

Richard blinked back the sudden sting of tears. After his mother died just as he turned thirteen, his father had never stopped mourning her. But unlike other men, his father had withdrawn into himself, carrying the shadow of lingering sadness on his shoulders for over a decade until it finally consumed him.

"I feel wonderful," his father replied with a rare smile.

Richard sat on the edge of the bed and regarded him thoughtfully. His father's bright eyes had faded with age, as had the zest for life.

Ah, his parents were so devoted to each other, so happy and so in love—an extraordinary love-match. Growing up, he had watched their affection and faithfulness to each other, the warmth of which spilled over to him, their only son. He remembered thinking he wanted that same kind of life—to love and be loved with such great devotion by the woman he would marry someday. His gaze wandered to Cassie.

The corners of her mouth lifted as her eyes met his. She was looking at him the way his mother used to look at his father from across the room. He smiled in return, stifling the sudden urge to reach over and hold her hand in his.

It had been such a long time since he had experienced the liveliness of her company, the laughter and camaraderie that came with her friendship, and the joy of spending time together doing the simple things they both loved. Ah, how he had missed those days, and how he regretted coming home too late.

Cassie. God, she was perfect, but already taken, by—out of all the people in the face of the earth—one of his best friends. And he—of all things—was bound in a betrothal to please his father who was dying.

He glanced at his dear father. Could he bear to disappoint him during his last few days on earth in lieu of pursuing his own happiness?

His mind drifted to Cassie. She was no longer free. Could he really act like a heartless, unscrupulous swine, throw away everything he had been taught as a proper gentleman, and steal her from a good friend who was more like a brother? Could he live with himself if he did?

He gazed at her, unable to hide the bleakness that suddenly crept into his heart.

Cassie's expression changed into concern. "Richard?" She tilted her head and searched his face. "Is anything the matter?"

"What? Oh—no." His eyes slid down to the large engagement ring she wore on her gloved finger, and he forced a smile, ignoring the burgeoning heaviness in his chest. "Jeremy—he's waiting for you in the drawing room downstairs."

JEREMY CHECKED HIS fob watch for the third time as he stood in the drawing room. Half an hour had passed since Cassie had gone to see the duke, and he was getting restless. His short but tension-filled exchange of words with Richard had left him feeling like a fool. Richard always had a way of assessing certain things—people included. He was not the sort who could easily be influenced, especially if the facts did not line up. When those piercing blue eyes of his had scrutinized Jeremy, he felt as transparent as his flimsy lies.

Jeremy glanced at his watch once again before he shut its elaborately engraved gold cover with a snap and slid it back into his waistcoat pocket. His patience for waiting at an end, he looked around for anything to keep him occupied and found himself staring at the large family painting on the wall.

He wandered over to the imposing portrait, flanked on either side by ornate Venetian sconces carved with bronze cherubs and intertwining vines. Splendidly dressed, the Duke and Duchess of Grandstone sat on a gilded couch ornamented with brass winged lions in what seemed to be the same room he was standing in. They leaned on each other, with the duke's arm around his smiling duchess, her hand resting on his knee, and they looked back at him with eyes filled with bliss.

Their only son, Richard, who appeared no more than two years old when the portrait was painted, wore a simple white button suit trimmed in blue and sat holding a small wooden horse on his mother's lap with a wide smile. The three of them personified the exuberance of a happy family.

Jeremy felt a twinge of envy. He wondered what it would be like to grow up in that kind of home. His mother had died when he was very young—of a broken heart, according to rumors, which may as well have been true, for his father was a scoundrel who repeatedly taunted her with his numerous affairs, including one with a pretty chambermaid.

After his mother passed, his father had left him under the care of tutors and governesses while he went on with his scandalous way. He barely knew his child existed, so Jeremy spent most of his childhood years in the company of servants, most especially Barton, who also worked as his father's butler at the time. Thankfully, Barton did what he thought was best for him by calling on Viscountess Carlyle for aid in raising him.

He was in desperate need of a family, craving any morsel of affection anyone could spare, which the kindly viscount, his lovely wife, and their wonderful children had given him aplenty. Rose Hill Manor became his second home. They treated him like their own and welcomed his daily visits with delight, which did not cease until he had to leave for University with Allayne and Richard. The viscount counseled him like a true father would, and the viscountess made sure his education and health were in order. For the first time in years, he felt wanted, needed, and loved.

The Carlyles saved his life.

And then one day, three years ago, he walked into Waterford

124

House and found his father dead with the gun barrel still lodged in his mouth and his hand on the trigger. Jeremy remembered standing there, frozen and emotionless. He did not know how long he remained staring at his father's lifeless eyes before Barton carefully guided him out the door and into the carriage, instructing the driver to take him back to Rose Hill Manor.

Damn his father to hell. Jeremy had gone into mourning to satisfy protocol, but he spared not a single tear for the lousy bastard. His drinking, womanizing, and gambling had bankrupted the coffers of Waterford Estates, leaving his son of barely twenty-one years to deal with the consequences. While his friends regaled themselves in Europe, he was left scrambling to save what was left of his inheritance. He used his share of the income coming from his overseas business ventures with Allayne and Richard to pay for his father's staggering debts, but even then, it was not sufficient to save Waterford Park from ruin.

The burden on his shoulders almost destroyed him. Out of sheer humiliation, he kept the real status of his finances from his friends. He had never felt so alone, so uncertain, and so frightened in his life. Were it not for Cassie, who continually pestered him and dragged him out of the house to Rose Hill every single day so her mother could fuss over him to eat his meals, he would have followed his father's example and pumped a bullet through his head.

May the rotten scoundrel burn in hell for eternity! If not for his devil's luck in attracting a good number of heiresses who not only willingly opened their legs but also their purses to help him put the financial disaster of Waterford Estates to rights, his entire patrimony would have been squandered amongst his father's shrewd creditors.

He flinched at the memory. He felt cheap, vile, and dirty. More than anything, he hated himself, but he had to do what he needed to do—and it paid off handsomely. His prowess for numbers and his keen eye for investments worked to his advantage. In a span of only over a year, he successfully restored Waterford Park to its former glory, making it one of the wealthiest estates in all of England today.

He had no regrets—except for the fact that he sold his soul to the very same devil who possessed his abominable louse of a father. Every time he indulged in his philandering ways, he saw more and more of his loathsome sire in himself. It would only be a matter of time before the tentacles of hell slithered and coiled around his neck in his sleep and collected his collateral.

"Jeremy?" Cassie's voice was like an angel's torch in the darkness that had enveloped him and saturated his thoughts.

He turned, and she slipped her arm through his, the way she always did for as long as they had been friends. "What are you doing here scowling at the Grandstones?" She tugged him to her side as they walked toward the door. "I apologize for taking so long. Will you have dinner with us at Rose Hill? Allayne was wondering about what you have been up to, and Mama and Papa wanted to see you. We can play whist afterward."

"Of course." He glanced at her as they waited for his coach by the entrance, his humor restored, and his mood substantially improved.

Cassie had already forgiven him for his behavior earlier like she always did. She was the ray of sunshine for his withered soul, the one who overlooked his faults and saw the potential beneath the rubbish that concealed the man he could become.

And what kind of man could he be? Could he be the gentleman of her dreams, the paragon she could look up to, the ally she could always rely on? Should he rise to the challenge and, for once, see himself through her eyes?

"What are you woolgathering about?" Cassie tapped his knee to get his attention as they sat opposite each other in the plush carriage.

He flicked his eyes at her, but instead of satisfying her with a reply, he simply gave her a little wink and a crooked smile.

CHAPTER NINETEEN

The fall of Prince Charming…

JEREMIAH WAS IN no mood to become Prince Charming. Certainly not at five in the morning, with his valet, Percy, and his butler, Barton, waking him up. A nocturnal creature who habitually stayed up and was more active late into the night, sunrise was his signal to retire—not to arise from the cozy softness of his bed where he lay dreamily on his stomach, stark naked under the covers.

"My lord." Barton shook his shoulder a tad more forcefully. "You wanted us to wake you up before sunrise so you could get ready for your appointment."

"You must get up, my lord." Percy patted his cheek. "I must help you get dressed, or you will be late."

Jeremy groaned and buried his face deeper in his pillows. What kind of malevolent entity had contaminated his wits for him to think that he could do this?

His mind, though a little foggy, may have been awake, but his entire body was dead asleep. He could not, for the life of him, make his limbs agree to the commands of his brain.

"My lord!" Barton's voice had taken a harsher tone, and he shook his lordship's shoulder almost violently.

"Wake up, milord, wake up!" Percy took his cue and struck his cheek with noisy, stinging half-slaps.

Good Lord, his servants had turned into sadistic brutes! Who would have thought they had the talent to beat him out of bed?

Jeremy moaned in annoyance and tossed himself on his back, scrubbing his face with his hand. At the moment, he felt more like the Prince of Darkness than Prince Charming in the flesh.

"My lord?" Barton peered at him. "Are you awake?"

"Do I look like I'm sleeping with my eyes open?" Jeremy snapped, arching his back with a yawn as he stretched his arms and legs.

"Let's get you ready," Percy said, motioning for Barton to assist him. They practically dragged him off the bed and flopped him on a fat chair by the fireplace. Within the next few minutes, Percy had him washed, shaved, and dressed, and by the time he had gone downstairs, Barton had his horse, Eros, saddled.

Jeremy inhaled the fresh morning air he seldom savored and urged Eros into a gallop. Cassie would be at the beach at this hour, doing God knows what. He would never understand the blasted chit. Why would anyone trade the warmth of a bed for freezing one's arse in the chilly ocean breeze? Hell, he did not know what she was about—and neither did he know what *he* was about, riding like an imbecile at this hour.

A sliver of light peaked in the horizon as he neared the coastline. Well, he had to admit, the colors of dawn and the vista of the ocean as the sun cast golden sparkles upon the water were breathtaking. He suddenly found himself looking forward to seeing the sunrise with Cassie.

The scene would have been perfect—but for the fact that Richard already sat next to her on the sand, both of them gazing out to sea like an old, contented couple.

Jeremy felt the lance of an unfamiliar emotion in his chest. After that mad scramble to get out of bed—was this the reward he deserved? Lord, but he could just strangle the little twit for ruining his sleep, and as for Richard—it would be quite the thing if he could bury him in the sand and intentionally forget about him.

Richard leaned over and whispered in Cassie's ear. The two of them burst into laughter.

Jeremy trampled the jealousy that mushroomed in his gut. What could be so funny about the wretched, frigid sea? Moreover, why was he acting like a damned jealous lunatic? Cassie and Richard had always loved mornings at the beach—he knew that. Well, then—what irrational motive made him think he had the right to be irritated by their closeness?

He must have gotten used to being the protective betrothed—yes—that must be it—even if their engagement was a farce. After all, if they were going to get away with their charade, he should be acting as if he was jealous—*right?* He urged his horse faster toward them.

Cassie turned at the sound of his approach. "Jeremy!" She waved excitedly.

He waved back and nudged Eros toward where Apollo and Artemis were, and dismounted.

"Jeremy! What are you doing up so early?" Cassie met him halfway with a big smile.

"I was just wondering about the same thing." He put an arm around her and squeezed her shoulder, and then on impulse, picked her up and twirled her around.

Cassie shrieked, laughing as he set her back on her feet. "What's gotten into you?" She twined her arm through his and led him toward where Richard sat on the sand, watching them. "Are you sure you won't turn into ash if the sun touches your skin?"

"Who knows?" He suddenly dipped her backward as they reached the spot where she sat. "I might turn into a monster instead! Aaarrr!" He playfully pretended to bite her on the side of the neck.

They both collapsed next to Richard in fits of laughter.

I AM THE luckiest girl in the world, Cassie thought as she sat down between Jeremy and Richard on the shore. True, she had not felt this happy in a long time, sharing the sunrise with two of her favorite people.

"I should be going." Richard brushed away the grains of sand that clung to his riding breeches. "Good to see you again, old chap." He gave Jeremy a single slap on the shoulder and started toward the horses, whistling for Artemis.

Cassie rose and caught up to him, asking with an expectant gaze, "Oh, but won't you join us for breakfast at Rose Hill?"

"No, thank you. Perhaps another time." Richard mounted his horse, his eyes shadowed, avoiding her gaze.

"Will I see you tomorrow again, then?" She cupped her hand over her brow to shield her eyes from the glaring sun as she looked up at him. His blond hair shone with gold flecks, waving in the wind, his profile carving a perfect outline against the clear blue sky. He was so handsome that he took her breath away.

He pursed his lips and fiddled with the reins before he replied, "Cassie, I think it's no longer proper for us to—" he drew a heavy breath and darted his eyes at Jeremy, "to be alone together."

"But—why?" Her chest constricted at the implication. She knew exactly what he meant, but she needed to hear the words from him.

His brilliant eyes bore into hers. "You're not eight, and I'm not fifteen anymore, Cass. You are betrothed to Jeremy, and I—to Desiree. It wouldn't—doesn't—look right."

"B-but—what about our mornings?" Cassie felt a lump growing in her throat. She swallowed it back, finding it harder to breathe.

"You can have our beach." He motioned at the stretch of coastline winding beautifully into a silver crescent.

"And where will you be?" Her eyes began to blur with unshed tears. Why did she feel like death was at her door, and she was about to lose someone special?

Richard shrugged, cleared his throat, and stared ahead. "On the other side of the bluffs." He flicked his chin at the steep headland jutting out into the sea, with islands of jagged rocks that divided the east shores of the Grandstone estates.

Cassandra saw her almost-perfect world imploding. "B-but—when will I see you again?"

He turned his gaze onto the ocean. "Whenever you wish, as long as you're with a chaperone, or with—with Jeremy. I will do the same. I will call on Allayne and visit you with him. It's for the best, Cassie." His voice had softened into a whisper, and she noticed the faint twitch of a muscle on his cheek.

"Richard—"

"Please don't—" he interjected with pleading eyes, tightening his hold on the reins as his horse snorted, impatiently swishing its tail, and moving its hindlegs from side to side, shifting the sand with its massive hooves. "Don't make it more difficult than it is. I don't want this to hinder our friendship—especially Jeremy's." He glanced at Jeremy, who was striding toward them before he raised his hand in farewell and turned his mount around.

Cassandra stood frozen on the spot as she watched Richard nudge Artemis into a gallop with his riding boot until they diminished into a speck in the distance. She did not notice the wetness on her cheeks until Jeremy offered her his handkerchief.

JEREMY HAD BEEN secretly watching them from a few yards away, catching small snippets of conversation carried his way by the wind. By the time Richard had left, he had a somewhat tentative assumption of what had transpired between them.

"What's this, brat?" He clamped his hands on his hips, annoyed and dismayed at the scene he had seen unfold. "Don't tell me you're crying over that idiot again!"

Cassandra mopped her face furiously with the square of fine linen and glared at him. "He's not an idiot!"

"Oh, yes—I stand corrected." He rolled his eyes heavenward and pointed a forefinger at her. "You're the idiot!"

"Shut up, Jeremy Huntington!" She angrily stomped off in the direction of the horses.

Jeremy caught up with her and spun her around by the wrist. "Don't you dare walk away from me, Cassandra Carlyle! It is about time someone tells you to stop making a fool of yourself because of Richard! Your mad obsession over him has become ridiculous!"

"I don't care!" She twisted her wrist and snatched it from his grip, moving away from him.

"Well, I do!" Jeremy held her back by the arm. "What in the devil's name do you see in him, brat?"

Cassie scrubbed her eyes with his handkerchief and blew her nose. "Everything," she said between hiccups. "He's intelligent, kind, decent, responsible, and I find him very handsome. He's a good man—a loving son to his parents, and a worthy friend." Her mouth curved into a pensive smile, even as more tears fell from her eyes. "He adores the sea and the sunrise like I do—and he's an excellent artist, too."

Well damn, Jeremy thought in exasperation. Save for the handsome and intelligent part, he lacked every other quality Richard had. He certainly had big shoes to fill—if he was serious about becoming Prince Charming.

He heaved a deep sigh. "I'm sure he's all that, but he's taken, brat. Let it go." He took the handkerchief from her and wiped a tear from the corner of her eye. "Besides, as far as he's concerned, he thinks you're likewise taken."

Cassie snatched the handkerchief back and scowled at him. "I know, but neither of us is married—yet." She lifted her chin in defiance.

Her vehemence elicited a pang of displeasure in his chest. For some unknown reason, he could not picture Cassie in another man's arms—even if it happened to be one of his best friends.

Now, where the hell did that thought come from?

Perhaps he had missed her while he was in London. Perhaps he did not have anything better to do, or he had gone mad and thought he was falling.

In love.

With *her*.

Jeremy muttered a curse under his breath and glared at Cassie—also known as the notorious *Piglet*—his little brat and dearly betrothed—who was otherwise smitten with *tiny prick*.

CHAPTER TWENTY

Princess Charming...

C ASSANDRA SAT ON a wing back chair in front of the fireplace in
her father's library with an open book on her lap, while Jeremy
slept soundly on the fat chaise across from where she was seated. She
had been staring at the same page for the past half hour, seeing not a
single word. She could not stop thinking about Richard. His sudden
aloofness earlier bothered her. But then—could she really blame him?
His betrothal to that condescending female and his belief that she was
betrothed to Jeremy had changed their friendship. And, as always,
given the task of coming to a wise decision, Richard saw the situation
as objectively as a man groomed to inherit the dukedom could. He
chose to do what was expected of him.

Would things be different if he had come home without a lady in
tow and without the news of her false betrothal? What would happen
if both of them were free and they saw each other for the first time—as
a man and a woman, as they had at the beach? Cassandra leaned back
in her chair and recalled their first encounter—the one in the meager
privacy of the little alcove at Almack's. The memory could still make
her insides quiver, and her toes curl. He had looked at her differently
then. His eyes smoldered when he slid his gaze over her. He beheld
her the way a man would a woman who was the object of his desire.

She had practically melted into a puddle under his heated inspection. However, instead of feeling offended, she felt desirable and

wanted—a woman who had the power to entice the man who captured her heart.

However—Richard had not known who she was back then.

Cassandra sighed and rested her head against the cushion of the high-backed chair. When she chanced upon him that morning at the beach, she waited for that same spark of desire in his eyes. She wanted him to kiss her—the way he almost had at Almack's. But instead, he smiled at her with warmth and tenderness in his eyes, the way he used to do when she was a little girl. And even though his open affection twisted her nerves into knots and sent her heart aflutter, it likewise reminded her of his sisterly fondness of her.

You are all grown up now, he'd said, but as she pondered more about the past few days they'd spent together—it occurred to her that he never attempted to behave outside of decorum the way he had in London—even when they were without a chaperone.

Did he really see her as a grown woman—or just a taller version of Cassie, his little piglet? Had the discovery of her identity extinguished his ardent desire for the unknown temptress she had personified during their anonymous encounters in London?

Cassandra set her book on the footstool and strolled toward the gilt mirror hanging on the wall over a half-moon enameled table near the door. She studied her reflection. Her nose was small and straight, and her long red-gold hair fell in ringlets about her face. She might not be as beautiful as the goat lady, but she was attractive enough and had curves in all the right places. Jeremy always said she was the prettiest girl in all of England—especially when he wanted to beg for some of her chocolate bonbons.

Richard had found her desirable when he did not know her identity, could it be possible for her to revive that passion in him all over again? How could she transform herself into an enchantress who could once more bewitch him? Was there a book she could procure that taught a lady how to seduce a man?

Her gaze found Jeremy sprawled carelessly on the chaise opposite her chair by the fireplace. After their morning at the beach, he had joined her family for breakfast, yawning in between bites of toast, ham, and eggs. She invited him to her father's library for a little bit of reading before he headed back home, but as soon as his body made contact with the soft, comfortable chaise, he had instantly drifted into a deep slumber.

Poor man. What had possessed him to wake up at dawn? He had even dressed nicely, was freshly shaven, and wore his favorite cologne. She was so surprised to see him—all crisp and clean, with his dark hair smoothly slicked and tied at the back. He did not look rakish at all. Indeed, he resembled a respectable gentleman.

She grimaced at the memory of him with not a hair out of place. She rather liked him better with his hair down and windblown. If anything, it made him look even more devilish and dashing. No wonder the ladies collapsed into vapors upon setting eyes on him.

Cassandra walked over to where he lay and frowned at the way his head angled awkwardly on one side. One arm and a booted leg dangled from the chaise, his longish black hair hopelessly tousled over his brow. She took a pillow and propped his head carefully against it, brushing the stray locks from his face. Then, she wrestled off his riding boots and gently set his dangling limbs back onto the chaise. She grabbed a throw from one of the chairs and spread it over him before sitting on the edge next to him, wondering what Jeremy would do if he were in her shoes?

She had watched him over the years, getting who he wanted—when he wanted. Not a single female was immune to Jeremiah Devlin Huntington—from the simpering chits to the matchmaking mamas—even the married ladies and grand dames worshipped the ground he walked on. He could charm a tree into submission if it had a skirt on it. How did he do it? Was there some secret code, some magic formula one needed to learn? But—from whom?

Her gaze settled on him as it struck her that the answer was right here, under her nose the entire time.

"Jeremy," she rasped in his ear. "Wake up."

Neither his serene expression nor his heavy breathing changed.

"Jeremy!" she said in a louder voice. "Wake up. I've something to tell you."

He replied with a groan and turned on his side, facing away from her.

"Jeremy!" She jostled his shoulder. "Wake up. I have an idea!"

He mumbled something that sounded like "go away" and pulled the throw over his head.

"I think I figured out what the problem is," Cassandra prattled on. "Are you listening to me?"

He replied with a grumble and what sounded like a muffled word not fit for a lady's ears.

"It seems I need to change my style." She yanked the throw off his head and held it fast when he tried to pull it back. "You see, I never really paid any attention to how important it was, but now I am stupendously enlightened."

Jeremy shifted without opening his eyes and snatched the pillow behind him, placing it on top of his face.

"I know you might think I am foolish and such, but I truly believe this could be the solution to the problem." Cassandra shoved the pillow away, letting it drop onto the floor. "You must help me with my plan. Jeremy—are you listening?"

She heard a muted curse and took that as agreement.

"Remember how we all grew up together like brothers and sister? Well, I no longer wish to be viewed as a sister. I know I had my season and had the opportunity to mingle with the highest echelons of the ton, but that was only because of you. They assumed you were interested in me, which fueled the ton's fascination over my person, and I became all the rage. But—Jeremy—" she shook his shoulder.

"Listen to me!"

He jerked his shoulder away with a growl and wrenched the throw from her grasp, pulling it over his head again as he curled into a ball.

"As I was saying," she tapped a finger on her cheek, "all those men desired me because of you, which is all wrong. I want them to want me because of me. Did you hear what I just said, Jeremy?"

His reply came in the form of a guttural sound and more stifled swearing beneath the throw.

"Oh, good—I'm glad you're paying attention," she pressed on eagerly. "Anyway, here's the plan. I do not want to be seen as a silly country girl anymore and go gallivanting about in breeches looking like a stable boy like Mama always says. I wish to be everything a man could long for! I want to talk, move, dress, and do things the right way—to be the most desirable woman I can be and become every man's dream! Yes, that is what you said about Countess Woolworth, and all the men follow her around like puppy dogs." She clapped her hands in delight. "Oh, Jeremy! Wouldn't it be divine if I could be like her? To be the most irresistible, enchanting kind of woman? Will you help me, Jeremy? Oh, please—will you show me how to do it—so I can seduce *Richard*?"

"What!" Jeremy sat up so abruptly that they butted heads and landed in a heap of tangled limbs on the carpet. "What the bloody hell are you babbling about?" he demanded in a voice that had escalated into a snarl as he rubbed his forehead, his immaculate hair now unbound and sticking out in all directions.

"Oh, Jeremy! Can't you see?" She framed his face in her hands and grinned widely. "You must teach me how to become Princess Charming!"

CHAPTER TWENTY-ONE

Capturing Princess Charming...

"NO! HAVE YOU gone daft?" Jeremy paced the floor in the library.

"But you're the only one who can teach me." Cassie trailed after him. "Please, Jeremy—this is a matter of life and death!"

"Gah! Life and death, my arse!" He paused to glare at her. "Since when did seducing an unsuspecting man become so dire to your person?"

"But it is! I can't live without Richard, and I'll just die if he marries that goat lady!" She followed him around the coffee table as he resumed his pacing.

"Then I'll go make sure we don't bury you in the pasture, so the goat lady will not bother your dead self," he snapped over his shoulder at her.

"Jeremy! I'm serious!" Cassie stomped her foot on the carpet.

He stopped and turned to face her. "What—do you think I'm jesting?" he yelled before moving toward the fireplace. "The answer is no, brat!" He flopped down on the chaise and grabbed his boots. "I used to think you had a brain inside that skull of yours, but now I see it contained nothing more than rotten mincemeat!" He angrily shoved his foot into one boot and yanked it violently, muttering, "What a preposterous proposition!"

"But it's the only thing that could work!" Cassie persisted, twisting her hands together fretfully.

"I don't want to hear any more of this madcap scheme of yours." He looked up and shook a forefinger at her.

"But—"

He stood up and smoothed his wrinkled clothes. "I'm going home to get more sleep. I don't want you showing up at my house and hounding me, do you understand?"

Cassie pursed her lips, plunked onto a chair by the fire, and sulked.

Ha! She can mope all she wants! Jeremy muttered under his breath as he marched toward the foyer. *I do not give a fig!*

"Jeremy! Are you on your way out, old chap?" Allayne rose from a chair as he passed the drawing room.

Jeremy paused by the doorway and pulled on his riding gloves. "Yes, I'm afraid I need a little bit more rest without your sister manipulating me into one of her obtuse plots."

"Oh? And what is she about now?" Allayne placed the book he was reading face down on a table and strolled toward him.

"The usual demented trickery on how she could snag Richard." Jeremy angrily jerked the edges of his leather gloves and flexed his fingers.

"I see. And what trickery is she scheming as of late?" Allayne leaned against the doorframe and crossed his arms over his chest.

"She wanted me to teach her how to seduce Richard." Jeremy yanked his coat from the rack and thrust his arms furiously into the sleeves.

"And you agreed?"

"Hell—no!" Jeremy adjusted his jacket collar with forceful tugs and scowled mightily at Allayne.

"Whyever not?" Allayne regarded him with an irritating, amused expression.

"What do you mean—why not?" Jeremy had the sudden urge to twist Allayne and Cassie's necks into a single braid. "Have you lost your marbles? Can't you see she's obsessed with Richard?"

"Actually, I believe that she believes she's hopelessly in love with him," Allayne replied with a maddening dimpled half-smile.

"I don't give a damn what she believes!" Jeremy threw his hands in the air. "Richard is not the right man for her."

"Oh?" Allayne raised his eyebrows. "And who do you think is—" He narrowed eyes identical to Cassie's at him. "You?"

Jeremy felt the rush of heat spread across his cheeks. He grabbed his top hat and adjusted it low on his brow to conceal his discomposure. "I'm tired. I must take my leave," he said in a voice that came out a bit too harsh for his preference.

"Certainly, and may I remind you, my friend," Allayne gave him a single slap on his shoulder as he opened the door for him, "I'm still a perfect shot."

⇶⤜

JEREMY STOMPED STRAIGHT to his study at Waterford House in a dark mood. He grabbed the decanter of brandy from the sideboard, poured himself a measure, and tossed the liquid down his throat.

What the hell was Allayne trying to insinuate? That Richard was a better man than he was? Or that he would put a bullet through his head if he had shown a romantic interest in Cassie? On the other hand—perhaps the blackguard meant both!

Jeremy poured another measure of brandy and swallowed it all in one gulp, ignoring the burning trail it left all the way down his belly. He felt insulted by Allayne's subtle insinuation, and he was angry at Cassie. She had certainly done it this time! Why couldn't she let go of Richard? What sort of fixation was this that afflicted her like a bloody disease?

Yes, he could accept the fact that Richard was the epitome of a gentleman in every way. His life had been perfect from the day he was born. He had probably done everything right since he started crawling in the nursery. Richard was his total opposite. Damn—if one compared Jeremy's accomplishments and the way he had chosen to live his life—he could never hold a candle against him.

Moreover, even though he had a definite advantage over Richard when it came to the ladies, he knew they only wanted him because he had a sterling reputation in bed, a high-ranking title to match, and was as rich as Croesus—aside from being blessed with his mother's good looks.

None of them really cared for who he truly was, how he felt, or what he thought about certain things. No one ever looked past the fancy trimmings surrounding him—the dashing Jeremiah Devlin Huntington, Marquess of Waterford: fashionable, wealthy, and debonair. None of them cared enough to reach deeper and find the real person behind the caricature society had created of him. None— except Cassie, who loved him only as a friend, and whose heart belonged to no one but Richard.

Perhaps he was the bigger idiot. Perhaps the moment had come for him to get out of Cornwall and travel to Europe. Perhaps time and distance would make him forget—and give him the much-needed motivation to find someone else. Jeremy put his glass down on the table and tugged the silk bell pull hanging near the side of his desk.

His butler, Barton, tapped on the door and entered a minute later. "Did you need anything, my lord?"

"Yes," Jeremy sat in his chair, leaned back, and crossed his booted feet at the ankles on top of his desk. "Have the maid bring up a supper tray for me. I am retiring for the evening. I do not wish to be disturbed."

"Yes, my lord." Barton glared pointedly at the dirt from his boots that had settled on the polished mahogany.

"Do not admit any guests—including Miss Carlyle." Jeremy ignored Barton's disapproving frown.

"My lord?" Barton tore his gaze from the dust marring the once spotless table and raised a silver eyebrow at him. "Even your betrothed?"

"You heard me, Barton. No guests—especially Miss Carlyle," Jeremy said in a firm tone.

"May I ask why, my lord, in case she does visit and inquires?" Barton's normally stoic face took on a look of befuddlement and curiosity.

"No, you may not!" Jeremy said irritably. "I grant you the authority to close the door on her face if she does."

Barton's chin went up, and his expression reverted to its usual lofty appearance. "Very well, my lord, just the door?"

"Out!" Jeremy stabbed a forefinger in the direction of the door. "And If I catch you accepting bribes from her—I'll reduce your station to a footman, am I clear?"

"Yes, my lord." Barton's face reflected not a single emotion or a speck of fear on losing his position as he bowed with a flourish. "Though I daresay those bonbons were rather excellent, milord," he said before hastily retreating out the door.

Jeremy glowered at his back with an exasperated shake of his head. The problem with older servants, who had been around wiping his nose and caring for him since he was a toddler, was they never could take their master seriously without being insolent.

He pulled some sheets of stationery emblazoned with his family crest from the desk drawer and began writing to his solicitor and stewards about arrangements to be made in his absence.

>⟫⟫⟩⟨⟨⟨

LATER THAT NIGHT, Cassandra pulled up her skirt and cloak above her knees as she climbed up the sturdy wooden ladder Jeremy's servants had prepared for her. Morton, the Rose Hill butler, had informed her this afternoon that his cousin, Barton, had sent a message, saying she was officially banned at Waterford House and the cost for her re-admittance would be no less than an extra-large box of chocolate bonbons.

Hence, Cassandra entered negotiations with the Waterford staff, with Morton acting as the chief liaison between her and Barton—the other side's mastermind. Within an hour, the bribe was paid, and necessary arrangements were made. In short order, a ladder was left in place, and the latch on the window to Jeremy's bedchamber was disengaged.

Cassandra pushed the well-oiled windowpane aside and slid into Jeremy's bedchamber. She knew how to navigate it even in the dark with only the soft flickering light coming from the fireplace, having visited it numerous times over the years with Allayne and Richard when they came over to play. For some odd reason, Jeremy never had the inclination to occupy the old marquess's bedchamber.

She slipped her hand in her skirt pocket to make sure she did not drop the ostrich feather she had stashed inside to wake Jeremy. He had been so upset when he left, and she had been distraught, for she hated quarreling with him. She could not bear to go to bed knowing he was angry with her; she just had to see him and appease his temper, and perhaps, make him laugh. Surely, he would forgive her once he saw the extra box of chocolate bonbons she had brought for him.

Cassandra tiptoed toward the massive bed, careful not to trip on any of the furniture. Thankfully, the low fire in the hearth and the moonlight streaming in from the windows provided some illumina-tion. She heard his heavy breathing as she got nearer, pulling the ostrich feather from her pocket with a stifled giggle.

As she came upon the edge of the bed, however, the laughter died on her lips. Jeremy lay sprawled on his stomach with a white satin sheet covering the lower portion of his legs—but other than that—he was stark naked.

Cassie could not remember how long she stood there gaping at him, the ostrich feather poised in mid-air. Aside from the sketches of couples in various stages of entanglement and undress in Allayne's naughty pamphlets, she had never seen a real man without a shirt before—much less without his breeches! She debated whether she should stick with her plan—or jump out the window.

Curiosity won.

Treading lightly on the carpet, she inched closer and climbed onto the massive bed, careful not to disturb him and grateful that he slept deeply. She crawled on all fours in a slow, cat-like motion and cautiously sat next to the poor unsuspecting man. Her gaze traveled the breadth of his shoulders. She had never thought of Jeremy as muscular, but now the evidence was right before her eyes. He had wide shoulders with lean ripples of flesh, and his arms were sinewy, boasting bulging biceps and a sprinkling of dark hair. Cassandra's mouth went dry as she followed the curve of his spine all the way down to his prominent bottom.

Good Lord! Her hand flew to her mouth as she spotted the two indentations right above the delicious mounds. Well-well! It seemed Jeremiah Devlin Huntington had dimples after all!

He suddenly stirred and flopped on his back in a single motion, arms extended over his head, his tousled black hair falling over his brow. The sheet slid further down and draped over his knees.

Cassandra froze in panic. She had never pictured Jeremy as a grown man. He had always been a young boy to her—her childhood friend—the same way Richard probably thought of her.

But now, sitting here with this outrageously virile male cast in the same mold as the god of love and desire, *Eros*—wasn't that the name of his horse? Her eyes darted in the direction of his proudly jutting sex, and she felt a flood of heat spread from her hairline to her cheeks, all the way down to her toes.

Sacred myrtles of Aphrodite! She fanned herself with the feather. Jeremy certainly was well-endowed as a prime-blooded stallion!

She dragged her gaze away from that most fascinating part of his anatomy and studied his broad chest, chiseled with well-defined muscles and thicker black hair tapering downwards into a dark line, ending in the area between his legs.

If her mother knew what she was staring at—at this very moment—she would have an apoplexy and would probably never wake up again.

Her fingers twitched with the unimaginable, utterly incorrigible desire to touch the forbidden fruit. Should she—or should she not?

Naturally, curiosity won.

She timidly reached out and touched a fingertip to the swell of muscles on his chest, delighting in the rough texture of the hair covering his smooth skin. He felt warm and smelled clean—a mixture of lavender, musk, and mint.

She trailed her finger lower, following the column of hair that narrowed, then flared into a groomed thatch of dark curls. She leaned in for a closer look and then gently poked the appendage with the pad of her forefinger. It suddenly twitched and sprang to attention, much like a startled serpent poised to strike. She recoiled so fast, she tossed the ostrich feather and fell back on her bum, causing the bed to rattle.

"I hope you find everything to your satisfaction, Miss Carlyle," Jeremy drawled, regarding her with a smoldering, heavy-lidded gaze and a heart-stopping crooked smile—which could very well be fatal enough to slay the wicked Queen and capture Princess Charming.

CHAPTER TWENTY-TWO

The Prince of Darkness...

I N HER ENTIRE eighteen years of existence here on earth, Cassandra Carlyle had never thought her short-lived life would end with death due to extreme humiliation.

She was caught where her finger—and her nose—should not have been impertinently prying, and at the moment, the question of what to do or say to justify her behavior had yielded not a speck of an excuse.

She stared warily at Jeremy, who was eyeing her with a knowing smirk. Never mind if he did not have any stitch of clothing on, the wretched man seemed not to give a fig. She must admit, he looked quite threatening in his state of undress and was not behaving like her Jeremy at all.

He was grinning like the big bad wolf, all hairy and sinewy and— she darted her eyes downward—monumentally *noteworthy* and profoundly *scary*. She knew he was going to take the bonbons, pretend to be harmless to a fault, then gobble up poor little Cassie in the scarlet riding cloak.

She leaned backward on her elbows, sinking deeper into the bed as he stalked her on all fours, like a dangerous beast sniffing at his feast. He was going to eat her alive—she just knew it—and he would start with her liver!

The hairy, scary, but remarkably attractive beast paused over her, propped his hands on either side of her head, and straddled her legs between his knees.

"What are you doing here, brat?" His voice even sounded different—deep and husky, as if it came from the bowels of the earth, sending shivers down her spine. "Did you come alone?"

What a clever question! She could just tell he would instantly swallow her whole if she admitted she had come by herself, so she shook her head in vehement denial.

"I see." His lashes swept upward, and he reached for something over her head. "You came with *Mister Feather.*"

Cassandra swallowed the alarm rising in her throat as he retrieved the fluffy ostrich feather she had brought and brandished it like a white flag for her to lay down her arms and avow surrender.

"And what, may I ask, did you and *Mister Feather* hope to accomplish?"

He brushed the soft, wispy plumes along her flaming cheek repeatedly, swirling it in mesmerizing patterns. The sensation made her stomach clench and jolt into a flip-flop, sending a flow of current through her frazzled nerves.

"N-n-nothing," Cassandra croaked, shrinking away from the teasing and trying to calm her roiling innards from attacking each other. There could be no mistaking it—she was absolutely certain that even though *this* Jeremy resembled *her* Jeremy, it was *not* him at all. This creature was possessed!

"Nothing, aye?" The devil's eyes narrowed into slits, and she sank further into the feather-filled bed as he bent his arms and rested his weight on his elbows.

He was much too close, oh, Lord—so close, she could feel the swelter of the fires of hell radiating from his skin. A heady, spicy, masculine scent exuded from his pores, disconcerting her sensibilities into an uproar.

"Are you saying that both you and *Mister Feather* are innocent?" He traced the outline of her earlobe lightly with the quill. "Hmm?"

Cassandra nodded, and then shook her head.

His breath fanned the little hairs that had loosened from her braid, tickling the side of her neck. Goosebumps rose on her arms—God Almighty, why was he looking at her with those dark, heavy-lidded eyes? She had never stared into them this intently before. Had they always been crowned with lashes so exceedingly thick and long?

He crinkled his dark eyebrows. "Yes-no? No-yes?" He smiled crookedly, and her gaze shifted to that delicious mouth. His lower lip was fuller than the upper, so sensual, yet so manly; it seemed to beckon her to sample what it tasted like.

Cassandra squashed that idea in mid-thought.

Since when did she think Jeremy's lips looked good enough to lick? Had the malevolent spirit instigated some underhanded mind-trick to tempt her to covet a kiss?

"Well? What is it going to be, brat?" He shifted his position so she could feel the entire length of his body pressed against hers. His hard chest flattened her aching breasts, and she could feel his heartbeat between their rigid crests. *Oh my, he was boiling hot—but he was naked and—and—eekk! What was that peck?*

She suddenly heaved him off her and scampered off the bed.

"What's the matter?" The devil who looked remarkably like Jeremy lifted an eyebrow and rose from the bed, unmindful of the glorious naked splendor he displayed in front of her.

She took one look at *that thing,* and her mouth desiccated into ash. She could swear—it had a mind of its own, for it was pointing directly at her.

Panic churned in her gut. Perhaps the devil could read her thoughts! She spun around so fast—she ran into a wall.

"Where are you going?" The ominous entity asked in that rich, velvety, devilish voice as he caught her, still wobbling dizzily from her collision with the plaster paneling.

"I-I-I—" she flinched, rubbing her bruised forehead, forgetting whatever lie she was about to devise, when he pinned her against the wall, holding her wrists above her head.

"Your *thing* is poking me!" She squirmed, but her wriggling seemed to make it prod even more insistently.

"Ah, yes," he replied with eyes gleaming like that of the Prince of Darkness. "That's what it likes to do."

"I-is that your t-tail?" she gulped, and perhaps he had horns, too?

"My tail?" He let out a hearty, evil laugh. "No, sweetheart, that's my snake."

"Y-your s-snake?" She stole a downward glance, but his torso blocked the view. "W-what is it doing down there?"

"It's looking for the Garden of Eden," his tone lowered into a baritone, and he nuzzled her neck, making her shiver.

"Eden?" Her heart pounded as unfamiliar warmth bloomed in the virginal depths of her core. "Where is it?" she asked breathlessly.

"Sweetheart," he whispered huskily, "it's underneath your skirt."

CHAPTER TWENTY-THREE

Lesson number one...

J EREMIAH, THE WICKED Marquess of Waterford, could not quite
fathom what to make of the young woman in front of him. All
women—with just one heart-stopping smile and a steamy, heavy-
lidded gaze, would have taken their clothes off and torn their pantalettes in half.

But oh, no—not Miss Cassandra Carlyle—also known as the notorious Piglet, the equally wicked brat. As soon as he had mentioned
where the Garden of Eden could be found, she had stared at him with
green eyes, big and round. Then, she began to chuckle—which
bubbled into a giggle—which eventually ended up with a hoot of
laughter.

"Oh, Jeremy, you oaf!" She slid her wrists from his grasp and
smacked him playfully on the forehead. "Garden of Eden, indeed!" she
chortled and pushed him away, giving his aching, massive erection a
swat.

Good God, but that hurt! Jeremy howled and covered his poor
member to protect it from another unforeseen assault. Of all the
females in the kingdom he would kill to defile, why, dear Lord, why—
did it have to be Cassandra Carlyle? She was a dangerous virgin, a
ruthless hoyden—a merciless castrator or, in this case—*castratress*
incarnate! If he survived the night and emerged in the morning with
his manhood and ballocks intact, he would tie her up spread-eagled in

a dungeon and show her how a real man made love!

"Oh no!" The merciless castratress reached out to pry away his hands. "Did I hurt you?"

"What the bloody hell were you thinking?" He swiped her fingers away from his most precious possession.

"Jeremy, I apologize. I did not mean to—"

He shrunk back from her. Did she think he would let her near his snake again? "Gah! Get away from me! What were you trying to do? Neuter me?"

"Nonsense. Let me see—" She took a step forward and dropped to her knees, unceremoniously prying his fingers off his forlorn, defanged viper.

"Cassie, will you please refrain from—"

She gasped. "Oh, Jeremy! I am so sorry!" She stared wide-eyed at his sex. "Oh Lord, I think I killed it by accident!" Her hand flew to her mouth. "I swear I did not mean to—"

"Cassie—"

"What are we going to do now?" she went on, oblivious to his discomfiture. "It's dead, isn't it? Should we bury it?" She poked his limp appendage with her finger as if to make sure it had truly departed this earth.

"Stop—"

"Oh, dear. But I am afraid we'll have to pluck it off first. Not to worry—I will help you. Do you suppose I can borrow a cleaver from Cookie?"

Jeremy uttered a chain of curses. Good, God! She was determined to geld him and turn him into a eunuch!

"That won't be necessary—"

She suddenly reached out and cupped his sex with one hand, then stroked it with the other. "You poor thing," she cooed. "I did not mean to clobber you on the head like that. Oh please, do not be dead. Would you please open an eye?" She frowned and glanced up at him. "Jeremy, do you know that your snake only has one eye? Quite an anomaly, don't you think?"

"Cassandra!" Jeremy growled and pulled his supposedly deceased member from her clasp. "That is quite enough, missy!"

Her face crumpled. "Please do not be mad at me, Jeremy. I was only trying to see if your snake—"

"This is not my snake!" Jeremy cursed so loud he was almost certain he had woken up the whole house. "This—" he grabbed his lifeless pecker in a chokehold, "is my cock!"

Cassandra lapsed into silence, looking thoroughly befuddled. "I'm confused," her fine brows snapped together.

"About what!" Jeremy snarled. Devil help him if this exasperating woman drove him to throttle her virgin self to death.

"You said it was a snake," she glanced suspiciously at his limp appendage, "and now you're telling me it's a chicken?"

Gah! The little dimwitted twit! He uttered several colorful expletives, reminding himself not to indulge in any more virginal trysts. Here he was, naked and exposed in all his male glory, balls bursting with the need for release—and all the woman wanted to do was argue about animals of the scaled and feathered variety.

Jeremy pursed his lips and narrowed his eyes at her. If he did not know any better, he would have submitted to the ridiculousness of the situation and bought into all of this supposedly guileless nonsense that she was blathering on about.

But something about it was not right.

Cassie might be a virgin and might act perplexed, but she was in no way naïve. She had been around him too long not to learn what went on beneath the bedcovers and had seen too much of Allayne's naughty pamphlets not to recognize a man's sex. Therefore—what was she doing here, poking at his cock, and at the same time, feigning innocence?

"Let me ask you again," he said in a sterner voice, all the more certain that the brat had come for a reason and was leading him in an orbit by his nose—she was a talented actress. "Why are you here, brat? And do not even think about lying. Believe me, I shall finagle it out of you until I reach the bottom of this scheme of yours."

"I-I brought you some bonbons." She extracted a small box from her skirt pocket.

"You brought me some bonbons."

"Yes."

"In the middle of the night."

"Yes."

"With *Mister Feather?*" Jeremy raised a dark eyebrow.

"I like Mister Feather." She glared at him.

"How did you get into my bedchamber?"

"I-I—" Her eyes darted to the open window.

Jeremy muttered a curse and peered outside. "Who gave you that ladder?"

"No one." She shuffled her feet and looked down at her shoes.

"How did it get here then?" Jeremy cocked his head to the side and crossed his arms over his chest.

"I don't know." She began to fidget with her hands and then hid them behind her back when she thought he had noticed.

He strode toward her and shook her shoulders. "You'd better tell me the truth right now, Cassandra Carlyle, or I'll dismiss all the servants in this house! Let me ask you again—what are you doing in my bedchamber?"

"I wanted to bring you some bonbons—"

"What about the feather?"

"I wanted to tickle you while you were sleeping—"

"And once I awakened?"

"Then I'd give you the bonbons."

Jeremy narrowed his eyes. From Grandstone Park to Rose Hill Manor and all the way to Waterford Park, everybody knew that bonbons were Cassie's currency for bribes. "You're bringing me bonbons in exchange for what, brat?"

"Nothing." She began to chew on her lower lip.

"For what?" He fairly snarled the words out.

"I-I was wondering, well—I thought, I might um—" she began to squirm and avoided his gaze, "apologize for being such a bully the other day and persuade you to t-teach me how to seduce Richard."

"Bloody hell!" Jeremy rammed his fist into the wall. He had never felt so angry with Cassie. He wanted to strangle her, ravish her, kiss her—suck the madness out of her head. An idea flickered in his mind. *Why not?* If she wanted him to show her some lessons in seduction, why couldn't he use the opportunity to seduce her himself?

"Well—will you do it?" she asked hesitantly. "I-I can bring more bonbons if you like."

Jeremy gave her a sly smile. "All right, brat, you win. Yes, I'll do it."

"Truly?" Her eyes lit up.

"On one condition." He ran a finger lazily along her jawline.

"W-what?"

"You must come to me." He lifted her chin and looked into her wide eyes. "Every night—beginning tonight."

"W-we start tonight?" she gulped.

"Yes." He trailed his forefinger slowly from her chin down to her throat, unhooking her riding cloak to expose the creamy, smooth skin above the neckline of her dress.

"Lesson number one." He let his finger continue its exploration along her décolletage. "Before you can learn how to seduce a man, you must first experience how it feels to be seduced."

He dipped his finger inside the neckline of her dress and circled her nipple, watching her eyes widen with a startled gasp.

CHAPTER TWENTY-FOUR

Lesson number one
(Part two)

C ASSANDRA KNEW THERE would be no turning back once she
managed to manipulate Jeremy into teaching her his magic
formula. She had played the fool for him—knowing exactly what a
cock was, and it wasn't a chicken! She had changed her mind a
hundred times before she got into his bedchamber and changed her
mind another thousand times again when he caught her, but none of
her pretense at innocence deceived him. He was too worldly, too
experienced, too sly, and too familiar with her not to know what was
going on inside her head.

Yes, she had successfully swayed him into giving in, so why did she
have the feeling that he had outmaneuvered her at her own scheme?

"J-jeremy—" His probing finger had left her incoherent, and she
did not even know why she breathed his name.

"Sshh." His lips followed the trail his finger had traced, making her
catch her breath and her breasts to heave upward, offering themselves
like sacrificial lambs for his inspection.

"Oh—" Her hand went up to restrain his as he hooked a forefinger
inside the scoop neckline of her dress and tugged it downward,
exposing a pink nipple.

"Sshh." He clasped her wrist and lowered her hand, tucking it
behind her back.

Cassandra gasped in shock as he took the hard peak in his mouth and suckled it, making her knees buckle. He supported her weight with a strong arm around her waist and swirled his tongue around the sensitive tip repeatedly until she was dizzy with wanting.

"Oh, Jeremy—" She buried her fingers in his thick black hair, wanting to say something—anything, but no matter how much she tried, she could not remember the words. She really ought to question his bold imposition upon her person, but her mind had gone numb, and her nerves had become frazzled. Furthermore, she found that she rather enjoyed whatever he was doing!

He released her nipple and rested his forehead against hers, with what she could only describe as wild, raw desire in his eyes. "Isn't this what you want?" he asked huskily against her lips.

"Y-yes, but—"

"This is how a man seduces a woman, sweetheart." He kissed her throat and cupped her breast, squeezing it through the fabric of her dress.

Cassandra could not think, could not breathe, could not speak—except to whisper the name of this devil. He overwhelmed her with his boldness, his strength, his maddening, masculine scent.

"Touch me." He took the hand he held behind her and placed it on his muscled chest as he ran the tip of his tongue along the outline of her earlobe.

"H-here?" Cassandra plowed her fingers through the coarse dark hair that covered his chest.

"Yes," he whispered and nipped her earlobe with his teeth.

Cassandra felt the heavy beating of his heart against her palm. His breathing quickened in response to her touch.

"Kiss it," he rasped against her ear.

"Pardon me?" She paused from exploring the beautiful hollows and slopes of his chest and looked up at him.

"Like this." He dipped his head once again and took her nipple in his mouth, suckling and teasing it until she thought she would go out of her mind and scream.

"I-is this really n-necessary?" she panted, feeling a hot tingle course down her belly.

He pulled away from her breast and cupped her face with his hands, gently guiding her mouth to the raised dark circle on his chest. "If you want to learn how to seduce a man, you must also learn how to please him."

Cassandra tentatively flicked her tongue at the hard nub and watched as Jeremy closed his eyes with a sigh of pleasure.

Her confidence grew.

She parted her lips and drew his nipple in her mouth, sucking and twirling her tongue around it, the way he had done to hers.

Jeremy heaved a deep breath and with skilled hands, swiftly unbuttoned her dress. She began to protest, but he silenced her with a searing kiss as his fingers expertly unlaced her corset in a matter of seconds.

Both articles of clothing fell on the floor, leaving her exposed, save for her thin chemise.

He pulled back just enough to rake his eyes over her, a satisfied smile playing on his lips.

She shivered with both fear and anticipation, unable to decide which emotion dominated her person.

Jeremy had suddenly turned into a man—a real man, before her very eyes. He no longer was the Jeremy she jested with, the childhood playmate who stole her chocolate bonbons, who conspired with her to turn the neighbors' fountains into bubbling froths, and raced horses with her along the shore.

He pushed the ribbons holding her chemise off her shoulders.

She instinctively caught the flimsy fabric to her chest before it slid down to join the rest of her garments on the floor.

He reached out to move her hands away. "Let me see you."

"I-I—" She suddenly felt unsure of what they were doing, and an overpowering urge to give up on her scheme loomed at the back of her mind.

"If you want to seduce a man, you must be comfortable to show him some skin," he drawled in that strange, sensual voice.

"What do you mean?" She hoped he did not notice the anxiety in her tone.

"A man's attention is enticed by womanly attributes more so than a pretty face."

Cassandra's heart thudded. He had spoken the magic words. She did indeed need an advantage over the goat lady's beautiful face. And she knew without a doubt that for her to stand a chance, she would have to show off her round bum and breasts.

She released her hold on the delicate material and watched the fire leap in Jeremy's dark eyes as her chemise fell away.

"You're beautiful!" He ran his hands from her shoulders, down to the sides of her breasts, to the waistband of her pantalettes, then back up again to cup her breasts.

All thoughts of Richard fled when he pressed her breasts together, circling her nipples with his thumbs before he leaned down and inserted his tongue into the tight cleft between them.

"Oh!" she gasped as he ran his tongue with languid strokes, dismayed to discover that another, more private part of her body yearned to be touched the same way.

"Sshhh," he murmured, his hands wandered to untie the ribbon sash of her pantalettes.

"Jeremy." She grabbed hold of her loosened drawers and pushed his impudent hands away.

"Yes?" He raised his head, only to trail more kisses from her shoulder to her neck.

"I-I think I have a stomachache." She inhaled the clean, lavender scent of his hair, unable to stop herself from caressing the longish dark mane with one hand, which, to her surprise, felt wonderfully soft between her fingers.

"Why?" He suddenly stopped his ministrations and looked at her. "Did you have anything that didn't agree with you?"

"No."

"Do you want me to ring for Barton so he can bring you something to make it go away?"

"It's all right. I feel fine now," she said, wondering why the sickness left as fast as it came.

"Are you certain?" He caressed her cheek with the back of his fingers, then dropped a feather-light kiss on the tip of her nose that rapidly progressed into gentle nibbling on her upper lip.

"Oh, no," she mumbled as he began to move his attention to her lower lip. "My tummy ache is back."

"Let me have Barton bring some—"

She vehemently shook her head. "I don't think that will work."

"Why not?" He arched a dark eyebrow and frowned.

She looked at him for a long moment before saying, "I-I think you're the one who's giving me the bellyache."

"Me?" His eyebrows flew upwards as he pointed at his chest.

"Yes," she gulped, confused and mystified by the new sensations she was experiencing.

He stared at her with incredulity, and then his lips tipped gradually on one side before he burst into deep, hearty laughter.

"What is so funny?" she scowled, missing the jest.

"Sweetheart," he reached for her hand and pried open the fingers gripping the sash of her pantalette, "that is not a tummy ache."

"Well, what is it then?" She glared at him, not pleased with being laughed at.

"That's the forbidden fruit." He undid the sash with a flick of a deft finger. "Aching for me to taste it."

CHAPTER TWENTY-FIVE

Jeremy's secret...

JEREMY KNEW WHAT a lucky devil he was to have the pleasures of heaven within his reach. He longed to bury himself in its soft clouds, savor the sweetness of its early morning dew, and listen to the siren song of the angel in his arms as they soared together in divine rapture.

His body yearned for the bliss of paradise, for the ecstasy of its wet, warm, and welcoming embrace. Every inch of his flesh pulsated with the desperate need for release and the craving to spill his seed in its fertile Elysian Fields.

He reached down to claim his piece of Eden, only to have the gilded gates close on his hand. No angels were singing—only a startled gasp and large green eyes filled with fright.

"Open your legs for me, sweetheart," he urged, but she compressed her thighs tightly together and shook her head.

"Let me touch you," he persisted, inflamed by the ardent desire to consume the forbidden fruit ripe for the picking within his grasp.

"J-Jeremy, no—" She clamped her fingers on his wrist and recoiled.

He paused in his advances and searched her face. Though her cheeks were bright pink, the rest of her person looked pale. She was shaking, wide eyes pleading—apparently from fear—of *him*.

His lust plunged into the depths of hell. He should have known that a devil like him had no place in heaven. What the hell was he thinking, anyway? Did he truly mean to debauch Cassie, his childhood friend, like a common trollop from the tavern? Had his morals plummeted so low that his behavior imitated that of his father? What kind of madness had possessed him to commit such wickedness—to take advantage of the only person who looked at him with genuine fondness, regardless of the blackness of his soul, without casting judgment or artifice?

"God, Cassie, I'm sorry—" He had never hated himself more than at this moment. "I didn't mean to frighten you."

She bit her lip, and tears welled in her eyes. "Jeremy, I know this is my idea, but I can't go on any further. Please do not be mad at me," she croaked, and his heart tugged at the corners. Here he was, a devious lecher about to ruin her—and she was more concerned about offending his feelings.

Her apology was almost his undoing. He should have known better and conducted himself in a manner worthy of her trust. And God, how she trusted him! She always forgave him no matter how abominably he behaved and loathed quarreling with him even for just a day—except for that time when he had embarrassed her in the fountain—Good Lord, did she make him grovel!

"Of course, I'm not mad at you." He picked up her clothes from the floor and placed them on the dresser. "Here, put these back on." He handed her the pantalettes and tactfully looked away as she dressed.

She put on her chemise, and he tied the ribbons on her shoulders while she held the flimsy fabric in place.

"Turn around," he whispered as she donned her corset, helping her lace the back with capable hands. When he finished, he reached for her dress and slid it over her head with her arms extended, fastening the pearl buttons from behind with the same efficiency.

"Thank you," she murmured, avoiding his eyes.

"Cass—look at me." He lifted her chin. "I'm sorry. I should not have done what I have done. I have no excuse for such behavior. You should not be here. I may be your friend, but I am also a man—and not a good one at that. Don't ever forget that I came from the same vine as my father."

Her expression changed. "Don't say that about yourself. You are not your father. I will not hear of it."

"Do you not realize that I could have ruined you?" He could not believe that after all that had happened, she would still defend his detestable self from himself.

"Of course I did!" she exclaimed with a frown. "I'm not daft, you know. I do know the difference between a chicken and a snake and a man's sex."

Jeremy stared at her. "And yet—you still ventured into my nest!"

"Jeremy." Her face sobered, giving him a look that made him feel like he was the one who was daft. "I know you'll never do anything to hurt me."

He wondered where on earth she got that line of thinking. God—if she only knew how close he had come to forgetting himself! "Let me take you home," he said with a resigned sigh. Cassie's unconditional trust in him made it all the more difficult to appease his nagging conscience. He dressed quickly, pulled on his boots, and rang for Barton to have his coach ready.

"I'll have the driver tie your horse to the carriage," he said as they waited for his carriage on the driveway when she told him she had slipped out of Rose Hill Manor on Apollo. "Don't come here late at night again—do you hear me, brat?"

"B-but what about my lessons?" Her delicate eyebrows wrinkled.

"No more lessons," he snapped, wondering why he could terrify most men with his temper, but no matter what he did or how horrible a fit of anger he threw, it never truly dissuaded her.

"All right," she mumbled, and he thought she agreed a little too easily to be believable.

"I mean it, brat," he said in a sterner tone, as their ride arrived, and the footman opened the door for them.

He handed her to the coach and then followed her in, taking his seat across from her.

"No—sit here." She yawned, patting the seat cushion next to her.

He scowled at her but did as she requested, hauling himself to sit by her side.

With another big yawn, she laid her head on his shoulder and slept all the way to Rose Hill Manor.

"Cassie," he whispered, nudging her gently as the carriage pulled up in front of the dark house. "We're here."

Her reply came in the form of a light snore.

The footman opened the door and pulled down the steps.

"Miss Carlyle is fast asleep." Jeremy shifted her weight onto his lap and lifted her toward the door. "Guide my footing while I carry her out."

After some maneuvering, he managed to complete the task without dropping Cassie or hitting her head on the doorframe. The footman ran up the door and, at his instruction, rapped the knocker lightly. Morton opened the door in a long robe and a sleeping cap.

"Is everyone asleep?" Jeremy peered inside the gloomy hallway.

"Everyone *was* asleep, my lord." Morton raised his bushy eyebrows and sighed, oddly unsurprised that his mistress was sleeping soundly in his arms at an ungodly hour.

"Excellent. I will take Miss Carlyle up to her room. You may go back to bed." Jeremy walked past him, heading straight to the winding staircase.

He carried Cassie with cautious steps to the second floor where the family resided, not relishing the idea of getting caught—especially by her brother. He would take on Richard anytime, but he would have to tread carefully with Allayne.

Jeremy cursed under his breath at the thought, pausing to glance around the darkened hallway. He tiptoed to the last door on the left-wing, turned the knob carefully, and peeked in to make sure Cassie's maid was not waiting for her before he entered the bedchamber. Then, he headed straight for her bed, stubbing the toe of his boot, and hitting his shin twice on some furniture along the way, before he finally deposited her on the mattress. After removing her cloak, shoes, dress, corset, and leaving her chemise on, he tucked her inside the blankets.

He sat on the edge of her bed for a few moments, smiling to himself. The minx slept through the whole ordeal with nary a whimper. Poor thing. She probably was tired and stressed from their encounter more than she cared to admit.

A twinge of guilt pricked his conscience. He reached out to brush away a stray strand of hair from her face, tucking it behind her ear. Since when did he develop some scruples?

A while ago, a little voice whispered in his thoughts. *When you began to see the highlights in her hair and started to notice the color of her eyes. When the mere scent and nearness of her took your breath away, and when you first realized she was all you needed—yet you would not give in because of your foolish pride.*

Jeremy filled his lungs with air, exhaling slowly in a long breath. He leaned down and pressed a kiss on her forehead, watching her for a while as she slept. His eyes drifted to his mother's ring on her finger. All at once, everything he had always known, yet denied ever existed—became clear to him.

"I love you," he whispered as he lifted her hand to his lips. "I'm afraid, Cassie, but I truly do."

Chapter Twenty-Six

Happily ever after
(The words of a fool)

"My lord!" A voice that sounded suspiciously like Barton's called, waking him from his dream of seducing Cassie. "Miss Carlyle has come to see you."

Jeremy groaned. "Tell her to go away."

"I did, my lord. But she nonetheless insisted that I tell you she will not be able to ride with you to the village today because she is on her way to visit Grandstone Park, and you need not rise to accompany her."

"So, what the bloody hell are you waking me for?" he snapped in annoyance, burrowing deeper into the covers, wishing he was nestled inside Cassie instead.

"She was adamant that I let you know she intended to practice the lessons you taught her with Lord Sunderland and see if they are indeed effective."

Jeremy sat upright on the bed. "What?"

Barton opened his fob watch and examined the time. "From the time I've been trying to wake you, my lord, I imagine she would've left more than ten minutes ago."

"Bloody hell!" Jeremy jumped off the bed, heedless of his nakedness. He had not intended to murder anyone and hang by the gallows, but as soon as he found her—he would wring the little twit's neck.

"Prepare a hot bath for me and call Percy. I need a shave. Have him prepare my attire for the day. Was Miss Carlyle riding Apollo?"

"Yes, my lord."

"Then, get my horse ready."

Several minutes later, Jeremy wandered into the second floor of Grandstone Park, peeking into every room along the hallway. Laughter drifted from a brightly lit room, and he peered through the partly open door, recognizing Cassie's voice.

He found her practicing the waltz with Richard, both of them humming an off-tune melody accompanying their steps.

Richard twirled her around, and she squealed in delight. They glided effortlessly across the floor, laughing, and looking into each other's eyes. Richard's gaze alighted on her décolletage.

Since when did Cassie purposely expose her breasts with a scandalous neckline on her dress? Jeremy wanted to pick up a chair and throw it at them. They were so engrossed in each other that neither noticed him standing by the doorway.

Cassie shifted and arched her back, lifting her female enticements for full inspection. She let them brush repeatedly against her partner's chest, boldly pressing even closer. Richard visibly swallowed, and his steps faltered.

Jeremy cursed under his breath. The brat had certainly lost her mind and turned into a trollop! He suddenly had the urge to drag her by the hair and give her bum a good spanking. His eyes darted to the firm bum in question. Richard's hand had most definitely progressed downward.

Jeremy gritted his teeth. Cassie did not seem to mind—in fact, she seemed to entice Richard's hand to that exact spot by wiggling her arse like a damned duck waddling! Jeremy changed his mind. Perhaps he could use a horsewhip instead and beat her!

Their dancing slowed until they all but swayed gently in the middle of the room. The laughter had gone, and now Cassie was staring at

Richard as if he were the King of England. She raised her chin and leaned closer. Richard's gaze dropped to her parted lips. Their mouths gradually drew nearer and nearer.

Jeremy cleared his throat loud enough to summon the entire British Cavalry. They sprang away from each other, swinging their heads at the same time to where he stood.

"Jeremy!" Cassie colored to a bright shade of crimson as he approached.

"Sweetheart." He pulled her to him and demonstrated his claim on her inviting lips. Richard could go to hell, and Cassie—well—he would have to strangle her later.

"You seemed to have forgotten your fichu." He released her from his kiss and glared at the exposed tops of her breasts as he unbuttoned his tailcoat.

Cassie's cheeks reddened even further. Jeremy shrugged off his coat and draped it over her shoulders.

"What brings you here, old chap?" Richard asked.

"I missed my betrothed's company this morning, and one of the servants told me she'd come to Grandstone Park." Jeremy narrowed his eyes at his friend, whom he now considered his rival. "Visiting—alone."

"Oh, but I came by to ask you to accompany me," Cassie interjected with a calming hand on his arm, her eyes wordlessly pleading with him not to make a scene. "But you were sound asleep, and I did not want to wake you."

Ah—so that is the real reason why she dropped by—to furnish herself with an excuse. Cassie gave him a small smile. Jeremy clenched his jaw and glowered at her. Hah! Obviously, she wanted him to be nice, but as ill-luck would have it, he was in no mood to be agreeable. "I precisely remember Barton telling me that you told him not to wake me because you did not need my company," he ground the words through his teeth.

"I-I—but you sleep like the dead, and I know you hate getting up before noon!" she snapped, snatching her hand off his arm.

"I had a nightmare last night and couldn't get back to sleep," Jeremy drawled in a satiric tone, meeting her wide-eyed gaze. "I dreamt someone sneaked into my bedchamber with a feather, looking for a snake."

Cassie paled, her mouth compressing into a thin line. Jeremy raised a taunting dark eyebrow, daring her to bring up the subject.

Richard glanced back and forth between them. "If you'll excuse me, I believe I have some important correspondence waiting for me." He bowed and took his leave.

Cassie wrenched Jeremy's waistcoat off her shoulders and threw it at him as soon as Richard's footsteps faded in the hallway. "You pigheaded oaf! Did you come here to embarrass me?"

"Embarrass you?" he exclaimed indignantly, catching his waistcoat with one hand. "You are well able to embarrass yourself without me, thank you very much!"

"And how—pray tell—do you think I managed to do that?" She placed her fisted hands on her hips. "We were just dancing, and you had to ruin the moment!"

"Dancing? Hah! Do you think I am blind? You were dangling your—your—" He pointed an accusing finger at her scrumptious-looking breasts.

"So? Wasn't that what you taught me to do?" She swatted his forefinger. "Didn't you say that if I wanted to seduce a man, I must be comfortable to show him some skin?"

Jeremy grimaced. *Well...she does have a point.* "Er, yes, but—"

"And didn't you say that a man's attention is enticed by womanly attributes more so than a pretty face?"

Jeremy cursed under his breath and scowled at her. The little hellion had him by the ballocks. "Yes, but see here—"

"You, Jeremy Huntington, are not being fair! You took my bonbons in exchange for lessons, and now you're telling me I'm an embarrassment? I did what you taught me, you dolt! And if you had not shown up, it would have worked! Richard would have kissed me, and I—I would have kissed him back!"

Jeremy drew a deep breath in vexation. Excluding the events that had transpired last night, hands down—that was the stupidest thing he had ever heard her say. He wanted to shake her and hammer some sense into her—anything to free her from this obsession with Richard. She had effectively made a fool of herself, and Richard—well, he never thought he would justify his actions, but Richard was a man. Given the right amount of temptation, he would most likely break any vow.

Something must be done. He simply could not let Cassie throw herself at Richard's feet. One of these days, the man's restraint would eventually break down and—

"And then, what?" he asked in an even tone.

"What do you mean?" Cassie lifted her eyebrows with a confounded expression on her face.

Jeremy pinned her with a look of reproach. "After you kissed him back—then what?"

"I don't know!" She turned her back to him. "Maybe he would realize he's in love with me and not with that goat lady. Maybe he'd cry off the engagement and ask me to marry him instead."

Jeremy felt his temper rise from hell and shoot to the high heavens. What she had just said—sounded even more stupid than the first. What was wrong with the girl? After all his attempts at distracting her from this madness, her pining for Richard had not been the least bit swayed.

"Cassie—that's the worst rubbish I've ever heard!" He angrily shrugged on his waistcoat and strode across the room toward the door.

What a nitwit he had been! How could he even think he could take Richard's place? How could he ignore the mountain of difference between them? Richard Christopher Radcliffe was the golden boy—the prized calf. Jeremiah Devlin Huntington was the black sheep—the unwanted son. He was a fool, nothing but a fool, to hope he had a chance to win the most beautiful princess in the kingdom.

Jeremy shook his head in resignation. As he reached the doorway, he paused with his hand on the doorknob and turned around to say, "Good luck to you, Miss Carlyle. I hope you'll live happily ever after." He slipped out the door and slammed it shut at her stunned face.

CHAPTER TWENTY-SEVEN

Revenge of the rake and the goat lady...

JEREMY SAT IN his study with an almost empty bottle of brandy in his hand. He was foxed to the gills, yet the heaviness in his chest remained. Cassie infuriated him so much that he could not think, could not function, could not even blink—without seeing her face. He hated wanting, needing, *loving*—anyone. No one wanted, needed, or loved him the way he loved Cassie. So why should he indulge in something so far-flung?

He swallowed the last of his brandy straight from the bottle and threw the empty decanter across the room. It collided with a loud crash on the marble mantel of the fireplace, sending splinters of broken glass all over the expensive Aubusson carpet.

Barton came charging into the room. "My lord! Are you all right?" His gaze darted to the glistening glass fragments scattered on the carpet.

"Do I look like I am?" Jeremy grabbed his quill, dipped it in the inkpot, and began to write.

"Is there anything I can do for you, my lord?" Barton asked with concern.

Jeremy immediately felt a twinge of guilt on his behavior. Barton had taken care of all his needs since his mother died when he was but a boy. He certainly did not deserve such boorish behavior from him.

"I did not mean to bite your head off." Jeremy raised both hands in apology. "But yes—I do need you to send this letter post-haste. I need it to arrive in London by tomorrow afternoon. I don't care about the cost—just ensure its prompt receipt."

"Yes, my lord." Barton took the letter and rang for a maid to clean up the glass.

Jeremy sat back in his chair. He had less than a fortnight left in this farce of a betrothal with Cassie. God help him if this outrageous scheme of his did not produce the results he expected. Inch by little inch, the idea of rusticating in Europe began to look more and more appealing.

⇛✦⇚

AT HER FATHER'S library in Rose Hill, Cassandra sat staring at the chess pieces in front of her. A few paces away, her brother reclined on a couch with a book, while her mother toiled on her embroidery by the fireplace. The stillness in the room aggravated her disposition. It had been three days since she quarreled with Jeremy, and his absence was beginning to take its toll on her. She had gone to his house every day to make peace with him, but he refused to receive her calls. She had tried to bribe Barton with bonbons to let her in, but even that route did not work.

Cassandra sighed. What else could she do? Jeremy had never been this vexed at her, and she could not bear it. She missed his company and his laughter and his crooked smile and their daily rides and—

"Cassie?" Richard, who had come to call on her and Allayne, peered at her from across the chess table. "It's your move."

"What?" She blinked at him.

"Your turn." Richard gestured at the chessboard.

Cassandra refocused her attention on the game they were playing. "Right—sorry."

"Is something the matter?" Richard cocked an eyebrow. "You've been very quiet."

"Oh, no, I'm fine." She gave him a bland smile. "I was just wool-gathering."

"I see." Richard watched her and gave her the impression he did not see at all, nor believe an ounce of her lie.

Cassandra squirmed in her seat. Richard always had a way of interrogating people and finding out what they were hiding. She avoided his gaze and moved her pawn without thinking.

"Does this concern your misunderstanding with Jeremy at Grandstone Park?" Richard asked in a casual tone as he studied the board.

"I—ah—"

Richard heaved a deep sigh and regarded her intently. "I should go see Jeremy and apologize. He had a right to be upset. We should not be alone together. It is highly improper. I must insist you visit Grandstone Park only if you are accompanied by him or a proper chaperone." He picked up his queen and moved it sideways on the board.

"Richard—" Cassie began as he reached for her hand on the table and patted it, just the way he used to do when she was a little girl.

"Cassie—please understand. Jeremy is my friend. He is like a brother to me—like Allayne. I must respect his wishes." He bestowed her with a fond expression for a little while, then squeezed her hand before he stood up, turning to say his farewell to her mother and Allayne.

Cassandra followed him with her eyes as he said his goodbyes to her father on the other side of the room before he left. She had always admired him for his sensibility and wit. He constantly knew the right thing to do and was disciplined and determined to a fault. When she was a little girl, she looked up to him for his guidance and clear-headedness. She felt safe with him as one would with a guardian.

Her guardian angel. She smiled at the thought of what she always believed him to be as a child. Unlike Jeremy, who relished breaking the rules and always laughed in the face of adversity. Who did everything his way, in his own time, no matter the consequences. Who was spirited and daring and passionate and beautiful and—

"He's got you on check-mate." Allayne pointed at the chessboard and tapped a finger on her nose, chuckling as he passed her on his way to return his book.

Three days later...

FROM THE WINDOW of his study, Jeremy observed the shiny black carriage with the ducal crest of Glenford pull into the long, winding driveway of Waterford Park, followed by two other coaches. He had been correct in his assumption that the lady would waste no time in traveling to Cornwall upon receipt of his letter.

Her arrival was of royal proportions—a mountain of luggage, three maids, and an army of footmen and outriders.

Jeremy rolled his eyes heavenward. Nine days was all he needed to survive Her Highness's exalted company. After that period, they could all go to Hades, and he would not give a fig.

"Lady Desiree Lennox, my lord," Barton announced from the doorway.

Jeremy turned to see the stunning goddess to whom Richard was betrothed standing by the arched entryway. "Lady Desiree." He smiled cordially, indicating the chair opposite his carved mahogany desk. "Please come in and have a seat."

She floated into the room with her nose in the air and took her place. "I hope I have not wasted my time in coming directly to this godforsaken part of the country," she said loftily.

Jeremy's amiable mood vanished. "You are welcome to leave if you intend to subject me to your disdainful attitude," he said in an icy tone and pointed at the door.

"Lord Waterford!" Lady Desiree abruptly stood up from her chair in outrage. "How dare you speak—"

"Let me make myself clear," Jeremy cut in. "I shall not hesitate to throw you out on your ear if you ever insult me in my own home again. Understood?"

Lady Desiree gaped at him.

"Understood?" Jeremy reiterated sharply.

Her haughtiness wilted, and she reddened, nodding her head with an audible gulp.

"Sit down." Jeremy flicked his chin at her chair.

She sat down obediently and placed her hands on her lap.

Jeremy took his seat and leaned back, crossing his arms over his chest. "As I mentioned in my letter, I have reason to believe that Richard is having a change of heart on your betrothal."

Lady Desiree paled. "He can't cry off—I'll be ruined!"

"Actually—" Jeremy said with a twist of his lips, "he can do whatever he wants."

"But—why?" Lady Desiree's eyes widened in distress. "Why would he do such a thing?"

Jeremy sighed and straightened in his chair. "I believe he has taken an interest in someone else," he said in a grave voice.

"Who? Who could have diverted him away from me?" Lady Desiree wailed, her demeanor and practiced detachment crumbling at his words. "Is she fairer than I? Does she have better connections? Or perhaps—a larger fortune?"

Jeremy rested his elbows on the desk and steepled his fingers. "She is far better than all you've mentioned."

"Who is she?" Lady Desiree asked in a voice filled with dismay.

"Miss Carlyle, my betrothed." He watched her mouth drop in shock. "Which is why I summoned you here."

"W-what can I possibly do?" She placed a shaking hand on her ample chest.

"I have a plan—but first, tell me the truth—do you love Richard?"
He pinned his dark gaze on her.

Lady Desiree lowered her eyes. "I was furious at Papa when I
learned he'd arranged for me to marry a man I'd never even met." She
swallowed, toying with her glove on her lap. "But then, Papa invited
him to dinner, and I admit—I was taken by his looks and fine manners." The corners of her mouth lifted a little as if remembering the
day. "He was so wonderful and attentive, and he looked at me a
certain way. I—I thought he liked me. Then, I found out he left for
Europe. He sent not a single correspondence to me while he was
away. I was devastated."

"So, you do have feelings for him," Jeremy said in a softer tone.

"Lord Waterford—" She raised her eyes and met his across the
table. "I have a number of highly eligible suitors who have asked for
my hand, but I never married—until Richard returned and asked to
marry me."

"I see." Jeremy leaned back in his chair and nodded slowly.

"My lord—I may not reveal my feelings due to the dictates of propriety ingrained in me from my upbringing." Her beautiful
countenance took on a look of conviction. "But I love Richard—more
than anything—which is why I am here."

"Well, then. I believe it's time to abandon propriety and win back
your betrothed and mine," Jeremy said with a satisfied smile. "Change
is in order. Now—here is my plan. Tonight, I need you to read and
study everything in this booklet." He handed her a leather-bound
journal. "And tomorrow, we shall start by amending your attitude on
how to re-capture your beloved Richard."

Lady Desiree inched forward and listened with interest as he ex-
pounded on his plot, nodding enthusiastically in approval, for it was a
brilliant scheme.

CHAPTER TWENTY-EIGHT

Revenge of the rake and the goat lady
(Part Two)

RICHARD LOOKED UP from his correspondence as his butler tapped on the door to his father's study before entering.

"My lord, Lady Lennox is here to see you," he announced, just as Desiree breezed into the room.

"Desiree!" Richard hastily rose from his chair, flustered and bewildered at her unexpected visit. "What brings you here?"

"Darling," she said in that melodious voice, rushing to his side with a warm embrace and a loving kiss on his lips. "How wonderful it is to see you."

Dumbfounded at Desiree's warm display, Richard darted his eyes at Gordon, who shrugged and rolled his eyes to the ceiling, quietly closing the door behind him.

"Er—is anything the matter?" Richard wondered at her showing up without warning and the sudden change in her behavior since the last time he had seen her. She had always been aloof, like most exalted ladies of her class—not the sort to profess feelings in public, much less show physical affection in front of other people—especially the servants.

"Nothing's the matter," she laughed, wrapping her arms around his neck. "I missed you, that's all." She pulled him close for another, more ardent kiss.

Richard could not quite believe he was kissing the same woman. This blond goddess in his arms brimmed with passion and sensuality, the two most important things that could stir the excitement in a man's blood.

"Desiree—" he said breathlessly against her mouth as their lips parted.

"Come." She tugged on his arm. "Let's sit over there and cuddle."

"Cuddle?" he repeated, perplexed. From the moment she walked through the door, she seemed to be a different person—free-spirited and filled with the promise of pleasure. He was having a hell of a hard time believing it.

"Yes—cuddle." She chuckled and led him toward the sitting area in front of the fireplace.

He sat on the loveseat, facing the fire, and, to his surprise, Desiree elected to perch herself on his lap instead of sitting next to him. She shifted sideways, grinding her delicious bottom against his lap, positioning her generous bosom directly in line with his vision.

Richard willed himself to focus on her face to quell the rising panic in his groin. Something odd was going on. Some kind of miracle had occurred during their period apart from each other to transform his cold-blooded betrothed into a sultry seductress.

"I'm so glad to be here." She cupped his face in her hands and showered him with tiny kisses.

"You are?" His puzzlement reached new heights. Desiree hated the country. In her own words: *Cornwall is unbearably bucolic and lacking in relevant entertainment.* He even remembered her saying, *I would never consent to live at Grandstone Park,* which fueled his growing resentment and ignited his regret in making a hasty decision in asking for her hand.

"Yes. I just realized how wonderful the air is and how beautiful and peaceful the countryside is." She looked into his eyes. "I think Grandstone Park will make a suitable home for us once we marry, and it would be a superb place to raise our future children."

Richard would have fallen out of the chair if she had not been sitting on his lap. "You want to live here?" he exclaimed. For obvious reasons, he could not quite picture the stylish and worldly Lady Desiree stashed away in the country, living a domesticated, non-sophisticated life.

"Of course." She gave him a tender kiss on the nose. "I'll be happy here as long as you're with me."

"Eh?" Richard raised a suspicious eyebrow, though he could not help the gladness that seeped into his heart. He had desired Desiree from the time they first met and wanted her for years, which was the reason he did not hesitate to ask for her hand in marriage. However, her indifference to the things he treasured and disdain for the home he loved quickly doused his passion, replacing it with disappointment and an utter sense of failure in not finding the kind of love and harmony his parents had.

"Are you certain?" He angled for some inconsistency in her response, in case he was missing something. Perhaps she was ill, or foxed, or had been taking some opiate drug, but her lucid disposition proved her clear-headedness.

"Yes," she sighed dreamily and circled her arms around his neck once more, bringing her delightful breasts against his chin.

Richard's thoughts careened to a more carnal nature. One sweep of his hand underneath her voluminous skirts, and he could insert a probing finger into her woman's flesh.

She shifted on his lap and pushed her bottom more firmly against the tautness of his now raging erection. Richard broke into a cold sweat. Desiree's long, tawny lashes fluttered, seemingly well aware of his predicament. She gave him a steamy gaze, which oddly reminded him of someone who his scattered brain could not pinpoint at the moment. The corners of her mouth lifted in a slow, heart-stopping smile. He had seen that smile somewhere—but now was not the time for him to ponder.

Richard swallowed the flare of heat that originated in his groin and eventually ended in his throat. The minx was most definitely seducing him—in every stimulating way—and she knew all the right moves. Where in hell did she learn how to enrapture a man with the promise of erotic delights to come?

"Desiree—" he began to protest, for although they were betrothed, it simply was not the thing to impose himself on her before she had the protection of his name.

She silenced him with a fervid kiss.

Richard's brain sank like jelly down to his loins, dragging with it the respectable principles of a gentleman of fine upbringing.

He slid his hands from her narrow waist to her breasts, circling her nipples with his thumbs through the fabric of her gown.

She gasped, pushing herself away from him with startled eyes. Then, as if realizing she had made a misstep, she quickly rebounded from shock by closing those arrestingly beautiful eyes and crushing her breasts firmly into his hands.

Richard needed no further provocation. He deftly peeled down the satin guarding her bosom, drawing a pink nipple in his mouth. She smelled of red roses in full bloom and tasted like warm honey, a delicious combination that fired his lust. He feasted on her breasts—generous, spilling over his palms, just the way he liked them. His mouth explored every inch of ivory skin, soft and yielding to his touch. But hell, it was not enough—he needed more, wanted more.

He had been celibate for too long. If he had not known she was a virgin, he would have bent her forward on the table, tossed her skirts up, and entered her from behind.

Richard immediately shook his head in an attempt to clear it, catching a deep breath to rid himself of his salacious fantasies. This was Desiree, his betrothed—not some wench at Madame Le Moreau's brothel. She was a lady and deserved to be treated as such. He must pleasure her in gentler, less vigorous ways.

He slipped his hand underneath her gown and traced the length of her shapely leg, going up and up, until he reached the triangular junction between her thighs.

Desiree suddenly stilled and caught his hand. "Not now, sweetheart," she whispered, and he wondered why she used a different endearment. He preferred the way she used to call him, *darling*, truth be told.

"There'll be plenty of time for you and me." She ran her fingers along his jawline. "I'll be staying for a fortnight."

"You are?" Richard felt his erection die a slow death at the thought of spending two weeks with Desiree, sitting around and doing absolutely nothing. She may have become an expert seductress, but that did not mean she had changed her other ways. She would never ride to the beach with him or visit the tenants, much less explore the beautiful countryside, for fear of getting freckles from the sun.

"Yes." She wiggled her bottom one last time, aggravating the ache in his balls bursting from the lack of ejaculation before she stood up and smoothed her skirts. "Oh—by the way—I've come across Lord Waterford on my way here and invited him and Miss Carlyle to join us for dinner if you don't mind."

"Of course not." Richard sighed as he watched her tuck her breasts back into her dress. Desiree indeed was acting strangely. She had truly invited Jeremy and Cassie? Desiree might like Jeremy—all women did—but she never liked Cassie! And as for her sudden amorous advances—he began to wonder who taught her the skills. Perhaps a widowed friend? An experienced governess? A paid courtesan? He mentally rejected the last choice.

Well, perhaps they would not end up doing nothing, after all. They certainly started on the right footing—and it was still early in the morning.

CHAPTER TWENTY-NINE

Revenge of the rake and the goat lady
(Part Three)

CASSANDRA STOOD HAND in hand with Jeremy as they waited in the drawing room of Grandstone Park for their hosts. She did not particularly have an inclination to attend the dinner tonight, but she did not wish to quarrel with Jeremy either. The only reason he started speaking to her again was because of the goat lady's invitation. And if that was what it took for her to mend fences with him, then that was what she must endure.

"I don't think this is a good idea," she whispered in Jeremy's ear. "Are you sure the goat lady is not cross with me anymore?"

"I suppose not." He glanced sideways at her. "She expressly mentioned that she wanted to invite you. By the by, will you please stop calling her goat lady? It's very impolite."

Cassandra raised one delicate eyebrow. Since when did Jeremy become concerned with what was polite or not?

She stole a fleeting look at him. Dressed impeccably in a dark blue superfine coat, matching trousers, dove-gray waistcoat, and an immaculate white shirt, he looked too well put together, dignified even—a far cry from the raw, rakish image he always projected. Thankfully, he left his medium-length dark hair unbound, falling to his shoulders in neat layers—otherwise, she would not have recognized him.

Cassandra frowned. If she was none the wiser, she would have thought he was taking after Richard's example: the picture of a perfect gentleman. She immediately squashed the thought. Now why would Jeremy want to do that? He looked fine just the way he was, which she personally preferred over this formal style that did not flatter his personality at all.

"What are you scowling at, brat?"

"You look strange," she said, appraising him from head to toe with a slight frown.

"I look strange—what on earth do you mean?"

She crinkled her nose. "You're dressed like Richard."

"Well, isn't that good?" He smoothed his jacket. "You do like the way he dresses, don't you?"

"Well, yes, but not on you." She shrugged and made a face to express her dislike. "I like the way you usually dress better."

Jeremy muttered a curse under his breath. He had taken the time to dress like a damned solicitor, ordered Percy to give him a good shave, and had him tame his normally windblown-styled hair—only to have the little brat fret that he looked strange.

Gah! What he needed to do to please this woman, he had absolutely no clue! She claimed to be enamored with Richard, so he tried to be like him—at least in the manner of dressing—and what did the little brat say? *You look strange.*

Then to drive the nail into the coffin, she said she liked *his* way of dressing better. May the Lord forgive his addled brains for the confusion, but wasn't she supposed to go all moon-eyed over him for becoming respectable-looking like Richard?

Devil be damned, but he would never understand women. He glared at the top of her head—especially this particular woman!

"There you are!" Lady Desiree entered into the drawing room on Richard's arm, a vision of elegance in red and gold. "I am delighted you joined us," she acknowledged Jeremy's bow. "The duke is indisposed, I'm afraid, so it will be just us for dinner." She took Cassie's hands in hers and said with a wide smile, "It's wonderful to see you again."

Cassie looked taken aback by Lady Desiree's unexpected cordiality. She cast a bewildered glance at Jeremy, but he merely shrugged and turned to greet Richard accordingly.

"Dinner is served," Gordon announced.

Lady Desiree placed her hand on Richard's arm, and they led Jeremy and Cassie into the formal dining room.

The room was opulent, as was the rest of Grandstone House. Portraits of landscapes hung along the exquisitely papered walls, and an intricately carved sideboard stood along the far end by the windows. The dinner table was wide and long, with ornate silver candelabras holding beeswax candles running along its length, fit for a large gathering. Lady Desiree sat on Richard's right instead of taking the opposite end of the table as was customary. The footman pulled out a chair for Cassie next to Lady Desiree, while Jeremy sat across the table on Richard's left.

CONVERSATION PROGRESSED EASILY over dinner. To Richard's surprise, Lady Desiree proved to be an excellent hostess. He had thought her obtuse before, for that was the persona she projected, but then in the few days they spent together after their betrothal, he never really did take the time to get to know her well. To his regret, he had come to the realization that, at the time, he had been selfish for wanting Desiree to amend her lifestyle in order to fit his, without consideration for the contrast in their upbringing. He had grown up surrounded by the beauty and serenity of the countryside, while Desiree had been raised in London, gracing the opulent ballrooms and mingling with the upper ten thousand. No wonder they could not reconcile their lifestyle preferences.

Richard watched Desiree over the rim of his wine glass as he took a small sip. He was mistaken for assuming her witless, for tonight proved she was quite articulate in several subjects. She diligently filled the awkward lulls with clever comments and directed the discussion on art and horseflesh—topics that everyone around the table enjoyed.

He observed in fascination as Desiree put their guests at ease. Though he was a bit mystified at her sudden congeniality towards Cassie, he nonetheless credited her for moving past the unpleasantness of their first meeting.

She made sure Cassie participated in the conversation by asking her many interesting questions about Rose Hill, her family, and other things Cassie enjoyed. It almost seemed like she had done her research, for, after a few awkward intervals, Cassie began to share freely the things she loved about Cornwall.

Richard sat back in his chair. Nothing could have pleased him more than seeing Desiree and Cassie address each other with civility. This truly was a good start. He began to feel a measure of appreciation for Desiree.

"Lady Desiree is an outstanding hostess," Jeremy said next to him as the footmen cleared the table and served the desserts.

"Yes, she is," he replied, surprising himself with the pride he felt for his betrothed.

"The food is superb." Jeremy picked up a chocolate-covered mallow and ate it all in one bite.

"Yes, it is," Richard concurred. Desiree's impeccable taste in fine dining contributed to the dinner's success. He noticed that chocolate bonbons were thoughtfully included in the dessert menu and wondered if Cook advised her that they were Cassie's favorite sweets.

"You're a lucky fellow," Jeremy said as he reached for a bonbon. "You'd be a fool to give Lady Desiree up."

Richard's gaze settled on the beautiful countenance of his betrothed—the same woman he had tried to avoid for over three years. She was laughing at something Cassie had said, and her eyes shone with a zest for life—something he had never noticed before. Her disposition seemed livelier and lighter her.

Richard nodded, starting to think that Desiree would indeed make a splendid duchess.

"I hope you're doing the right thing, and your other lady-love is worth it," Jeremy said between bites of chocolate. "Because if you decide to cry off the engagement, it will not take long for Lady Desiree to find another suitable prospect."

"What are you talking about?" Richard snapped out of his cogitation.

Jeremy reached for another chocolate in the shape of a heart. "You said you met someone else. I remember you mentioning it to Allayne and me at the Templeton soiree." He stuffed the bonbon in his mouth and licked his fingers. "I hope she's worthy enough for you to give up Lady Desiree."

Richard inhaled sharply, and his eyes darted to Cassie, who was engaged in conversation with Desiree. She looked lovely in her emerald green gown, and he could not believe how grown-up she had become. Had he really been gone that long?

Long enough not to recognize her, a voice at the back of his head said. He was so smitten by her that he had agreed to a tryst at that damned fountain. Luckily, he had lost his way, otherwise—good God! He inwardly cringed at what could have happened next. If he had only known who she was then—there was no way in hell he would even touch a hair on her head!

Richard shuffled his feet under the table. He remembered how shocked he was when he found out that his mystery princess was none other than Cassie—his little Piglet! That discovery certainly doused his desire in cold water—and though his attraction to her lingered, it nevertheless forced him to reconsider everything.

Cassie glanced at him and smiled before her eyes shifted onto Jeremy, who was devouring all the chocolate bonbons at an alarming rate.

"Leave some for me!" She slapped his hand as he reached for another one. Laughing, both of them tugged at the silver platter playfully back and forth.

Richard could not help but chuckle. The scene was a familiar occurrence throughout their childhood. While Jeremy teased Cassie to no end—sometimes to the brink of tears—he spent most of his time cheering her up and fending off Jeremy's torments. Could it be that nothing had changed?

Richard straightened in his seat. Could he have misjudged his true feelings for Cassie? Could his possessiveness over her have been influenced by her betrothal to Jeremy? He could not deny that the announcement of their betrothal had left him feeling powerless to protect her if things between them did not go well. And he certainly was *very* protective of her.

Moreover, he felt as if he had been replaced—the same word Jeremy used when they confronted each other in his art studio. Cassie thought he had replaced her with Desiree—and now, he just realized that he truly felt like she had *replaced him* with Jeremy!

Richard saw a flash of light in the murky tunnel of perplexity in his brain. Could this be possible? To love someone with such possessiveness and protectiveness—*yet not be in love with her?*

He fended off Jeremy's fingers from the platter and pushed the sweets toward Cassie, who beamed at him, then stuck her tongue at Jeremy—just like all the other times when he rescued her from his pestering.

"In my opinion," Jeremy said as he gave up on trying to get the treats back, "Lady Desiree will make you a perfect duchess."

Richard could only but agree. Even now, he could clearly see her standing by his side, managing his vast, complex households and hosting parties for peers of his rank. To his consternation, he could not imagine Cassie coping with the magnitude of a duchess's responsibilities. She was too young and carefree—and did not have Desiree's training and maturity.

"Darling," Desiree placed her hand on top of his, "Miss Carlyle and I are going to leave you and Lord Huntington to your port. We shall be in the drawing room when you're ready to join us."

"All right." He briefly squeezed her fingers, and to his amazement, he delighted at the blush that crept up her cheeks in response.

⟫⟫⟪⟪

Jeremy sought Lady Desiree's eyes as he and Richard joined them later. She was turning the pages for Cassie while she played the pianoforte. Jeremy gave her a secret signal as she glanced in his direction.

"Darling, why don't you turn the pages for Miss Carlyle while I ring for some tea?" She motioned for Richard to take her place.

"Of course." Richard moved to the spot she vacated.

"You've done an excellent job," Jeremy whispered as Lady Desiree pretended to offer him a cup as the servants brought in tea in exquisite porcelain pots decorated with hand-painted flowers and gold gilded scrolls. "Were my notes of use to you?"

"Oh, yes, my lord." She snuck a quick glance at Richard and Cassie over her shoulder. "The journal you gave me has helped me tremendously in understanding Richard's likes and dislikes. In fact, I am aiming to join him in his early morning rides at the beach and other activities he prefers."

"Good." Jeremy pretended to laugh at what she had said to discourage suspicion from the other two people in the room. "And have you tried the—er—ah—*other things* I gave you precise instructions on in the journal?"

Her cheeks bloomed into a considerable color of pink. "Yes," she muttered with visible bashfulness. "I daresay your directions are quite astute."

"Yes, they are—though I advise you not to go beyond the limit unless you are certain Richard reciprocates your feelings." Jeremy casually strolled toward a chair and sat as Cassie ended her piece and stood up from the piano.

⫸⫷

CASSIE HAD BEEN watching Desiree and Jeremy beneath her lashes as they conferred with each other while she played the pianoforte. Since when did those two share such a friendly *tête-à-tête*? What were they talking about? And why was Jeremy whispering? What was so funny about what she said? Oh—and now she is blushing? How dare he flirt with the goat lady with her in the same room! Was he trying to seduce her? Had he forgotten that they were supposed to be betrothed?

Hah! She most certainly needed to uproot his underlying motive! If she discovered that Jeremy was making overtures of a carnal nature, she would twist his ballocks and tie them in a sailor's knot with his snake!

Jeremy caught her gaze and winked. Wink all you want, you devil incarnate! She frowned at him in response.

He raised a black eyebrow and blinked innocently.

"What were you and the goat lady talking about?" she rasped in his ear.

"Nothing," he replied coolly.

"What do you mean—nothing?" She glared at him until she thought her eyes would pop out. "She was blushing. I saw it with my own two eyes. Don't you dare trifle with me, Jeremiah Devlin Huntington!"

"Oh, that." He stretched his arms and crossed them behind his head, and shrugged.

Cassie had the sudden desire to pull his hair and pinch him until he squawked. "You're trying to seduce her—I can tell! But let me make this clear—it is not going to happen. I'm your betrothed—"

"My betrothed?" he interjected smugly and regarded her with those lazy eyes that made her feel as if she was naked. "Since when?"

Cassie opened her mouth then closed it again with a gulp. He was right. Their betrothal was nothing but a farce. She had no claim over him, and in less than a fortnight, their fake engagement would come to an end. The thought made her pause. Why was she depressed all of a sudden? Wasn't this the plan all along? For Jeremy to cry out from their betrothal, and for her to be free at last with her reputation intact? She gasped at the unexpected pain that lanced in her chest. For the first time in her life, Cassie felt the sting of fear and vulnerability of losing Jeremy—deep in the confines of her *supposed-to-be-enamored-with-Richard* heart.

CHAPTER THIRTY

Miss Cassandra Carlyle's secret…

Cassandra peered out into the darkness from the window of the moving carriage, wondering what in the Hades was wrong with her. She was exceedingly peeved with Jeremy for flirting with the goat lady after dinner, and she could not fathom the reason why. Why would she give a fig if he fawned over Desiree?

She cast a black glance at the wretched man in question, who leaned precariously against the window with his booted limbs sprawled on the luxurious velvet squab across from her. He looked peaceful, lulled to sleep by the gentle swaying of the carriage.

Cassandra sighed. No one loved his sleep better than Jeremy. If it were possible, he would ride his horse with his eyes closed, and if she did not harass him every morning, he would never rise from his bed until past noontime.

Perhaps his penchant for rest had something to do with his quick mind—for it utterly amazed her how he could manage his estates with meticulous attention to detail. And perhaps, all that slumber may be the secret to his youthfulness—for no one in England could look as vital and devastatingly beautiful as Jeremiah, sleeping naked in his bed.

A small smile curved on her lips. Good Lord, but that was close! She had almost given up her virtue to the dear, devilish man. If he'd insisted and kissed her one more time in that maddening way of his, she would have lost her head and let him have his way.

But she knew Jeremy would never hurt her nor touch her against her will. Despite his licentious reputation, he was a gentleman deep within that hardened heart of his. And even though he seemed cynical and indifferent to the world around him, beneath that strong exterior was a man who needed the most love and constant reassurance.

The coach lurched, and he slid further sideways, a lock of dark hair falling on his brow. Cassandra's fingers itched to brush it away, but she clenched her hand instead and looked away. What in the bloody earth was wrong with her? Since when did she begin contemplating too much about Jeremy?

She stole another glance his way. Well, perhaps she could just prop a pillow for him to rest his head. She would despise herself if he acquired a crick in his neck in the morning.

Two pillows, a loosened cravat, and several gentle strokes through his thick dark hair later, she found herself unable to tear her gaze away from his face. He truly was a breathtakingly handsome man.

Did he have the same effect on the goat lady—even if she was betrothed to Richard already? But why should she be bothered by such a ridiculous thing, anyway? She rolled her eyes. What concern did she have about whom Jeremy bedded? She never did care a jot before; why would she give a hoot now?

Because you do, a voice from the inner recesses of her mind whispered.

Cassandra twiddled her thumbs and glanced at the darkness outside. Was that the reason why she was so vexed when he dismissed that fountain tryst as if nothing had transpired between them? She'd stared at the canopy of her tester bed that night for hours—ruminating, wondering why she felt even more disappointed by Jeremy's insouciance than the fact that she never got the chance to steal a few moments with Richard.

Wasn't that the real reason why she refused to see him for three days straight—and more—if the cad had not shown up to grovel at the

Templeton soiree?

Cassandra sighed. She could never bear to quarrel with him, then go to bed without knowing everything was right between them again.

Somewhere between the rhythmic movement of the carriage and the sound of Jeremy's breathing, a shaft of revelation illuminated the secret depths of her heart. Cassandra's eyes moistened, and she pressed trembling fingers to her lips. Allayne had been right all along.

She had been clinging to an impossible dream—the ridiculous notion of a knight in shining armor who was the very embodiment of perfection. Who would never hurt her, fight with her, or make her cry; who would be dependable and faithful, and would never look at another girl; who would kiss her morning, noon, and night, and love her forever. She had been chasing a figment of her imagination, a non-existent hero—to escape the true but imperfect man of her dreams.

Richard, her childhood idol, the only semblance of the ideal man she envisioned—was never the one.

She had been waiting for *the wrong prince.*

She leaned over and dropped a kiss on the bridge of Jeremy's nose, lightly cupping his cheek with her hand. "It was you all along," she whispered, caressing the fine shadow of his beard with her thumb. Now that she had finally acknowledged her feelings, the leaded weight on her chest lifted, and she could finally breathe, could finally see the light, like the sunrise at the beach, the dawning of a new day.

"I think I love you," she said softly to the dear, wonderful man before her, who was ensconced in a deep slumber. "I'm afraid, Jeremy, but I think I really do."

A warm teardrop slid from her cheek as she moved closer and closed her eyes, planting a tender, loving kiss on his lips, careful not to wake him.

When she opened her eyes again, she found herself staring into a pair of magnificent dark eyes. None of the devilish glint was there, but they were shining, nonetheless.

Her heart ricocheted in her ribcage at being caught in her most vulnerable state as Jeremy sat up and faced her.

"Say it again," he whispered huskily, lifting her chin as he reached out to brush the wetness her tear had trailed on her face with his thumb. "I want to hear you say it again." He pulled her onto his lap, buried his face in her hair, and held her in a tight embrace.

CHAPTER THIRTY-ONE

The proposal…

JEREMY HAD NEVER thought that he could experience such elation with the mere mention of those three silly little words. After all, he couldn't count the number of women who had professed their love for him, uttering the same words in his ear—and yet, he could not remember a single instance when any of it mattered.

But this time, with Cassie in his arms, whispering, "I love you" against his cheek, the bleakness of his world infused with sunshine; his worthless existence suddenly had meaning. The path before him had unfurled, and he could see the rainbow in the distance, beyond which beautiful, happy children with dark hair and bright green eyes beckoned.

He gazed at her. She had been crying. He framed her face with his hands and brushed away a tear that cascaded down her cheek with his finger. A smile rose on the corner of his mouth.

"I-I'm sorry." She tried to pull away from him, but he kept her in place. "You must think I'm a ninny—" She reddened and let out a bland chuckle that he knew was out of embarrassment at being caught in making such a declaration. "I know, you don't love m—"

He cut her off with a kiss.

And gave her his all. Told her everything she needed to know, everything he wanted to say—in a single kiss so passionate yet so gentle, so sensual yet so sincere.

Gradually, her discomfiture subsided, and she melted against him, twining her arms around his neck. He cradled her on his lap, stroking her back as he explored the depths of her mouth. She tasted so sweet, so delicate, her body yielding so softly against his hard chest that his head reeled with unfamiliar feelings. Possessiveness. Tenderness. Love so great it made his heart ache.

"I love you, too," he whispered against her lips as he released her from his kiss.

Her eyes moistened once again.

"Stay with me at Waterford Park tonight." He slid his fingers beneath the fall of her hair on her nape and kissed her elegant neck.

"Yes," she muttered in his ear.

Minutes later, he carried her into the master's bedchamber, unmindful of Barton's eyebrows that lifted past his hairline, though he wisely abstained from speaking at his lordship's warning glare.

Cassandra sighed as he gently set her in the middle of his enormous bed. His pristine white pillows and linens smelled of him—clean and masculine, wrapping her in a cloud of musk that was Jeremy's alone.

He undressed her—slowly—between kisses. After tossing her satin slippers off the bed, he slid her garters off and rolled her stockings down in a leisurely fashion, skimming his fingers along the length of her legs. "Lovely," he murmured before he pulled her to a sitting position and began to unbutton the back of her dress.

He tossed her gown in a swirl of emerald silk over a nearby chair and then proceeded to unlace her corset, swiftly followed by her chemise and drawers, each article disposed of with steadfast efficiency over every available surface.

Cassandra met his hungry eyes as he raked his gaze at her nakedness. He deftly unpinned her hair and let it fall in a shining tumble of red-gold curls over her shoulders, all the way down to her waist.

"You're exquisite." His eyes lingered on her breasts, then slid further still, to feast on the auburn curls between her thighs.

She was completely exposed to his inspection while he was still fully clothed.

"Undress me," he said as if he had heard her thoughts.

He slid off the bed and removed his boots and stockings, then stood waiting for her by the edge of the bed.

She kneeled on the mattress in front of him. He was so tall that even with the height of the bed, the top of her head barely reached his shoulder. She reached out to push his dark blue evening coat from his broad shoulders. He took it from her and tossed it on the floor. She began to unbutton his waistcoat. The expertly tailored garment joined the rest of the clothes on the carpet. His fine lawn shirt followed, baring his muscular chest to her admiring gaze.

She plowed her fingers into the mat of dark hair sprinkled across his chest. Good Lord, but he was gorgeous—like a mythical warrior come to life. He took a sharp breath and led her hands down to his trousers.

Her fingers shook as she fumbled with the silver buttons. His hands alighted over hers. She glanced up at him with questioning eyes.

"I love you." He raised her fingers to his lips. "There's no need to be afraid."

"Jeremy—" she began, looking uncertain, her eyes pleading for guidance on what she should do.

"Sshhh." He kissed her. Then, he gently pushed her down until she was lying on her back on the mattress with her legs dangling over the edge.

His mouth traveled the length of her throat, trailing kisses on her shoulder before capturing her nipple. Cassandra gasped at the maddening sensations he invoked as he swirled his tongue around the sensitive skin. He suckled her breasts hungrily, filling his hands with their softness—kneading, squeezing, until she was dizzy with uncontained passion.

He traced his path back to her lips with his mouth, claiming them with a fervent kiss as he rid himself of his trousers. He lowered his body unto hers, the hardness of his manhood pressing against her belly.

Cassandra never thought in a million years that she would have a sudden, uncontrollable craving for that mischievous snake of his, but she did—urgently so. She reached down and cupped him.

Jeremy released her mouth and stared at her with startled eyes.

"D-did that hurt?" She certainly did not intend to murder it again.

"No," he breathed, sliding off her to lay on his side. "Let me show you." He placed his hand over hers and wrapped her fingers around his member.

She watched his lids flutter, a look of ecstasy on his face, as he guided her hand up and down his rigid length.

"You like this." She glanced down as she stroked him. Even now, after seeing it beforehand, she was still amazed at the size and girth of his sex—a terrifying notion indeed, if all those naughty pamphlets were to be believed. Surely, she could not accommodate him—she just could not see how it was possible.

A tiny drop of moisture beaded on the tip of his manhood. Without a thought, she scooted downward and flicked her tongue on it.

"Cassie." His breath peaked, then he let it out in a hiss through gritted teeth. "That felt so good. Do it again."

Eager to please him, she did as he requested, twirling her tongue slowly over it this time.

"Kiss it," he rasped, "the way you kissed me."

Cassandra could not quite understand what he meant, but she must have done the right thing because Jeremy suddenly tensed, closed his eyes, and held his breath when she took him in her mouth—and pretended that his snake was his tongue.

A moan that almost resembled a growl escaped from his lips, and she found herself on her back, pinned beneath him. He pushed her legs apart with his knees. She would have been petrified if not for the tender look in his eyes as he settled himself over her body, the coarse hairs on his chest and legs tickling her skin.

He returned his attention to her breasts, all the while rubbing the length of his sex against the triangle between her thighs. She closed her eyes at the warmth and urgency that bloomed in her belly. Is this what desire felt like? A constant ache that would not go away—unless it was satisfied?

"Ah, Cassie." Jeremy shifted, trailing his warm tongue over her stomach and dipping into her belly button. "You're intoxicating," he whispered against her skin as he moved further down.

Cassandra stole a glance at his dark head. Surely, he was not headed for—

He effortlessly pushed her knees up and spread her thighs wide. Cassandra would have jumped off the bed if not for her captive limbs. This could not be right. "Jeremy—"

"I want to see you," he interjected without looking up and parted her cleft with his thumbs, his eyes glued to her—her—

She struggled to cover herself. He brushed her hands away and, to her mortification, touched her—*there*—with his *tongue*. Her soul must have somersaulted in the air because that was how she felt, except her body stayed right where it was, writhing on the bed. Good Lord, what was he doing? She shivered as pleasure lanced into her core. He was licking her most intimate secret, torturing her with the power of a thousand feathers.

She arched her spine and muffled a scream with the back of her hand, unable to distinguish if the butterflies in her belly all came awake or if what she was feeling was another stomachache. His wicked onslaught was sheer torment—but she wanted more—she did not want him to stop. A mixture of agony and delight escalated in her belly.

"Tell me if this hurts," he said, and she reluctantly peered down to see one long finger disappear into her woman's flesh.

"What are you doing?" she gasped, but her protest drowned in the delicious sensations playing inside her silken walls.

"I'm pleasuring you," he replied huskily. "Tell me if it hurts, and I'll stop." He inserted another finger, sliding in and out in a mesmerizing caress.

Cassie lost her voice—and her senses—when his tongue joined his wicked fingers in exploring the recesses of her feminine cleft. Her legs turned into jelly, and every inch of her skin prickled.

Then, just when she thought she had sunk into the very depths of the ocean, he circled his tongue around the most sensitive part. A burst of pleasure shot straight to her core, and she threw her head wantonly from side to side. Her thighs quivered, and her toes curled, every stroke of his tongue making her pant in excitement.

She slowly opened her eyes and found Jeremy smiling down at her. "W-what was that?" she asked.

"You had your release." He kissed her forehead and tucked a stray curl of hair behind her ear.

"W-we copulated?" She looked down at his still massive erection.

"Yes, but not all the way." He cupped her breast and twirled her nipple with his thumb.

"I-I don't understand—" She blinked in befuddlement.

"You're still a virgin." He said with tenderness in his eyes.

"You didn't—?"

"No."

"Why?"

He sobered into such a state of seriousness that she began to worry. Perhaps she had gone about it all wrong?

"Marry me," he said with earnestness.

Jeremiah Devlin Huntington, the most notorious rake in all of England—looked utterly frightened and vulnerable.

Her heart skidded to a halt at his words. This time, there was no pretense between them. This time, he was asking her to be his wife for real.

"Please, Cassie—will you marry me?" His face dissolved into such boyish fretfulness that she had the sudden urge to shower his beautiful, beloved face all over with kisses.

She traced the anxious line of his brow and kissed her favorite spot instead—the bridge of his perfect nose. "Yes." She rested her forehead against his. "Yes!"

CHAPTER THIRTY-TWO

The day after...

C ASSANDRA WOKE UP to the bright sliver of sunlight dancing on her
face that peeked through the heavy draperies in Jeremy's blue
and white bedchamber. She shifted a little and gazed at the man
sleeping next to her. He was on his stomach, a muscled arm draped
possessively across her waist, his heavy breathing ruffling the hair on
top of her head. His black hair was hopelessly tousled.

She reached out and gently pushed the stray strands away with her
forefinger so she could have a better look at his beloved face. He was
asleep, his mouth curved in a small smile as if lost in a blissful dream.
She pressed her lips softly on his chin, marveling at the feel of his skin
roughened with day-old stubble. The poor man must have been too
exhausted from last night because he did not even stir nor make a
sound.

Cassandra let her gaze wander around the master's bedchamber. It
was the same room Jeremy had when they were children, but he had
made substantial improvements to it. The walls to the next room had
been removed to open up the space and make it larger. Another room
was converted into a sitting room and fitted with an opulent mahogany archway carved with lion heads for access.

Cassandra turned her gaze back to the handsome, peaceful countenance of her betrothed. Why it had taken her forever to realize she
loved him, she did not have a clue. She just hoped that he would

remain faithful.

Her stomach growled. Lord, but she was hungry!

She carefully rose from the bed, washed her face, and put on her clothes, fixing her hair as best as she could, before she headed downstairs. Barton would probably have an apoplexy if he found out she was still here, and the servants would gossip to no end, but she did not care. They were betrothed—this time for real. And if the servants had any sense, they would keep their mouths shut or else—no generous bribes, and certainly, no bonbons would be forthcoming.

To her dismay, not a scrap of food could be found in the breakfast room. She glanced at the clock on the mantel. Half-past ten. Rose Hill would have had a full buffet of toast, sausages, ham, bacon, and eggs by this time. But then again, the Marquess of Waterford dawdled in his bed till past noon, a good enough reason for the servants to serve breakfast at lunchtime.

She smiled to herself. Her mama would certainly swoon if she knew where she had spent the night. But not to worry—she could always borrow a horse from Jeremy's stables and ride into Rose Hill, and everyone would think she had just come back from her early morning outing.

She decided to go to the kitchen. As she passed the foyer on her way to the servants' stairs, she heard voices coming from the vestibule leading to the main door.

"I'm sorry, but his lordship is still abed, my lady," she heard Barton say. "Would you like to leave your card and perhaps a message?"

Cassandra wondered who could be calling on Jeremy—and a lady at that! She peeked from behind the life-size bronze sculpture of Achilles and was surprised to see the impeccably dressed woman standing on the doorstep, partially blocked from view by Barton's tall, lanky frame.

The goat lady! What could she want from Jeremy?

"Yes, thank you," Lady Desiree was saying. "I just came by to return this. If you could please let him know that I will not need it anymore and that I deeply appreciate all the help he extended to me."

Cassandra craned her neck to see her hand a small package to Barton, wrapped in black muslin and tied with red yarn.

"I shall relay your message to his lordship, my lady." Barton took the package from her and bowed before closing the door.

Cassandra hurriedly tiptoed to a corner and hid behind the wall, listening to Barton's footsteps as he crossed the foyer. She peered from her hiding spot to see him walk down the hallway and open the first door to the right—Jeremy's study.

He came out a minute later with a quick nod at Barney, the footman, who stood on guard by the door.

Cassandra waited until Barton disappeared in the long hallway leading to the other side of Waterford House, which was as grand as Grandstone House before she came out of hiding. One could get lost in the passages and the staggering number of rooms.

She had always wondered how Jeremy could live in such an enormous home by himself. He had a full staff but never held any parties, save for the dinners he hosted with only her family as guests.

Cassandra stifled a giggle as she approached Barney the footman who was standing in all seriousness in front of Jeremy's study room door. He was a little older than Jeremy and had often accompanied him when he visited Rose Hill.

"Hello Barney." She beamed at him.

"Good morning, Miss Carlyle." He inclined his head and blushed. He seemed to do that a lot these days.

"Barney, could you go to the stables and ask the groom to saddle a horse for me?"

"Of course, my lady," he agreed without hesitation.

"Thank you. I'll wait at the front." Cassandra watched him leave, then darted her eyes at the study room door.

She tried the doorknob. It was locked. She pried a pin from her hair and jammed it into the keyhole, jiggling it a little here and a little there—just the way Jeremy had showed her years ago when they were trying to steal bonbons from Cook's pantry—until she heard a faint click. The door opened without difficulty. She slipped into the room.

Jeremy's study was large, the walls paneled in mahogany and lined with books on business and all sorts of industry. The room was dark and very masculine, with leather chairs, a black marble fireplace on one side, and a side table laden with decanters of port, whisky, and brandy. She had never been in this room, and for the first time, Cassandra saw a glimpse of the other side of Jeremy. This chamber symbolized his real world as a man—the place where he put his sharp mind to use and made a fortune.

Her eyes alighted on the massive desk situated before a large window overlooking the grounds in the center of the room. On top of it, papers and correspondence were neatly stacked in groups. The muslin-wrapped package sat right in the middle. Cassandra moved toward the table and touched the red string binding it. No, she really should not. She had no business snooping around Jeremy's study. She withdrew her hand and took a step back. But—why did the goat lady say she would not need it anymore? What could it be? She debated with herself whether she should go ahead and investigate or run out of the room before Barton and Barney discovered her caper.

Curiosity prevailed.

With a glance toward the door, she hastily untied the ribbon and unwrapped the package, and discovered a small leather-bound journal that looked personal—much like a diary. Why would Jeremy lend this book to Desiree? She skimmed through the first few pages. The bold handwriting was Jeremy's—she would recognize his penmanship anywhere.

Her eyebrows snapped together as she read the first few lines. Why was he cataloguing Richard's habits, likes, and dislikes? Then, she noticed a thin silk ribbon inserted in between the pages in the middle section. She opened the journal to the section marked. Her eyes widened upon reading the title.

Seducing a Gentleman. Her fingers shook as she proceeded to read the contents. *Step one—If you want to learn how to seduce a man, you must also learn how to pleasure him.* The rest of the instructions blurred as hot tears prickled her eyes. How could Jeremy be so cruel and do this to her? The book fell with a dull thud on the carpet as she stifled the sobs erupting from her throat with the back of a shaking hand, stunned by the hurt and betrayal inflicted by the one person she trusted and loved the most.

JEREMY WOKE UP with a smile on his face. He had slept so well—the first time in weeks. Today, he planned to go to Rose Hill, speak with Cassie's father, and ask for her hand. Then, he would set out to see about procuring a special license so they could get married as soon as possible. They might have had the shortest engagement—with most of it faked, but he could not wait any longer. After last night, all he could think of was finally making her his—legally—or he would die of unfulfilled desire.

He stretched and turned to reach for Cassie beside him but was greeted with crumpled white sheets and an empty space. "Cassie?" He pushed himself on his elbows to look about the room.

Only the chirping birds and the distant hum of the ocean answered him. He sat up and raked his fingers through his tousled hair. Where could she have gone? He glanced at the clock on top of the mantel. Half-past twelve. His disappointment immediately subsided. Cassie had always been an early riser. She must have ridden to see the sunrise or might have gone downstairs to have breakfast.

Jeremy reached for the bellpull by the corner of the bed to summon his valet, then paused with his hand hoisted in mid-air. The leather-bound journal he had lent to Lady Desiree was on top of his bedside table. But that was not what made him ill to his stomach. His mother's ring rested atop the journal, the gems sparkling from the sliver of sunlight peeking through the draperies and casting a rainbow of colors around the room. The same ring he had given to Cassie, the only girl he wanted to marry.

CHAPTER THIRTY-THREE

Pumpkin and the viscount
Seven days later...

C ASSANDRA WATCHED HER mama and papa as they settled themselves on the chairs on either side of her bed. She had cried buckets and refused to talk to anyone, locking herself in her room until her mother finally threatened to cut off the delivery of her food, beginning with her bonbons.

"What is the matter with you?" her mother scolded. "You're not sick, yet you pretend to be ill, and you're not mute either, yet you won't talk! You've sequestered yourself in this godforsaken room, and I'll tell you this right now, young lady, if you don't make yourself go downstairs and have luncheon with your family, I'm going to have that beast of a horse of yours sold to the highest bidder!"

"But, Mama!" Cassandra threw a helpless glance at her father, who shrugged and settled himself more comfortably in the nearby chair with a yawn.

"Does all this sulking have something to do with that profligate friend of yours?" Her mother stood up, placed her hands on her hips, and began to pace back and forth. "He's been asking for you every hour for the past six days, driving the entire household mad! Whatever quarrel have you two gotten yourselves into, now? I am sick of the both of you. Truly, my hair will turn gray, and I will die if this squabble of yours does not end!"

Cassandra crossed her arms over her chest. "I never want to see him again, Mama."

"Then—why can't you get out of bed and tell him so yourself? The man will not go away nor listen to anyone, not even your brother! He has been brooding in the library and will not touch his food at dinnertime, except for the wine. As to why you cannot act like a well-bred young lady and speak to him so we could all have some peace around this house is beyond my comprehension!"

"I don't want to speak to him—ever." Cassandra averted her eyes.

The viscountess threw her hands in the air and swiveled her gaze at her husband. "Did you hear that, George? Did you see how impertinent this daughter of yours has become?"

Her father answered with a loud snore.

"George Carlyle!" her mother screamed at the top of her lungs.

The viscount winced with a startled snort.

"For God's sake, George, did you doze off on me?" The viscountess peered at her husband from across the bed.

"Eh?" He muffled a yawn with the back of his hand. "Of course not. I was just—"

"This is all your fault!"

The viscount glanced around the room and pointed at himself. "Me?"

"Yes—you! You have condoned your daughter's behavior and let her run amuk like a hooligan behind my back. You talk to her! I am going to lie down. I need smelling salts." Her mother fanned herself furiously with her hand and left the room in a huff.

Cassandra and her father looked at each other.

"Well—since your mama has disowned you for the day," the viscount sighed and stood up from his chair, sitting next to her on the bed, "why don't you tell your papa what this is all about?"

Cassandra traced the embroidered monogram on her pillowcase. "Oh, Papa, I hate him!"

"Pumpkin," her papa said in a gentle voice, "you always say that every time you quarrel with him."

Cassandra shook her head. "But this is different. I never, ever, want to see him again."

"I'm sure you don't." Her papa took her hand and regarded her with kind eyes. "It's all right, you don't have to tell me anything if you don't want to."

She burst into tears.

Her father shifted closer and hugged her, rubbing her back soothingly. "You know, pumpkin, he has been coming here, bringing you all sorts of flowers. The drawing room is beginning to look and smell like a mausoleum. He has been genuinely miserable. Now, if you truly do not ever want to see him again, why don't you put the man out of his misery? Go downstairs and tell him when he comes back. I am sure he will understand. Perhaps he will even move on and find another friend—or even get married. Countess Libbey's daughter is quite lovely. Perhaps your mama can arrange an introduction."

Cassandra grimaced, blowing her nose on the handkerchief her father supplied. "She's too timid and frail. Jeremy will never be interested in her."

"What about the Earl of Templeton's daughter? Her name escapes me, but I heard she's a beauty."

Cassandra rolled her eyes. "She also thinks she's a princess—not at all suitable for Jeremy."

"Hmm. You may be right." Her father rubbed his chin. "He does favor ladies who are spirited and capable. He has quite a brain in his head, so he would prefer someone who could match his wit and keep up with all those amusing schemes of his. Ah—but why am I troubling myself?" The viscount patted her hand and rose from the bed. "I do believe he has had his eye on a particular lady for quite some time now."

"He has?" Cassandra sat up straight, flustered at this new information. "Who?"

"Oh, a lady he constantly called on and danced with when he was in London." Her father waved his hand with nonchalance. "Titian hair, expressive eyes, exceptionally beautiful, quick-witted. I know her father very well—handsome old chap." He smiled at her and strolled toward the door.

"Papa—wait!" Cassandra tossed the blankets off and crawled toward the edge of the bed. "Tell me who she is!"

The viscount paused and looked over his shoulder. "Oh, don't concern yourself, my dear." He shook his head as he turned the doorknob. "You don't ever want to see him again, remember?"

Cassandra frowned in consternation. Of course, why would she care? In fact, she did not even want to hear about it!

"Now—get dressed and come down for luncheon," her father said before he slipped out the door. "Your mother will drive me to an early grave if you don't."

CHAPTER THIRTY-FOUR

Choosing the one...

LUNCHEON, THANKFULLY, HAD been a short affair. Her mother forbade her to go back to her room, so she decided to take Apollo for a gallop instead. A week had passed since she had ridden him, and he was restless, kicking at the ground and brimming with pent-up energy.

She rode through the woods in the direction of the pond on the border of Rose Hill and Grandstone Park. God, how she relished the wind on her face and the blur of trees as she and Apollo sped down the path. She felt better already, though she missed Jeremy terribly. The past seven days had been hell. She could not eat, could not function, could not sleep—without crying and thinking about him.

Many times, she was tempted to run down the stairs and rush into his arms—especially when she could hear the echo of his voice, arguing with every servant in the house to let him into her bedchamber. Only Allayne and her father could pacify him with kind words and more drink; Allayne had bellowed in exasperation when he demanded she get out of bed and fix their petty misunderstanding at once.

Oh, if only they knew! Reading that journal almost killed her. How could Jeremy do that to her? How could she ever trust him again? She should never have let herself fall in love, should have never invested her heart in someone like him—who could hurt her without a qualm when the next girl with a pretty face came around.

Cassandra drew Apollo's reins and winced. In her distraction, she had forgotten to wear her riding gloves, and her hands were sore from gripping the leather straps. She dismounted next to the tree they used to climb as children and let Apollo graze on the grass near the pond.

The old wooden ladder was still nailed to the tree trunk, and she clambered up the steps until she reached the thick, wide branch hanging over the water.

"Well, hello there! Are you visiting my tree?" She heard a familiar voice call out to her as she reached the top.

"Richard!" She held on to the nearby branches and treaded her way to where he sat. "What are you doing here?"

"I took a dip in the pond." He scooted a little to give her some space. "I missed coming here."

"Me, too." She sat next to him.

"Remember these?" He pointed at the markings carved on the branch.

Cassandra chuckled. "Oh! Yes!" She studied the rough heart shapes she had engraved on the wood when they were children, containing the letters R and C.

Richard cleared his throat. "Listen, Cass, I've been meaning to talk to you about what happened in London—"

"It's all right—" Cassandra felt a rush of warmth in her cheeks, and she lowered her head to hide her discomfiture.

He took her hand and gave it a little squeeze. "No—I sincerely apologize for my behavior. I was a fool not to recognize you."

Cassandra shrugged. "I don't blame you at all. It had been ten long years, and I looked nothing like the eight-year-old you left behind. You couldn't have recognized me even if you walked into Rose Hill manor and saw me there."

"I'm sorry for being too forward. I thought—"

"You thought I was someone else," she chuckled, then regarded him for a moment before saying, "I wished I was someone else."

"I wished you were someone else, too." His lips tugged at the corners. "But as it turned out, you were my little piglet—my treasured friend who was more like the sister I never had."

"I wish I could say the same, but I was more determined to marry you, then." She laughed softly, tracing the heart markings on the branch with her forefinger.

"What's this?" Richard reached out to touch the tarnished brass ring on her pinky finger. She had worn it for so long that she had forgotten it was even there.

"My wedding ring—with you." She gazed at the memento she'd treasured for so long. "Call me silly, but yes, I held on to it over the years."

"How can I call you silly—" he slipped his fingers inside his shirt and pulled out a gold chain with a tarnished brass ring strung through it, "when I kept mine, too?"

Cassandra gasped, covering her mouth in surprise. She cupped the ring dangling from the gold chain identical to the one on her palm. "You never forgot." She raised bewildered eyes to meet his.

"Never, except for one thing," he smiled. "That my little piglet would grow up to be a princess."

Cassandra reflected for a moment. "It's funny, but it was the same for me. I always thought of you as a fifteen-year-old boy. I never dreamed you'd grow up and be a giant man."

"I suppose we were both stuck in the past." He grinned sheepishly.

They both laughed.

Finally, Richard paused, peering at the water below as he once again cleared his throat. "Cass—Desiree wanted me to ask you—if you would be her bridesmaid."

"Me?" Cassandra waited for her heart to break, but she felt nothing except a longing for a certain someone with long dark hair, magnificent eyes, and a crooked grin.

"Yes." Richard turned to look at her. "Desiree is an only child like me. She needs someone, a sister to stand next to her—and she picked you."

"So—you are finally getting yourself leg-shackled." She searched his handsome face.

"Yes." He nodded, swinging his feet back and forth. "I think—I'm falling in love with her."

Cassandra's smile disappeared. She felt a familiar loss, the same one she experienced when all three of them left for Oxford.

"Don't look so sad." Richard elbowed her playfully the way he always did years ago when they used to sit in this same branch and dangle their feet over the pond below. "We're not moving away. We're staying at Grandstone Park."

"You are?" Cassandra's spirits instantly lifted.

"Yes, and I have Jeremy to thank for it. Desiree confessed that he helped her. She even showed me the journal he gave her. Jeremy wrote explicit instructions for her to follow and practice in front of a mirror." Richard shook his head and chuckled. "I should have been furious, but Desiree did it because she loves me. A lady of her standing would never agree to do such a scandalous thing unless she loved someone so badly that she was desperate to win him. Do you know that she even forced herself to wake up early in the mornings to go riding with me?"

"Truly?" Cassie tilted her head at him, a twinge of envy in her heart for having someone else take her place.

"Yes, she even challenged me to a race along the beach. The other day, she insisted on coming with me to visit the tenants, taking the time to get to know their families and listening to their concerns." Richard shook his head. "I knew Desiree did everything to please me. Her resolve to show how much she loved me made me see her in a completely different light and brought us closer together. Later on, we had a good laugh about that outrageous journal. For once, Jeremy's demented scheme proved useful and successful."

Cassandra swallowed the lump in her throat. They laughed about the journal? Richard should have been insulted, enraged to find his privacy invaded and enumerated like a shopping list! But, as usual, Richard always saw the wisdom in everything. He dealt with the circumstance in an objective manner, heard what Desiree had to say, took the time to understand everything from her perspective. Why couldn't she handle things in a grown-up way like him? She felt like a child—an idiot—for running off and refusing to talk to Jeremy.

"Cassie—Desiree said Jeremy helped her because of you. He thought he was losing you—*to me.*" Richard's eyes alighted on her bare hand. "I don't see your engagement ring on your finger."

"I-I—" Cassandra stared at her lap, a sudden spring of tears flooding her eyes. She wiped them frantically with the back of her hand.

"You broke it off," Richard said in a somber voice and peered at her. "Is it because of the journal?"

She nodded, trying her best to stifle another flood of tears.

Richard took her hand and clasped it between his warm hands. "My mother used to tell me this story on how she chose to marry my father." A pensive expression crossed his face. "It is a tradition in our family for the parents to select the best match for their children. My mother had many suitors, but her parents favored two gentlemen whom they wanted her to wed. She was asked to select between the Duke of Pennworth and my father, who was heir to a dukedom and a marquess at that time. My mother said she was enamored with the duke, who was a paragon and the most handsome man she'd ever seen, but at the same time, she was very fond of my father, though he was a rake and a little immature."

Cassie listened closely, thinking of Jeremy at the same time. She'd been a fool for nothing.

"Grandmama noticed Mama's predicament and summoned her. Over a cup of tea, she told Mama the story of how she solved her dilemma over two suitors." Richard paused and plucked a leaf from a nearby branch, letting it fall like a feather buffeted by the gentle breeze onto the pond below.

"What did your grandmama tell your mother?" Cassandra turned her gaze toward him.

He smiled. "Choose the one who loves you the most." He gently squeezed her hand. "And that was how my mother chose my father, who may be of lesser rank and consequence, but he was absolutely devoted to her." Richard paused for a moment before continuing, "Jeremy loves you. That man will do anything for you to the point of dishonoring himself. I admit I was skeptical at first and did not approve of your engagement. And it was not because I did not trust him—I do, as a friend and associate—but I just didn't trust him when it comes to *you*. Now I am confident the man is determined to make you happy for the rest of his life."

She covered her face with her hands.

Richard put an arm around her shoulders and sat quietly with her, the way he always did when he had comforted her as a child.

After several moments, when she had regained her composure, they made their way down the tree.

"Go to him," Richard said with a quick hug before they parted ways.

CHAPTER THIRTY-FIVE

Losing Prince Charming…

CASSANDRA URGED APOLLO into a fast gallop toward Waterford Park. She felt buoyed, her burden eased, as everything came into focus. She wanted nothing else but to see Jeremy, to kiss him, hold him, tell him how sorry she was, and how much she loved him.

Barton opened the door just as she dismounted. She rushed to the steps. "Is his lordship in?"

"I'm sorry, Miss." Barton swallowed, his usually unruffled demeanor cracking and his face taking on a troubled look. "But his lordship left with his valet at dawn for London to see his solicitors and board a ship for Europe."

"Europe?" Cassandra felt her breath whoosh out of her lungs. "Where in Europe?"

"Er—I'm not at a liberty to tell, Miss," Barton replied with evident concern. "He was very adamant to keep his whereabouts confidential."

"How long will he stay there?" Cassandra quelled the urge to break down in a fit of tears in front of Barton. Jeremy had never before left without telling her—and worse forbade his servants to inform her of his destination.

Barton cleared his throat. "Indefinitely, Miss. He asked me to close Waterford House and retain a skeleton staff. I had the distinct impression that he will not be coming back anytime soon. He assigned the management of all his properties to his solicitors and stewards."

Cassandra stifled the rising panic in her chest. She wanted to scream, to fling herself to the ground, and cry her heart out. Jeremy could not walk away from her like this. He was too dear to her, too essential to her existence that she would cease to breathe if she lost him. No—she would not let him leave! She would follow him all the way to London—or Europe—anywhere in the world if that's what it took.

"How many hours has it been since he left?" She paced in front of Barton, her resoluteness to find him becoming stronger by the minute.

Barton pulled out his fob watch. "Nine and a quarter hours, give or take, Miss. He is scheduled to board a ship five days after today."

"Did he say which ship?" Cassandra asked in earnest.

"I'm sorry, Miss." Barton shook his head. "He skipped that particular detail."

"I'm going after him," she said in a firm voice.

For the first time in her life, she saw the starchy, ever-somber Barton smile. "Barney will escort you, Miss, and I will send word to Rose Hill about your plans." He turned to call out instructions to Barney, who nodded and dashed off to change into riding clothes. "I assume you will be on horseback all the way to London. You will need some blunt for food, coaching inns, and several changes of horses. Please take this." He handed her a purse full of coins.

"Oh, Barton, thank you!" Cassandra exclaimed. "I promise to pay you when I get back."

"That won't be necessary. The money is his lordship's household fund he left for me to use in his absence. If you succeed in bringing him back, I shall no longer be needing it. Good luck to you, Miss." He inclined his head and gestured to another footman to bring her horse closer to the steps as Barney trotted toward them on his borrowed mount from the stables.

Five days later
Temple, London

JEREMY WALKED OUT of his solicitor's offices with a massive headache and in a very black mood. The man had piled a mountain of paperwork in front of him to sign, but he was in no frame of mind to sit for hours poring over documents, and he had lost his temper. The poor solicitor had quivered in his chair and promised to send the paperwork to Europe instead as soon as he was settled.

He rubbed the back of his neck. He was tense and irritable—even his valet, Percy, avoided him whenever he could. His alcohol consumption had increased to a frightening degree, while his eating had markedly decreased. Within days, the fit of his trousers and coats had loosened quite a bit, and without the constant nagging from Viscountess Carlyle to finish his meals, his weight continued to plunge.

He could not get Cassie out of his mind. No matter how much he drank, he could not forget about her. The sweetness of her lips, the scent of her hair, and the taste of her feminine softness—adhered to him like a second skin. She was all around him, like a persistent ghost haunting every waking moment and every erotic dream.

His footman opened the door and lowered the steps of his carriage.

"Take me to the docks," he called to the driver before disappearing into the interior of the coach.

CASSANDRA HANDED THE reins of her horse to Barney then pushed into the throng of people boarding the *Citadel* for France. They had searched every ship bound for Europe on the docks but failed to locate

Jeremy and Percy. The *Citadel* was the largest and last ship on their list, and her hope was fading fast. If Jeremy was not on board, then his ship had most likely already sailed. She expunged the fear that suddenly gripped her heart at the thought of losing Jeremy. She was dirty, tired, and aching all over, but she could not give up. She must not give up.

"Your pass, Miss?" One of the ship's crew asked as she crossed the ramp.

"I'm looking for the Marquess of Waterford." She covertly handed him a gold sovereign. "I'm his betrothed."

His eyes widened at the generous reward she handed, and he quickly pocketed the coin. "First class on the upper deck. The marquess is occupying a suite of cabins on aisle A. Take those stairs." He pointed in the direction of the stairway leading to the private cabins and waved her on.

Cassandra practically flew up the steps. As soon as she reached the upper deck, she wasted no time in finding aisle A. The top of the stairs opened into a hallway dividing the upper decks into two sections. Mounted on a wall, a sign indicated where she should go. She turned in that direction and wove through the servants carrying their masters' luggage. Ladies and gentlemen socialized in groups along the narrow, crowded corridors, oblivious to the hustle and bustle around them. By the time she climbed up another short set of stairs and found Jeremy's rooms, she was out of breath.

She knocked on the door, but no answer came forth. After pounding on the door harder for another minute, she turned the doorknob, and it opened. She rushed inside, peeking in each tiny adjoining room. In the small dining area, she found a half-full glass of brandy—the kind Jeremy liked. His cologne lingered in the air.

He was here. An immediate sense of relief washed over her. She rushed toward the doors. He probably had gone out to get some air. She scoured the entire upper deck, but she could not find him anywhere. She went back to his rooms. Nothing. She ran down to the middle and lower cargo sections, and still, she could not find him.

On her third way back to his rooms, she bumped into the same sailor she had bribed earlier.

"I'm sorry, Miss, but you must disembark." He pointed at the massive sails rising from the ship. "We are about to set sail."

Cassandra frantically shook her head, panic swiftly rising in her gut. "No, please—I must find the marquess—"

A deafening horn sounded from above.

"I'm sorry, but that is the final signal for passengers to board and for everyone else to leave the ship." He took her arm and escorted her back down to the ramp. "I will send word to the marquess that you were looking for him, Miss—?"

"Carlyle," she replied as men raised the anchor and untied the ship from the ramp posts.

Within minutes, the massive vessel had pulled away from the harbor and steadily glided onto the waters. Cassandra stood on the edge of the ramp, watching it become smaller and smaller in the distance. She wanted to cry, to scream at the top of her lungs.

Jeremy was gone.

She had let her beloved Prince Charming slip away.

Her legs buckled from sheer exhaustion, and she collapsed in a heap of crumpled lace and silk on her knees in the middle of the wooden gangplank. She could not think, could not move, and did not know what else to do—and so she wept.

CHAPTER THIRTY-SIX

The wrong prince...

JEREMY HAD BEEN so distraught the moment he stepped inside his cabins aboard the *Citadel* earlier. He had paced around the tiny sitting room, sat, drank, stood again, and worn a path on the carpet as he wandered aimlessly in the cramped space.

The hopelessness of mending his relationship with Cassie troubled him greatly, and the thought of their betrothal coming to an end tore his heart into pieces. He could not stay still; he must do something—anything, to distract himself from jumping overboard or putting a pistol to his temple. Yes, just like his father, the foolish bastard! He slammed his fist on a nearby table. He was no different from him after all.

Jeremy walked back into the dining chamber and poured himself another glass of brandy before resuming his pacing around the room. His valet, Percy, watched him quietly from the corner where he was sitting for several minutes before he finally suggested they take a walk outside.

They strolled from one end of the ship to the other, explored the small saloon, the bridge, and the upper and lower decks. When they had run out of places to roam on board, Jeremy told Percy he wished to get off of the ship and take a stroll along the harbor boardwalk. He must have been so lost in his thoughts because Percy had to shake his arm to tell him that their ship had blared the final boarding horn.

But as he watched the massive sails rise on the ship's masts and unfurl into enormous flags billowing in the wind, his steps had become heavier and heavier. Percy urged him on—they were quite a distance away, but his pace had gradually slowed until he just stood there, staring at the ship from the boardwalk.

He could not make himself go. He may as well die if he did. So, he kept standing right where he was, watching the great ship as it pulled away from the dock and smoothly sailed out to sea.

"My lord." Percy pointed at someone sitting atop a horse not too far in the distance. "Isn't that Barney, your footman?"

CASSANDRA COULD NOT remember how long she had been kneeling on the ramp, crying her eyes out, but she did not care. People kept stopping to ask if she was all right, but she simply shook her head and buried her face in her hands. The life had gone out of her. She could not even utter a word, much less pick herself up.

She sat back on her heels and stared out into the water. The ship was no longer visible. A flood of tears blurred her vision, and she knew, with deepest regret, that her heart had left with him. How odd it was for her to have found love and gone through it all backward. First, it was her wedding, then her betrothal, after which was the proposal—followed by the realization that the right man had been in front of her all along. The only thing she had to do was open her heart and choose him over a silly childhood fantasy.

Now, as it had come about, she had lost him—her tormentor, her best friend, the man she genuinely loved—her Jeremy. She had indubitably made a muddle of everything.

A cool breeze blew on her face, and a shadow shaded her from the glaring sun.

"Pretty dress, brat," Jeremy's familiar drawl penetrated her empty, discordant thoughts.

She kept her gaze fixed toward the horizon, where the ship had disappeared, refusing to listen to her imagination. Her head ached, and her mind was in such a state of disarray, it must have been playing mean tricks on her.

"Who did your hair?" Jeremy's voice whispered in her ear. "You look a fright, but I like it."

She squeezed her eyes shut, refusing to heed to the sound of his voice.

"Come on, brat." A hand cupped her chin and turned her head. "Look at me."

He felt so warm—so real.

She slowly opened her eyes and found the most magnificent pair of dark eyes gazing back at her. "Jeremy?" she said in a small voice, gaping in disbelief.

"I love you too much. I could not leave." He brought her fingers to his lips, and his eyes filled with tears.

"My God, Jeremy!" She flung herself to him, wrapping her arms tightly around his neck. Her heart must have done a pirouette in her ribcage because she could feel it dancing with renewed vigor, infused with the strength of her love for him.

"Oh, Jeremy, I love you so much," she said tearfully, burying her face in the curve between the side of his neck and shoulder. "Don't you ever—ever, frighten me like that again!"

"I'm sorry, love, I wasn't thinking straight. I—"

She silenced him with a fervent kiss. "I'm sorry for refusing to see you," she whispered against his mouth. "But I'm here now, and I don't want you to wander away from me again."

They embraced for a long time, neither of them saying a word.

Finally, Jeremy pulled away and looked into her eyes. "Does this mean you'll still marry me?"

She framed his beloved face in her hands, her heart shining in her eyes. Dear God, how she loved this man!

"You're the one I love the most," she whispered, "and I want to spend the rest of my life having you to love and to hold, to indulge and to spoil, to obey everything you ask for, with kindness and without a grudge, forever and ever." She smiled into his eyes. "Yes, I will marry you."

"You sound like Reverend Jeremy," he grinned, his gaze dropping to her lips. "Wise chap—that one."

And they kissed right there, in the middle of the busy ramp, amidst the loud cheering from the eavesdropping crowd.

EPILOGUE

Eight years later…

L ADY CASSANDRA WATERFORD, Marchioness of Waterford, sat on the veranda of her magnificent home with her parents, the Viscount and Lady Carlyle, and her friend, Desiree, the Duchess of Grandstone. Leaning against the balustrade was her brother, Allayne, who was watching the game of catch on the sprawling grounds below.

"George, don't you sometimes wonder if Allayne envies his friends?" Lady Carlyle glanced at her husband over the rim of her teacup. "After all, he is the only one who is still unmarried, the poor darling."

"I'm sure he does," the viscount replied, placing his own cup on the table. "I can't imagine how lonely he is without a special someone by his side. But do not fret, my dear. Your match-making days will soon be over."

"They will?" Lady Carlyle's eyes lit up, and she sat up straighter in her chair. "How so?"

"I have a secret plan." The viscount grinned as he picked up a lemon cake from his plate.

Allayne cleared his throat and turned to face his parents. "You do know that I can hear you perfectly well from where I'm standing." He glared at the co-conspirators, who regarded him with innocent expressions. "The two of you need to stop this." He shook a finger in their direction. "I am tired of being foisted at every husband-hunting chit in England. Pray—leave me alone, or I will run away and reside with Cassie and Jeremy. When I am ready to marry, you will be the first to know."

"Humph. Let us hope we have not turned senile or turned our toes up by then," Lady Carlyle muttered under her breath as she took another sip of tea.

"And that would be my signal to withdraw from this conversation and pack my belongings." Allayne touched his forelock in a salute to bid his parents farewell, then jogged down the balcony steps to join the game on the lawn.

>>>><<<<

IN THE GARDEN below, Jeremy and Richard, now the Duke of Grandstone, were playing catch with their children.

Edward Devlin Huntington, the Waterfords' first born son and heir, threw the ball at Joshua Royce Radcliffe, heir to the dukedom of Grandstone, and twin to a beautiful, younger—by two minutes—sister, named Diana.

"That ball should have been mine!" Diana shrieked. "Papa! Edward is ignoring me again!"

"So what?" Edward yelled, brushing his long dark hair from his forehead with the back of his hand and glaring at her with emerald green eyes. "You're so clumsy, you shouldn't even be playing ball!"

"Edward!" Jeremy threw a warning look at his son. "Apologize to Diana at once!"

But before anyone could stop her, little Diana had marched over to where Edward stood and gave him a nice big kick on the shin.

"Ow!" Edward screamed, shoving Diana as he danced around on one foot with a limp. "I'll kill you. I promise I will!"

"I'll kill you first—milksop!" Diana yelled, retaliating with a forceful push that sent Edward staggering backward, landing on his bum.

"Edward! Diana! Stop this right now!" Allayne immediately intervened before the two got into more fisticuffs.

"Come here, young lady!" Richard grabbed his daughter by the arm and gave her a resounding lecture about good manners.

Her older brother, the perfectly behaved Joshua Royce, crossed his arms over his chest and shook his head with a resigned sigh as he watched the ludicrous spectacle.

Up on the veranda, Cassie and Desiree hollered their disapproval of their children's behavior and demanded they sit on separate corners, ejected from the next game.

"Does this scene remind you of some people?" Viscount Rose remarked to his wife.

"God help us." The viscountess rolled her eyes heavenward. "It's starting all over again."

About the Author

Veronica Crowe is a dentist, entrepreneur, and author of The Silver-eyed Prince, Guardian and Commander, and Son of the Redeemer, from the Highest Royal Coven of Europe series under the pen name, VJ Dunraven.

Veronica loves reading and writing urban fantasy and historical fiction books and has recently finished The Wrong Prince, and The Viscount's Heir, both books from the Heirs of Cornwall series, set in the Regency era. Currently, she is in the process of writing the third installment, My Only Earl.

In her spare time, Veronica enjoys photography, designing, and running a myriad of enterprises to generate small contractual jobs for stay-at-home moms, students, retirees, or people who have talent and potential but need a little boost. She credits her work ethic from her dad, who rose from humble beginnings and became one of the most successful dental practitioners and entrepreneurs in his city. The best advice Veronica loves to share from her dad is, "Discover your gifts and use them wisely to inspire people. Believe in your power and strength. Remember that criticism and disappointment are just words. You can always hit "delete" at any time."

Made in the USA
Middletown, DE
13 March 2021